Secret Signs

SECRET SIGNS

T. J. Waters

GALLAUDET UNIVERSITY PRESS

Washington, DC

Gallaudet University Press
Washington, D.C. 20002
http://gupress.gallaudet.edu
© 2010 by Gallaudet University
All rights reserved. Published 2010
Printed in the United States of America

Library of Congress Cataloging-in-Publication Data

Waters, T. J.
Secret signs / T.J. Waters.
p. cm.
ISBN-13: 978-1-56368-473-9 (pbk. : alk. paper)
ISBN-10: 1-56368-473-X (pbk. : alk. paper)
1. Interpreters for the deaf—Fiction.   2. Political consultants—Crimes against—
Fiction.   3. Assassination—Washington (D.C.)—Fiction.   I. Title.
PS3623.A8692S43 2010
813'.6—dc22
2010035208

T. J. Waters is represented by Bob Diforio
Diforio Literary
7 Indian Valley Road
Weston, CT 06883

Prelude

GRETEL STOOD quietly as he worked. Brent fussed over her. The pretty pink ribbon. Her nails. The long strokes of the brush. He applied the finishing touches with one hand while the other furiously tapped away on a Sidekick messaging device. An electronic beep from the device elicited a laugh.

A pair of headlights pierced the shop's front window to signal the old lady's arrival. Gretel fidgeted wildly, knowing her return home was imminent. Home with the woman who fed her treats and coddled her like a person. As dog's lives go, it was hard to beat. The big Buick pulled into a parking space by the front door.

He put the Sidekick in his pocket and opened the door for her as he'd done a hundred times before. Gretel's excitement was palpable.

"Oh my sweet girl," the old lady exclaimed. "You're such a beautiful thing! Oh my! You've truly outdone yourself. She looks great."

He stood by beaming silently, an artisan of animals, quietly accepting the praise of one of the few people who really understood why he'd ever gotten into this line of work.

"Oh my baby is so pretty," she said. "Yes she is! Yes she is!"

He picked Gretel up off the stainless steel table and lowered her gently to the ground. French poodles are by no means light, but he'd long ago learned that the old lady was not fond of quick movements, and intentionally slowed down his actions to accommodate her. She was a good client who tipped well. And her happiness meant a bigger tip when she wrote the check for his services. Everyone left the shop satisfied.

"You do such wonderful work," she said, presenting the check with one hand while accepting the leash with the other. He offered again to deliver Gretel but knew enough not to oversell. Make the

1

offer, but don't push—the freedom to drive was important to her, and she might easily mistake a repeated offer as an affront to her skills and competence behind the wheel.

"Don't be silly! I'm perfectly capable of picking up my girl. I know you deliver, but I was in the neighborhood."

A lie they both accepted with smiles. Word games are commonplace between shop owners and customers, men and women, rich and poor, old and young. This pair crisscrossed all of those demographic dimensions—and probably more.

They had little in common, yet she was his favorite customer, one of the first when he opened the shop. She'd stayed with him through thick and thin, mistakes and missteps, as Brent learned the business side of his trade largely through trial and error. She'd taken it in stride and remained patiently resilient through it all—a near-perfect client.

Although they were alone today, she surreptitiously pressed three twenties into his hand as if she were hiding it from some unseen menace or IRS henchman. It was a game she adored. How sly could she be? A bit of private theater between them, meant to be fun as well as financially rewarding for Brent.

A loud metallic click reverberated through the shop when he locked up behind her. He stood there patiently as he always did, waiting until she disappeared in the distance before turning out the lights. He checked his Sidekick one more time for a message.

Nothing.

Brent crammed it into the back pocket of his jeans and placed his white smock on its hook on the way to the back room. He unlocked the heavy steel back door and propped it open with a brick. His pickup truck sat right outside.

He turned to the white-faced German shepherd in one of the cages and opened the door to attach a leash. He didn't need it at all but wanted to keep in the habit of not having an open door and a freely roaming animal. He enforced the rules even on himself. It made him a better businessman. After all, that's what he was. A self-made businessman. In control of his shop, his life, and his future. An entrepreneur.

He lowered the truck's lift gate and patted it once. Long familiar with the routine, the dog hopped aboard and walked calmly into the cage bolted to the bed. Brent removed the leash, locked the cage, and turned back to the door.

As he walked back in to turn off the lights and lock up, the shepherd barked. A loud series of barks and yelps, followed by a low growl. The dog clawed at the cage door's latch.

Brent flipped off the lights and double-checked his stock of cleaning and grooming supplies for tomorrow. He turned around to the back door and the truck. The dog's agitation confused him.

"What's up, buddy? There a raccoon out there again?" he asked.

The dog's fur pointed in every direction as it jumped up and down in the cage. He didn't understand the dog's antics and kicked the brick aside to close the door.

A figure stepped out of the shadows behind him. One gloved hand slipped under his chin while the other seized the crown of his head. Their synchronized twist snapped his neck and dropped his body to the concrete floor.

The intruder unfolded a black tarpaulin on the ground and rolled Brent's body into it. He stood the lifeless cocoon on end and lowered it into the truck's bed next to the cage. The dog's head hung low in a rare expression of fear. It sniffed the tarp apprehensively but kept its gaze on the intruder. Predators respected other predators across species. Admiration for skill, risk, and reward—and for the privilege of continued existence—survived even among so-called domesticated animals.

Except, perhaps, for humans.

The killer closed the heavy steel door and ensured it had locked securely. He slipped into the truck's cab and drove off into the night.

Chapter One

AMY KELLEN stood in line at Starbucks, staring across the room at a small crowd of customers. They were animated, talking and roughhousing, clearly a group that knew each other well and enjoyed each other's company. She could easily be one of them. In her mid-twenties, slim, her hair pulled back in a ponytail. She was dressed for work—khakis, a V-neck sleeveless shirt, and a blazer. Appropriate, but not overdressed. She preferred it this way—"professional casual" she liked to call it.

As the long line snaked forward, her eyes cut over again to the assembly of people huddled around five nearby tables. Their conversations were loud, full of laughing and camaraderie, not at all concerned about anyone overhearing them. Quite the contrary—they appeared willing to let anyone join the club. She allowed one last glance their way before she stepped up to the counter.

"Hi, Amy! Bagel today?" the barista asked.

"No, I've got to go. I've got an appointment," she replied.

"Drinking and driving, huh?"

"Yeah, sort of," Amy answered after a short pause to catch the double entendre.

"Why don't you stay for a meeting sometime?" he asked, throwing a glance at the growing crowd of people.

Amy's reply was unconvincing. "I'll try. I promise."

The barista didn't ask for her order. Amy's visit on Tuesday was so routine the staff didn't need to hear it—they knew it by heart. She was the coffee equivalent of Norman walking into Cheers— "grande cappuccino" with four raw sugars. Amy paid for her drink and stepped down to the receiving area as she glanced once more at the energetic crowd. Sure looked like they were having fun.

A section of tables was roped off, and two people were hanging a large banner across one corner of the store: Deafcoffee.com in bright yellow text on a blue background. No way anyone could miss it. The laughter died down as a young man stood up on a pedestal and motioned for quiet. He attracted the attention of two patrons next to Amy as they waited for their drinks.

"What's that?" one of them asked the barista.

"It's a coffee club for deaf people," Amy explained without prompting. The barista looked at her and smiled as he returned to his steaming milk.

"No kidding," the young man replied. He noticed Amy for the first time. Five feet seven or so; 125 pounds including the purse. Her tan was a fifty-fifty blend of sun and spray, carefully applied over an athletic frame he only now fully appreciated. Her makeup was flawless—clearly what she spent the most time on—hazel eyes framed only faintly with liner, with an equally understated hint of color on her cheeks. Today her auburn locks were pulled back in a ponytail. "Are you with them?" he asked.

"No," she replied. "Well, yes, sort of. I mean, no, I'm not *with* them. I mean I know a little about them, but no, I don't know any of them."

The young man's face reflected his confusion. Even the barista looked dazed as he placed Amy's cappuccino on the counter.

"It's complicated," Amy muttered. She walked past them and out the door as the meeting got under way.

AMY SETTLED down in front of a large computer monitor in a small room at All Hands Video Relay Services. A camera atop the monitor stared directly at her. When engaged in conversation, her deaf caller was seated in front of a similar monitor, and his or her face filled the screen. A small picture-in-picture inset allowed Amy to see what the caller could see of her on the other end of the link. She'd initially found it very unnerving to see herself like that. But soon she accepted it for what it was—an assurance that her signs were visible to the person on the other end of the line. She hardly gave it a thought anymore.

She took a deep breath and adjusted the headphones. The adjustment was an automatic gesture; adjusting her mindset to the emotional needs of each caller was far more difficult. In fact, more often than not it was emotionally draining. She reminded herself that all down the hallway of the office complex, dozens of other video relay interpreters had to address the same feelings.

Video relay had made great strides in replacing the old Telecommunications Devices for the Deaf, the previous means for connecting the hearing and Deaf communities. TDDs were limited to text only, and were incredibly slow because typing and reading a conversation took a long time. The Internet changed all of that.

With high-speed video compression and Voice over Internet technology, it was possible for a deaf person to speak with a hearing person as if they were in the same room. It meant the Deaf community was more fully integrated into mainstream society.

American Sign Language is the primary language for over a million people in the United States, the fourth most common language behind English, Spanish, and Chinese. Unlike these languages, however, facial expressions, body movements, and placement of the signer's hands play important grammatical and contextual roles in the communication process.

As with regular phone services, the Federal Communications Commission regulated Video Relay Services. There were a number of firms in addition to All Hands contracted to provide the service, and offices were popping up in major cities throughout the country. Interpreters worked in shifts based on the ebb and flow of worldwide telecommunications, adding additional staff as patrons used the service more and more every day.

The deaf callers had to be comfortable in allowing the interpreter, a complete stranger, into the most intimate parts of their lives. Legal entanglements, lover's quarrels, a sick child at school, anything that commonly took place in the hearing world similarly took place within the Deaf community. The services were designed to remove any dissimilarities between the hearing and non-hearing worlds' calls—both should be convenient and private.

Enough reflection, Amy thought. Time to get to work. She pushed the cord off her leg and checked to see it was plugged in properly. It snaked down to a Rolm Series 412 commercial telephone receiver that was tied into the office's master computer server. A microphone stuck out of one earpiece on her headset and reached to within a couple of inches of her mouth. Facing the camera and monitor, Amy tapped the keyboard to route her first call of the day.

A boy of about twelve years old filled the screen. Amy's smile became wide and bright, her demeanor almost giddy.

"Hi, Wes!" she signed. He waved, signing back, but didn't speak. "Hi, Amy!"

The number for his call entered her computer and was routed through the phone system. After two rings someone picked up the other end of the line.

"Hey, Wes!" filled her headset.

Amy adjusted the headset volume down and signed to the camera. "Are you coming over to practice?"

"I can't," Wes replied in sign as he pouted. "I'm grounded."

"Don't be a chicken," she signed. "Sneak out of the house for crying out loud!"

"I can't," Wes signed.

"Come on! You would totally get away with it!" Amy spoke the words aloud, matching the intensity and enthusiasm of the speaker so her young caller would pick up visually all of the subtle nuances of his friend's rebuke. "I'm serious, dude, nobody has anything like this out there! You'll get past the semifinals into the regionals without breaking a sweat!"

Wes's response was fast and eager. Unlike Amy he was not speaking aloud—he only signed, which she then articulated aloud into the microphone.

"You guys practice without me tonight. I'll come by your house on Saturday before the tournament starts. Nobody can beat *us!*" she relayed.

ON ANOTHER call, Amy's face was dour and accusatory. The monitor framed a stern-faced man in a gray power suit and red tie. A huge bookcase overflowing with law books towered behind him. He appeared aggressive and angry as he forcefully signed to Amy, his hands audibly slapping into each other at times.

"My client will not accept a settlement offer of $400,000. Your client was legally drunk at the time of the accident, and we feel certain a jury will find in our favor. We're prepared to show not only the police videotape but also additional film that shows your client drinking and driving at another party a couple of nights later," Amy articulated into the microphone. A tinny high-pitched squeal on the other end of the line suggested opposing counsel was not overly enamored with these intentions.

DURING THE next call Amy's eyes became red, her signing interrupted by a frequent need to wipe away tears. She tried desperately to hold her emotions in check, to make it simply a job, but it wasn't working. She pushed through, hoping she wouldn't have to excuse herself from the call, and interpreted the devastating information coming through the headset.

"It's called non-Hodgkin's lymphoma. A cancer of the immune system," she signed, her throat tightening even in a whisper. "If we'd caught it earlier we might have better options. I'm sorry. I'm afraid all we can do is make her as comfortable as possible."

The woman on the screen sobbed openly at the worst news of her life. Amy ached to offer words of consolation, perhaps sympathy or encouragement, but knew she could not utter a word of her own. Rigid FCC rules bound video relay interpreters to a code of silence— they were to function like a piece of equipment, nothing more.

LATER IN the afternoon, Amy interpreted for an attractive young coed who tried to sign while also holding a cookbook and a glass of wine. The girl smiled mischievously.

"You should make shark steak kabobs on a bed of rice," Amy interpreted. "But let him grill—guys love fire! Afterwards, a little dessert in the Jacuzzi . . ."

Amy finished as the young woman reached for her wine. The delighted laughter of new love filled her headset.

AN EIGHTEEN-YEAR-OLD boy's piercing eyes filled the screen. Amy leaned in toward the camera to similarly fill his screen with her high cheekbones and long nose.

"Let's go," she signed. "Let's do it!" She giggled and signed simultaneously. "I can't believe we're getting married! Pick me up in an hour. If we miss that flight we're screwed!"

Amy relayed the young man's reply. "Don't you have to be twenty-one to get married?"

"No," Amy relayed from the voice in her earpiece, "you only have to be twenty-one to get into the casino . . ."

AMY REMOVED the headset and walked out of the relay room into the main hallway. She saw shadows against the frosted-glass doors behind which dozens of other phone calls were taking place. The routine capriciousness of daily contact between couples and coworkers, enemies and friends, families and strangers, was very draining. She'd only been in the job a few weeks, and the spectrum of human emotion poured into her lap every day continued to amaze her.

She entered the break room and purchased a Coke and a Milky Way candy bar from the vending machines before sitting down next to her pal Kathy Maynard.

"Wow!" she said, exasperated. "As a parent I sure hope someone would tell me if my daughter was eloping to Las Vegas!"

Kathy continued thumbing through the latest issue of *Vogue* as she spoke. "I think Celia's a little young for that. You've got a ton more worrying to do about other things before then."

Kathy and Amy had been friends in college, and when the time came to find a new job, in fact a new *career*, Kathy had been there for her. A true friend by every measure.

"Still! Married at *sixteen*? You want to call her parents and yell 'Lock her up!'" Amy replied.

"I don't think the FCC would appreciate that. Remember, when the call starts, you are just . . ."

". . . a dial tone, yeah, I know," Amy said. She sure would have liked to help with some of the gut-wrenching situations she'd communicated today. She shook her head. "I would just hate to be that poor woman when she wakes up tomorrow."

The FCC mandated that nothing a video interpreter ever heard on a phone call could be repeated to another party. Even if the conversation revealed a crime, they could not contact authorities. Interpreters were thrust into their callers' most intimate secrets. Because the FCC rigidly enforced this code of silence, callers were ensured their conversations were as secure as if they were conversing in person. The penalty for revealing a conversation was a felony, and prosecutors were certain to make examples of any interpreter foolish enough to be loose-lipped.

"Makes you realize what good dirt priests get to hear. They've got to be tempted from time to time," Kathy said.

"Aren't priests supposed to be experts at resisting temptation?" Amy asked.

"You would hope," Kathy replied.

"Hopefully they're more disgusted than tempted. I've seen stuff I never want to think about when I leave here," Amy said.

"I just had one of those," Kathy said. "Whole call—naked! Not Brad Pitt naked, either; more like . . . Larry King naked! I kept stumbling because I couldn't force myself to watch real closely."

"I know that guy! Thin, stringy hair, big lips, and a tattoo of a . . ."

". . . penguin over his groin! That's him!" Kathy sighed. "That's my Howard. I'm totally going to marry that guy someday! Fine, upstanding member of the community there, boy!" she joked.

"Yeah, well, speaking of *community*, I've got to get back in there. See you later."

Amy stood up and retrieved her drink can and candy wrapper, placing them in a nearby garbage can.

"Want to grab a drink after work tonight?" Kathy called after her.

"No, thanks. I can't. I've got plans," Amy replied.

Kathy eyed her suspiciously. "What kind of 'plans'?" she asked.

"I'm going to Whitaker's rally."

"Going to or working?"

Amy paused, unsure how indignant she wanted to appear. "I can do both, you know," she said finally.

"You aren't going for politics, you're going because you don't want to be alone! Why don't we get a drink?" Kathy asked.

"They hired me! I can't bail on them—they need an interpreter or the people won't know what's going on—they won't know the issues."

"You aren't going for issues, or for people. You said you wanted a job here so you could have a more normal schedule, yet you're still doing community interpreting."

"It's just a rally. It's no big deal," Amy said. She rolled her eyes and walked out of the break room. Kathy leaned out toward the hallway to yell.

"Reconsider that drink!"

WALKING THROUGH the cavernous Walter E. Washington Convention Center in D.C., Amy was taken aback by the grandeur of presidential politics. Banners and signs covered every square foot of wall space. Marquees directed delegates and representatives to break-out rooms all over the building. There were strategy sessions, seminars on grassroots movements, and tactical overviews of door-to-door campaigns. Every avenue of possible vote grabbing appeared covered, though the election was still months away.

She approached community interpreting with relish; perhaps because it was more personal than VRS work. No technological barriers between her and the community. Unlike an intimate conversation between two people, today she would interpret in front of an audience of thousands. While the speaker might be flamboyant and the subject matter a stretch of the truth (as she often thought was the case in politics), it didn't put her in the middle of something that tugged at her heart. She could remain relatively dispassionate.

Amy entered the auditorium and found her way down front to the stage. Because she had an all-access badge on a lanyard around her neck, the security guards barely acknowledged her and simply waved her through to the churning sea of humanity setting up the stage equipment. She walked to the back where the dressing rooms were and stopped to ask a production assistant for help.

"Excuse me," Amy said. "I'm looking for Mr. Whitaker's campaign coordinator, Jackie Hodge. Do you know where she is?"

"Yeah. I think they're tweaking his speech for the run-through when we get all this finished. Third dressing room on the right," he replied.

"Great, thanks."

Amy found the correct door and knocked. No one answered. She opened it and entered timidly.

"Hello? Ms. Hodge?" she called out.

As she stepped into the room, the bathroom door suddenly flew open. Jackie Hodge half tripped into the room.

"Oh my God, Glenn! I'm going to walk like a cowboy all night!" she exclaimed.

Hodge was a voluptuous dirty blonde in her early thirties. She was also naked as she wrapped her wet hair in a towel. Behind her, presidential candidate Glenn Whitaker jumped back into the shower he and Hodge had just stepped out of. Hodge spun around.

"Amy! Oh my God! You're early! I, uh, I . . . can you give me a moment?"

Amy turned around and pulled the dressing room door closed behind her.

GLENN WHITAKER was a man in his element. Pounding the podium

13

in front of a capacity crowd of thirty thousand people, the political pro had them right where he wanted them. Putty in his hands.

Amy was stage right, interpreting for a group in the front two rows. Jackie Hodge kept her distance along a nearby wall.

"What has happened to this party?" Whitaker bellowed. "What has happened to our basic values? Where is the high moral ground this party was built on?"

Amy stole a quick glance at Whitaker and cut briefly to Hodge, never slowing down her interpreting.

"Ladies and gentlemen, I promise that if you make me your presidential nominee I will return your party to you! I will bring back something called *accountability!*"

He gestured to quiet the screaming crowd.

"People are not accountable for their actions anymore. This is not the country I grew up in and it's not the country I want to raise my children in."

A brief expression of disdain slipped across Amy's face.

WHEN THE rally was over, Amy milled around backstage waiting for her check. An attractive woman walked up to her.

"Excuse me. I just wanted to introduce myself. I'm Sharon Whitaker, Glenn's wife."

Jackie Hodge, who was walking up with Amy's check, stopped short.

"Very nice to meet you," Amy replied, offering her hand.

"I just wanted to thank you for coming out tonight and providing this service to people. I think it's really important."

"That's very kind of you to say."

"Have you met my husband?" Sharon asked.

"I've seen him, but not formally met him, no," Amy replied.

"Jackie!" Sharon called to Hodge. "Have you seen Glenn? Is he in the shower?" Sharon turned to Amy. "He must shower three times a day!"

Hodge's face bordered on panic as Glenn Whitaker walked up to the group.

"Glenn," Sharon said, "did you meet Amy Kellen, your sign language interpreter?"

Whitaker turned white.

"What's wrong with you?" Sharon asked him.

He looked through all three women as the analysis paralysis seizing his brain manifested itself in lockjaw and a perversely awkward silence.

"I'm sure he's exhausted after the workout he had tonight," Amy offered. Hodge's eyes widened when Amy stuck out her hand. "Very nice to finally meet you. I've heard," she said, glancing at Hodge, "so much about you."

Whitaker hesitated, unsure how to react.

"Great to meet you as well, Amy." Pause. "Thank you *very* much!"

"Not at all," Amy smiled back at him.

Amy turned to Hodge and accepted the envelope with her check.

"Ride 'em, cowboy!" she muttered under her breath as she walked off.

Chapter Two

At All Hands the next day after the morning break, Amy put her headset back on and tapped a key on the computer to route the next call.

"All Hands VRS. May I have the number you want to call?"

The monitor popped to life. A large black man filled the screen. The scene behind him was disgusting. Trash was piled around the La-Z-Boy recliner he was fully reclined in, his feet up in an almost horizontal orientation. Several small children scurried around him, oblivious to the trash that covered the floor. The man began signing.

"I want to call a bridal shop," he said.

Amy nodded, seeing the number come in through the computer. It was a 704 area code—Charlotte, North Carolina. She tapped a few keys on the computer to finish making the call. Clicking filled her ears.

"Michael's Bridal—can I help you?" a woman's voice asked.

"Yes. This is interpreter 112 with All Hands VRS. I have a video relay call for this number," Amy said. "Are you familiar with Video Relay Service?"

"Of course. Happy to help," the woman replied.

"Go ahead, sir," Amy signed to the man in the chair.

"Hello. I'd like to order several dresses from your catalogue, please," he signed. Amy relayed the message.

"Certainly, sir. I can help you with that," the woman replied. "Can you give me the catalogue number?"

"5-0-7-0-0-0-6-5," the man read out.

"Great. What would you like to order?" she asked.

"I'd like five of the Forever Memory Collection series forty-five and five of the Precious Times series ninety-nine. I'd like the forty-

16

five series in white and the ninety-nines in ivory if that's possible. Sizes 8 through 10," he said.

"We can certainly do that. Is there anything else?" she asked.

"Yes. I'd like ten pairs of the Dominion open-toe shoes and ten pairs of the closed-toe. I need them in two pairs each of 7, 7½, 8, 8½, and 9."

She repeated the order back to Amy, who signed it to the man in the recliner. He nodded his agreement.

"Do you have the Trinity veils available in both white and ivory?" he asked.

"Yes. We have both in stock. Five of each then?" she anticipated.

He smiled widely. "Yes, thank you. I think that's all I need."

She repeated the order back to him. "How would you like to pay for this?" she asked.

"Visa," the man replied with a flourish. He provided the card number, expiration date, and three-digit security number. The woman repeated it back for his confirmation. In a moment the transaction was done.

"Would you like this shipped?" she asked.

"Please," he replied. "The address is 4213 Greenway Drive, number 145, Chattanooga, Tennessee, 37411," he read from a piece of paper. Amy heard the woman repeat the series back to her through the headphones and once again confirmed the information with him.

"Thank you for your order," the woman said.

"Thank you," the man replied. He turned off his computer link with a remote control.

Amy sat back. Why in the world would he need ten wedding dresses? He didn't look like a businessman. And why didn't he use a tax identification number if he was purchasing product to resell? He was paying retail and ordering straight from the catalogue. Oh well. She'd given up trying to understand people, their odd ways and purposes for calling each other. It rarely made a lot of sense to her.

Then again, her own phone calls wouldn't make much sense to anyone else, either. Even in her short period with All Hands she'd figured out that most conversations were clipped. Not that people were rude or trying to be evasive. Most people simply use a type of linguistic shorthand full of historical context known only to them. Everyone has so little time. When they are on the phone they try to be efficient, relaying the maximum amount of information as quickly as possible.

She keyed the computer to pull in the next call from the queue.

"Good afternoon. Thank you for using All Hands VRS. How can I help you?" she signed.

Amy's face tightened. She had come to recognize a fair number of callers. Working regular hours, she would inevitably synchronize with certain people's schedules. For some, there were business calls to be made. Others were stay-at-home moms with quiet time while their kids were at school. Still others were shut-ins or otherwise not busy during the day, with little else to do but pick up the phone and call someone.

Sammy was one of the latter. He was about forty-five years old, hard looking, never impolite, but definitely not someone she'd invite to dinner. He was a real weirdo. Not rude, but not friendly, either. Habitually disheveled, his greasy hair was combed over to one side. Today his shirt was unbuttoned all the way to his very hairy belly. Oversize hearing aids protruded from his ears.

"I'm placing an international call to Eastern Europe," he signed. "I trust that won't be a problem?"

Amy signed back. "No, not at all. Go ahead with the number. Who are you calling?"

"His name is Lenny. He knows how this works," Sammy replied.

In Amy's headset, a gruff voice answered the ringing telephone line.

"Yeah?" A thick but nonspecific accent filled her ears.

"It's Sam. How are you fixed right now?" Sammy signed. Amy repeated the question into the microphone.

"You call me in the middle of the damned night, you psycho-pathic shit?"

"It's not the middle of the night where I am. That's the only place that counts," Sammy said.

"The hell you say. I got plenty of other clients."

"They don't pay you the way I pay you. Answer the question. How are you fixed right now? Anything new?"

"Yeah. I've got some new stuff. I think you'd like it," Lenny said.

"Different from last time?"

Sammy picked up a photograph from a pile on the table nearby. Pornography. A child in a suggestive pose. Amy felt her stomach heave.

"It's dangerous to move this any way other than the Internet. You're the one at risk of being caught—not me."

"That's what encryption is for," Amy forced herself to relay.

"Do you want something from inventory, or were you interested in a custom product?" Lenny asked.

"Custom."

"I'll send a picture or two. You decide who you want."

Amy heard tapping on a computer keyboard through her headset. A moment later Sammy's computer emitted a soft tone. He looked at the laptop.

"Got it," Sammy reported. He printed the photograph on a nearby printer, unconcerned that Amy could see it.

"They're good," the thick accent said in Amy's ears. "They're young. You want to place an order then, yes? Something special?"

"Sure, why not?"

A pause.

"Who would you like to see? What would you like to see done?" Lenny asked.

Sammy held up a picture. "This one. Carmen. How about her?"

"She's very cute. Very innocent. What would you like?"

"Tie her up."

"Anything specific?" Lenny asked.

Amy's revulsion was palpable. It was all she could do to continue. She wondered if she could possibly fake a glitch in the system and

19

end the call, but knew the pair would just reconnect with another interpreter.

"Yeah. I want video, not just stills. I like the crying."

"You want her to cry out your name? That's pretty popular."

"Sure," Sammy said, "why not?" He was touching himself now, stroking his crotch with one hand when not signing. "You're sure she's innocent?"

"*In every sense of the word* as you Americans like to say," Lenny replied.

"We've got a deal. How long to deliver?"

"Around two weeks, but it's not cheap."

"Cost is not a factor."

"I'll let you know a more concrete delivery time in a day or two. There might be more expenses. Incidentals, you know."

"Don't even think about jacking up the price," Sammy replied, glaring from the monitor as he abruptly terminated the call.

THE OFFICES of grief counselor Dr. Reginald J. Brown were thoughtfully decorated. Muted fabrics with soft textures and colors. At the same time, there was a flavor of individuality to the decor that was clearly from outside the Beltway. The office was a beautiful but unabashedly masculine reflection of the low-country marshlands of South Carolina. Photos adorning the room reflected life on the shrimp boats of Beaufort. Reggie Brown had an MD from Wake Forest and had completed his clinicals at Johns Hopkins, but the boy knee deep in mud in the many black-and-white photos was still very much a part of the grown man sitting nearby. He wasn't ashamed to show it off.

Instead of the high-backed leather chair that so many other clinicians used, Reggie Brown preferred Pawley's Island wicker chairs. A good bit cheaper, a lot cooler in the summer, and an all-around icebreaker when new a patient showed up. It was easier confiding in a man who was so open about his own past. One could literally watch him grow up on the walls around the room. Hokey to some of his highbrow power elite clients in Washington, perhaps, but he wasn't hurting for business.

Amy sat across from him; a glass-topped wicker table was between them, with two iced teas on it. He pulled his notes out of a file.

"So, how are you today?" he asked.

"I'm OK."

"You don't look OK."

"There was this creepy caller at work earlier."

"Anything you want to talk about?"

"I can't. Besides, I was screwed up before I went in."

"Doesn't say much about our sessions."

She made a face. "You know what I mean."

"Did you really think you weren't going to be affected by this?"

"No, I just didn't expect it to be this . . ."

"Personal?"

"I guess."

"He was your husband. You should be sad, especially around the anniversary of his death." He paused for a moment as he considered a different tack. "How's the weather treating you?" he asked.

Her gaze fell to the floor.

"I'm better," she said quietly.

"Rainy season's started."

She nodded her reply.

"Don't you think we should talk about it?"

"No. I want it to go away. I've been dreading this," she replied.

"A year is a milestone," he continued. "It's time for you to move on with your life."

Easy for you to say, she thought. Not wanting a confrontation, she chose her words carefully.

"I don't know how."

He leaned back in the chair and shuffled the file on his lap. Pursuing this line of inquiry was clearly going nowhere. He decided on a different approach.

"This new job of yours. Tell me about it. Do you like it?"

"It's OK. I've only been doing it a couple of months. Sometimes I feel like a hack."

"A hack?" he repeated. "Why would you feel that way?"

"Jeff's gone. He was my only real link to the Deaf community."

"So without him you don't matter?"

"I don't think so, no."

"Seems a little stereotypical to me," Brown observed. "So why not forge your own identity?"

Amy shifted uncomfortably in her chair. "What do you mean?" she asked.

"Jeff was deaf. I understand *his* connection. But now that he's gone, you need your own identity."

"Meaning?"

"You need to find a reason to remain part of that world. Being an interpreter is your new profession, but it's disconnected from your life, the life you have now. You need a purpose."

"What kind of purpose?" she asked.

"Establish Amy Kellen as her own person. Find something important to the community and seize it. That way you're not referred to simply as someone's wife, but as Amy Kellen—a member of the community by choice versus chance. You had career aspirations before Jeff's death. You can't change things halfway. You need to jump into your new life with both feet firmly planted—like you're planning to be there a while."

SEVERAL INTERPRETERS were enjoying lunch in the All Hands break room. A television at the front of the room featured all five of the current Democratic presidential front-runners bickering among themselves. A reporter closed with an interview with DNC chairman Chris Billings.

"It's going to be a difficult decision not only for the delegates, but also for party leaders. We've got to get our muscle behind the right candidate to take back the White House. That means not fracturing over multiple candidates and diluting the momentum we've built up over these past few months," Billings said into the camera.

"Mr. Billings's concern over keeping the party focused on a single candidate is going to remain a tough sell until a clear majority of the delegates have indicated who they want to see run for president," the reporter concluded.

Amy stood up from the table and tossed the remains of her lunch into the trash can. A boring day, like so many before. It was stable—no travel involved, no exposure to the elements—but it was pretty darn dull a good bit of the time. She was not one to spend a lot of time on the phone with her own interests or issues. Having to interpret the same for others was much more tiring than she'd anticipated.

She closed the frosted-glass door of her VRS room and settled into the chair. She put the headset in a comfortable position and smiled into the camera as the next call came in.

"All Hands VRS; how can I help you? Oh, hi, Mr. Kensington. How are you this afternoon?" she asked.

Harold Kensington, the former attorney general to two presidents, now senior consultant to a presidential hopeful, stared ruefully into the camera.

"Good day, Amy. I'm well, thank you. How are you?" he said.

"Great, sir. How can I help you?" she signed.

"I've got to call Chris Billings. The number is coming through now."

Amy checked the phone and waited for someone to answer on the other end.

"Good evening; this is All Hands VRS. I've got a call from Mr. Harold Kensington to Mr. Chris Billings," she said into the microphone.

"This is Chris Billings," a voice replied.

"Good evening, sir. I'm video interpreter number 112 for Mr. Kensington. I believe you're familiar with our service, is that correct?"

"Yes, thank you," Billings replied.

"Very good. Please begin your call."

"Evening, Hal. How'd the polling plan work out today?" Billings asked.

"The plan is fine," Kensington answered. "It's the result that bothers me. We're spending a pile of money on this and not getting any real bang for our buck."

"You can't win an election without data, Hal. We've got to have numbers. The party can't pick a candidate until we know what the people want." Chris Billings's words filled Amy's ears as she signed.

"Ah, don't give me that crap," Kensington replied, waving his hand. "Polling data isn't about the people. It's about winning. That's what elections are—winning."

"I understand that, Hal, but there are other candidates. If you don't think the polling supports you, maybe it's best for your man to drop out."

"You'd like that, wouldn't you?" Kensington glared into the monitor. "Thompson can win, Chris. And you know it."

Amy was taken aback—she'd never seen him look like that before.

"We can't put the party muscle behind someone until all the facts are in."

"Chris, I suspect you recall that I spent a few years in military intelligence when I was young. We used to run honeypot operations in Germany back in the cold war days. We recruited hookers, cleaned them up, and gave them some training, then set them up as mistresses for key East German leaders. A messy bit of business, but it was a messy time. Always got good intel from them, but it came at a heavy price. The hookers always had the information before we did and could act on it faster. You never could trust them. Know what I mean?"

A white-faced German shepherd walked into view behind Kensington. He reached down to pet the animal, but missed.

"Hey, Champ. How you doing?" Kensington said. "How was the groomer's today, huh? Geez, you look terrible, buddy."

Kensington turned back to the camera and resumed talking.

24

"I'm not talking about polling. I'm talking about saving our money and best strategies until closer to the election. We're burning bucks and bandwidth arguing among ourselves right now. We've got to save something for the fall sweeps or the electorate will just tune us out," Kensington signed.

"Media campaigns are important, Hal. You've got to keep that electorate engaged."

"Engage them, but don't overwhelm them! We've been switching subjects every day. I'm having trouble remembering what all we've worked on."

"Hal, if you're not comfortable with the way the campaign's going, I don't understand why you don't . . ."

Without warning, the German shepherd suddenly jumped up and clamped its teeth on Harold Kensington's throat. The old man jumped in surprise. His eyes widened in panic as he fell onto the floor.

"Oh my God!" Amy yelled.

"What's that, Hal?" Billings asked through the earphones.

Kensington thrashed around, his office chair slipping away on its rollers. He knocked aside a small tray, sending coffee and a pastry flying out of sight. He grabbed handfuls of fur, pulling furiously on the dog, but to no avail. He punched the animal several times, but because he was lying on his back, his strikes were glancing at best. The dog pulled him to one side. Kensington's left arm was too close for an effective punch, the right arm too far away. He flailed wildly, unable to get his legs underneath him to stand up. The dog was too strong.

"Did the connection drop off, ma'am?" Billings asked in Amy's ear.

She was transfixed, frozen in horror. Her muscles refused to act.

As Kensington grew tired, the dog moved again, and was now standing on his chest. His jaws were still locked tight on the old man's throat. His fur stood on end as his claws ripped into the expensive fabric of Harold Kensington's suit.

"Oh my God! Stop! Stop!" Amy yelled again as she pounded her fists on the screen. She hopped out of the chair and put her face only inches from the monitor. She reached for the phone but stopped. Could she legally cut off the connection herself? She looked back to the monitor and started again for the phone, only to stop again.

"Hal? Are you there?" Billings asked impatiently.

Amy sobbed as her hands covered her face. She didn't know what to do. She didn't know how to help. How could she just sit there and do nothing? There must be some way to stop this animal.

"What the devil is going on over there?" Billings asked tersely.

Amy pulled off her headset and let it drop to the ground as she stared up at the ceiling.

"Somebody help me!" she screamed.

Chapter Three

DETECTIVE MIKE Seers stopped, as he always did, and took a good long look around the crime scene. "Heartbeat moments," they had called it at the police academy. Take a few heartbeats when you first arrive at the scene and look it over. Soak it all in. This was the sole purview of an investigating officer. It was a private moment, an ethereal link between him and the victim. He could never explain it in a report, nor describe it to a jury. It was his and his alone. It deserved his quiet respect.

Mike Seers understood respect. It had been whipped into him as a child, and he'd channeled that knowledge to whip young officers into shape in the service. He still sported a close-cropped military-style haircut despite the fact that he'd not worn a uniform in over twenty years.

He refused his captain's repeated requests to wear a tie, preferring a button-down shirt and sport coat. Younger detectives chided him about his coats being older than they were. In some cases, they were correct. But Seers didn't mind. He bought quality, and unless he decided to start running marathons in the pouring-down rain, a well-made sport coat should be more than up to the task of his meticulous manner.

He didn't rush, didn't hurry. Sometimes criminals counted on that—investigators rushing through things and not being thorough. He was unquestionably thorough. He took his time and made sure i's were dotted and t's were crossed. He'd never lost a case on a procedural technicality, nor on cross-examination in court. He did his homework. That homework always began with a measured, silent sweep of the scene as soon as he exited his car. Today would be no exception.

Police tape held back the growing crowd of neighbors outside Harold Kensington's stately Georgetown home. A collective gasp echoed across the street as the coroner's staff wheeled Kensington out the front door on a gurney. Several people made the sign of the cross and whispered quiet prayers.

Inside, crime scene technicians made quick work of Kensington's office. A small pool of blood stained the Persian rug in front of his VRS machine. They photographed the entire scene, cataloguing everything they took and finishing in less than thirty minutes. There wasn't much evidence to compile. His own dog had killed him. It was pretty cut-and-dried.

Detective Seers spoke into a police radio outside the house. "I'll get statements over here and check into it." He turned off the radio. "Damn!"

A man walked toward him in an apparent daze. His eyes were red and glassy from crying, but the expensive coat and tie were a dead giveaway. Political consultant. Somebody's handler. Seers stopped him.

"Can I help you?" he asked.

"I'm Dan Banducheck, Mr. Kensington's aide."

"What can you tell me about this?" Seers asked.

"Nothing. I can't believe it happened."

"The police called you?"

"Yes. He had an in-case-of-emergency entry on his cell phone listing me and one of his sons as primary contacts."

"And the dog?" Seers asked.

"The police already had him locked in the mudroom. I've not even seen him."

"You're here often?"

"I've been Harold Kensington's aide for almost two years, since Phil Thompson conned him out of retirement. He's had that dog forever. I can't believe this happened. There's no reason for it."

"So, there are no witnesses?"

"When I came in, the machine was still on. He was apparently in the middle of a VRS call."

"VRS?"

"Harold Kensington had been losing his hearing for several years. It was the main reason he retired. He was still in full control of his faculties. The man was scary sharp. Phenomenal intellect. He used the VRS to place phone calls."

"What's VRS?" Seers repeated.

"Video Relay Service. It connects a deaf caller to a hearing caller through an interpreter on a video link over the Internet. It's made phone communication a lot easier for deaf and hard of hearing people. It's really quite something," he effused.

"Did you have any trouble communicating with him?"

"No. I've learned a fair amount of sign language."

"And you used this VRS for phone calls with him, too?"

"Sometimes. He can't hear over a regular telephone, even the type where you can boost the volume way up. People on the other side of the room could hear the call, but he couldn't. That's when we learned about VRS."

"He was deaf but had a cell phone?"

"He was a proud man, Detective. He carried it, but in truth he only used it for text messaging. He had the same number for ten years, and hated the idea of giving it up. Have to keep up appearances in politics—otherwise you're perceived as weak."

"Got it. We should probably pay a visit to this VRS facility to see what they can tell us. I'd like you to ride along if you don't mind. I'm going to need an experienced ear, or—I guess more correctly—an experienced eye to help me sort this out. Show me the lanes in the road, if you will. Is that a problem?" Seers asked.

"Not at all," Banducheck said. "Happy to help any way I can."

AMY SAT at the break-room table with a cold cloth draped across her forehead. Her eyes were puffy, her cheeks flushed. The other interpreters had been coming in and out as the call volume allowed, simultaneously trying to learn what had happened and to console their colleague. Kathy was sitting with her, as she had been since Amy's blood-curdling cry emptied every VRS room in the office.

All Hands site manager Carol Burdick brought Seers and Banducheck into the room. Carol was in her late fifties, a short Italian grandmother who was both mother hen and slave master to her young charges, finessing her matronly advice with a firm hand of control. She pointed Amy out to Seers.

"OK, Miss . . . Kellen. What can you tell me about the victim?" Seers asked.

"She can't tell you anything!" Carol said as she positioned herself between Seers and Amy. Seers was taken aback.

"Beg your pardon?" he asked.

"She can't tell you anything. The FCC forbids interpreters from discussing the content of a call, the callers, or anything they've heard," Burdick said.

"She's right, Detective. The law is very specific. They cannot repeat anything they saw or heard," Banducheck offered.

Seers eyed him closely. "Let me guess. You're a lawyer?" he asked.

Banducheck nodded. "Afraid so. But if it helps you any, I passed on private practice and got into politics instead."

"No," Seers said, "that doesn't help. Moreover, it doesn't leave me many options."

"Can't I just . . ." Amy started.

"No! Don't say a word," Carol retorted.

"The protection afforded by the FCC rules on video interpretation is one of the reasons Hal felt so confident about continuing to work even after his hearing failed," Banducheck explained.

"He was such a nice old man," Amy said quietly.

"Yes, he was," he said. He extended a hand to her. "I'm Dan. I've seen you on-screen a few times."

"Yes," Amy replied. "I recognize you as well. The police called you?"

Banducheck nodded. "You saw what happened?" he asked.

Amy nodded back.

"That's great. You saw the incident but can't shed any light on what happened," Seers interrupted. "OK, forget the conversation for a moment. Did you see the animal kill Mr. Kensington?" he asked Amy.

Her face flushed again. "His name is Champ. He loved that dog," she whispered.

"What's that?" Seers asked, moving closer to her.

"He babied it. I can't believe it did that to him."

"Did you see . . . Champ . . . a lot during calls?" Seers asked.

"Yes. He was always around," Amy replied, as Dan nodded in agreement. "He was always gentle and loving to that old man. And he was the same to Champ. His wife is dead, his children grown and gone. Champ was all he had at home."

"Was there anything unusual about him tonight?" Seers asked.

"Don't answer that!" Carol said. "Don't say *anything* about Mr. Kensington's appearance."

"I meant the *dog*. What was the dog like?" Seers said.

"He looked disheveled. Unkempt. Mr. Kensington took good care of him. Maybe too good. It looked like Champ had gained some weight. I guess Mr. Kensington didn't have time to properly exercise him, what with the campaign and all," Amy said.

Banducheck's gaze fell to the floor; possibly he felt guilty about agreeing with her last point. Seers continued writing his notes.

"Detective, I've got about ten thousand phone calls I need to make. If you don't mind, I'd like to get going," Dan said finally.

Seers stared at him a few seconds, considering. "Yeah, I can't see any reason to keep you. I don't think there's anything you can really contribute in here."

He motioned to one of the uniformed officers standing around the table.

"Can you take Mr. Banducheck back to Kensington's place, please?"

Banducheck stuck a hand out to Amy. "I'm very sorry you had to see that tonight," he said.

"Thank you," she replied softly.

The officer and Banducheck passed a man on his way in through the front door.

He was tall, in his mid-thirties, with wavy, shoulder-length hair. He was neatly dressed—a dark suit and tie against a white shirt. Kathy eyed him admiringly, despite the solemn circumstances. Carol Burdick jumped to her feet.

"You can't just come waltzing in here. What do you want? Are you with the press? Get out of here!" she yelled.

He reached into his pocket and produced a brown leather wallet containing a badge. "Heath Rasco, U.S. Secret Service," he said.

"Secret Service? Was Kensington under protection?" Seers asked.

"No, but his boss is. Harold Kensington was the chief political strategist for Phil Thompson's presidential campaign."

"So, if he's not under protection, why are you here?" Seers asked.

"Oh, the service thought I might be useful," Heath said.

"Why?"

"I have a unique insight into the Deaf community," Heath replied. He pushed a lock of hair back to reveal a hearing aid.

"A *deaf* Secret Service agent?" Seers asked incredulously.

"Sure. I blend in. Everyone in the service wears an earpiece," Heath replied.

"Everyone whispers into their cuffs," Seers muttered.

Heath pulled up his sleeves. "Sorry to disappoint you, Detective. I don't even have a secret decoder ring."

"You don't appear deaf to me," Seers noted sarcastically.

"I hear enough, Detective. I'm not deaf—call it 'hard of hearing' if you like," Heath pointed out.

"What's the difference?" Seers asked.

Heath flicked the bifocals hanging from a lanyard atop Seers's chest with one finger. "Roughly the difference between wearing glasses and being blind," he said.

Carol and Kathy exchanged glances, impressed.

"Great," Seers noted. "How are you supposed to help?"

Heath ignored him and addressed the interpreters around the table. "Good evening, everyone. I'm sorry for the trouble you've had tonight. I promise to make this as quick and painless as possible, OK?"

Amy nodded.

"Phil Thompson took a crash course on ASL. He's pretty good. Harold Kensington asked me to get involved with Thompson's security detail since I could help foster communication between him and the service. I also helped Mr. Thompson with his signing. I know the Deaf community pretty well. I'm a native, born and raised here. I'm a Gally grad," he said.

"A what?" Seers asked.

"Gallaudet? Really?" Kathy responded.

"The Deaf school?" Seers asked.

"Yes. I majored in criminology and psychology. I started out in computer and telecommunications fraud before moving into special services. My specialty is interpreting body language for law enforcement."

"That must be interesting. Do you work much with people like Detective Seers?" Carol asked.

"Though we use many similar methods and tactics, we tend to chase after very different kinds of people," Heath said.

"What do you mean?" Kathy asked.

"Detective Seers deals mainly with localized threats. There may be a nutcase on occasion, but they are usually sloppy and make mistakes. Isn't that correct, Detective?"

"Yes, for the most part," Seers replied.

"The Secret Service, on the other hand, deals with a lot of rational psychopaths. They don't make stupid mistakes, so we have to force them into making smart ones they're unprepared for."

"How do you do that exactly?" Carol asked.

"We have a number of ways," Heath replied. "For instance, do any of you know what a 'tell' is?"

"*Tell?*" Kathy repeated.

"A movement or mannerism that tells another person something about you without you saying a word," Heath replied. "Secret Service agents try to recognize tells to identify the one guy in a crowd that might be planning an attack."

"Sounds like a lot of black magic to me," Kathy offered.

"Not really. You spend your days face-to-face with a lot of people. It might be useful to you. Let me show you how it works."

Heath took a piece of blank paper and drew a face on it. Then he bisected the face horizontally and vertically, cutting it into four quarters.

"Pay attention to where someone looks when they talk to you. You can gain quite a bit from the direction their eyes move."

He scribbled on the paper and turned to Seers.

"Detective, I'm going to ask you three questions. Lie to me with one of your answers."

"OK," Seers replied. "Shoot."

"Where were you born?"

"Phoenix, Arizona."

"What is your favorite dessert?"

"Chocolate cake."

"What was the color of your first bike?"

"Red."

Heath scribbled in three of the four quarters on the paper. He circled the lower left quarter.

"You lied about the dessert. What's your real favorite?"

Seers's face lit up. "Hey! That's right! Wow! How'd you do that?"

"It takes more effort to lie than to tell the truth. More importantly, lying takes place in a different part of the brain. To recall a memory, people often look up and to the left."

"Really?" Carol asked.

"It's not a precise science, but it's a useful field technique to help determine if someone is telling you the truth. Obviously we can't strap every potential wacko on the street to a lie detector to find out if he plans to shoot the president. So we have little techniques like this to help us weed out the normal weirdos."

"So how do you know if someone's lying?" Seers asked.

"When they fabricate a memory, people generally look down and to the left," Heath replied.

"That's awesome," Kathy said, smiling.

Detective Seers flipped his notebook forward a few pages.

"Do you mind if I take a few notes?" he asked.

Everyone looked at him.

"It could be useful for this Damato case I'm working on," he added awkwardly.

"Sure, write it up all you want. But I've also got some cheat sheets I use in training in my briefcase. Why don't you all take one?" Heath said.

He handed out several. Seers folded one up and placed it in his jacket pocket.

"Well, I think we've taken up more than enough of your time. Any more questions, Detective?"

"Not right now. Ms. Kellen, I'd suggest you go home and try to relax. If you think of anything you're allowed to tell us, please give me a call." He handed her a business card. "My cell is on the back."

Heath followed Seers out of the office and closed the door behind them.

"I don't think you'll get any more, not that she said much to begin with," Heath said when they were far enough away.

Seers flipped through a few pages of his notebook, looking back toward the office before responding.

"Do you think she can handle this? Can she get counseling without talking about what she saw?" Seers asked.

"I don't know. This technology is so new; I doubt anything like this has happened before. Maybe her doctor can prescribe something for her. You know, help her sleep?" Heath suggested.

AMY ROLLED around on the bed. It was 2:38 according to her bedside clock. She couldn't sleep. Couldn't get the scene out of her mind.

The awful image of Champ with his jaws clamped tightly on Harold Kensington's throat. What would possess him to do that?

She hadn't interpreted for Kensington in several weeks, which was in itself unusual. He was a very busy man. Lots of people wanted to talk with him. She'd been privy to conversations with the White House, several big-name national news anchors, even heads of state in Canada and Britain. It was all very exciting. Most were related to Phil Thompson's presidential bid, but others were just longtime friends of a man who'd helped many people over the course of his career.

And she'd watched him die. She had done nothing, other than scream like a child. She rolled over again, unable to shake the incredible guilt she felt. She pulled up on one elbow and punched the pillow over and over.

She'd done *nothing*.

She couldn't imagine what must have gone through his mind, knowing she was there watching, expecting her to do something, *anything*, to help him. Did he think about his children? Were they in his final thoughts? Was he thinking about the unfinished business of Thompson's campaign? Did he think Chris Billings would do something when he didn't continue with the call? When did he realize that he was going to die with Amy looking right at him?

She rolled back to the other side of the bed and shivered at the thought. He'd had to be looking at the camera, desperately hoping that she would somehow help him. Instead, she'd simply sat there, watching, offering no assistance while a man she'd come to know and admire died a horrific and lonely death.

She buried her head in the pillow so her sobbing wouldn't wake Celia. She prayed no one would ever know how she'd let Harold Kensington down.

AMY SPREAD the morning paper across the kitchen table as Celia played energetically on the floor nearby. Amy had barely slept a wink all night, her headache magnifying the stupor she already felt. She jumped when the phone rang.

"Hello?" Amy mumbled.

"Hey! How are you?" Kathy asked.

Amy glanced at the newspaper's front-page article about Harold Kensington's death. The caption below Champ's picture noted he'd been placed in a kennel awaiting a judge's decision on whether he should be put down as a violent animal.

"I'm OK," Amy said finally.

"I can't *see* you, but I can *tell* you're lying," Kathy said.

Amy allowed a tired laugh.

"Didn't sleep much, huh?" Kathy asked.

"No, not really. When Celia wasn't crying, I was dreaming about Champ biting down on that poor old man."

"What are you doing now?"

"Reading the paper. I can't believe he's dead. His address is in here—he only lived a few blocks from me."

"Amy . . ." Kathy said.

"How could he live so close by and I didn't know it?" Amy asked.

"You don't exactly hang out in the same circles. You didn't have much in common," Kathy pointed out.

"I guess."

"He was an interpreting client. I'll grant you that living nearby probably got you a lot more work with him since you could be available quickly as long as you had a babysitter. And yes, I know he liked to use you for his VRS work, too. Whenever he popped up in my queue he would ask if you were working."

"Really?" Amy asked. "That's so sweet."

"Listen, you need to get out. Get this out of your head for a little while."

"I can't. Celia's . . ."

"I'll come get Celia. I don't have to be in until three and we could hit the playground. You could take a nap," Kathy said.

"I don't want to sleep. Every time I close my eyes I see it over and over."

"Maybe Detective Seers was right. Maybe you should see a doctor," Kathy replied. She paused. "Did you tell Dr. Brown about it?"

"I can't. You know I can't."

"You don't have to give him the gory details, just the fact that you saw someone die," Kathy said.

"You think it could affect me somehow?" Amy asked.

"I can't imagine how it wouldn't," Kathy said. "I know it would affect me, and I didn't lose a husband last year."

"Yeah, maybe," Amy said after a moment.

She folded up the section about Kensington's death.

"Do you want me to pick up something for you?" Kathy asked.

Amy eyed Champ's picture on the folded-up newspaper. She hesitated before speaking.

"No. Actually, there's something I'd like to do today. I'll take you up on your offer. If you can watch Celia, I'll run a few errands. It won't take long."

"I'll be over in a little while," Kathy said.

"Thanks."

AMY WALKED hesitantly in front of the cages of barking dogs. She had never liked animal shelters. Too much noise. An employee training a dog nearby addressed her.

"Can I help you?" he asked. His voice was airy and slurred. A deaf person's voice.

Amy involuntarily jumped, scaring them both. She blushed.

"Yes. Do you work here?" she asked in sign language while mouthing the words at the same time.

"Yes," he replied, happy for a visitor who used ASL. "I'm Jim Skelton. What can I do for you?"

Jim's voice was very similar to her husband's in tone and tenor. It was reassuring and relaxing to hear it again after a year without Jeff.

"Hi. I'm Amy Kellen. I'm looking for the German shepherd the police brought in the other night," she said.

"It's locked up," he replied.

"I know. I was just hoping to see it."

"Are you the owner?"

"No, it's just, that is, I was just hoping to see it. That's all," she said uncomfortably. She had no idea what this would accomplish, but somehow felt compelled to at least see the dog—as if seeing Champ could help her understand why he had attacked his beloved owner.

Jim Skelton looked around—they were alone. He gestured for her to follow as he unlocked the door. A lone dog was inside the enclosure of a quarantined area, caged separately from the other animals.

"Here he is," Jim signed.

Amy stared. Champ appeared even more disheveled in person than he had on the monitor.

"I don't understand how he—" she started, when the dog suddenly leaped up against the cage at them, growling and baring his fangs. They both jumped back.

"Down!" Jim yelled.

"Oh my God!" Amy cried.

The dog tried to climb the chain-link cage, digging his paws into openings, saliva slinging everywhere as he barked.

"I don't understand what's going on!" Amy cried.

The dog bellowed, leaped up on the gate, fell backward, and then jumped again, biting at the wire.

Amy ran out of the kennel.

Chapter Four

It had been a mercifully quiet shift at All Hands. After helping a teenager on a homework assignment with his tutor, Amy prepared for her next call. Kathy tapped on the door and stuck her head in.

"You've got a call on hold. Line four," she said.

"Who is calling me here?" Amy asked.

"Not the office line. The relay number. Someone asked for interpreter 112," Kathy explained.

"Oh, OK," Amy replied, looking over at the blinking phone console.

"You're starting to get established. That's great!" Kathy said.

"I don't know about that," Amy replied.

"Hey, it usually takes years before an interpreter gets 'by name' requests. Usually it's for a particular expertise, like a deaf Spanish speaker who needs to call a hearing English speaker, so they want a bilingual interpreter. Some folks set themselves up as subject matter experts for scientists or academics—whenever the language is industry exclusive or highly technical. I met a guy at a conference last year that specialized in Klingon and traveled to all the Star Trek seminars around the country! Or maybe you just have a fan," Kathy quipped.

That made sense. But Amy was still new and didn't have any particular specialty—just a few clients from her community interpreting days who occasionally called through her just to stay in touch. It was good for them—and quite frankly, it was good for her, too. Nice to see friendly faces every now and again.

She punched line four on the phone system and spoke into the microphone. "All Hands video relay. This is interpreter 112. Can I help you?"

"I got ripped off!" a voice bellowed through her earphones. Amy winced and turned down the volume.

"Excuse me! Please don't yell. I'm wearing earphones. I'm sorry—who do you want to call?" Amy asked.

"I don't know. You made the call! You tell me!" the woman replied, still talking way too loudly for Amy's preference. "You people are ripping off small businesses! I want my dresses back!"

Amy frowned. What was this woman talking about? "Ma'am, I don't know what you mean. I haven't purchased any dresses."

"Not you. Someone you interpreted for ordered a bunch of dresses a few days ago."

Amy interpreted a lot of phone-based catalogue orders. She vaguely remembered someone ordering dresses. "Who are you again, please?" Amy asked.

"My name is Diane Similton. I own Michael's Bridal in Charlotte. You helped me with an order last week for ten dresses that were shipped to an address in Tennessee."

Amy thought again. "Five white, five ivory—is that right?" she asked, wondering how she'd misinterpreted the order.

"Yes! I want my dresses back!" Diane repeated.

"Back, ma'am?" Amy replied, not expecting a return to originate from the store rather than the customer.

"That credit card was stolen," Diane continued. "I shipped ten dresses to the address you gave me, and it's not a real address."

"What do you mean—'not a real address'?" Amy asked.

"It's one of those private mailbox places. You know, a print shop, mailbox, and shipping joint. But the addresses people rent sound like homes or private businesses," Diane explained.

Amy knew them. She even had one. Jeff had set it up when they were traveling so that their mail didn't fill the box at home and alert people that they were out of town. It was a good safety mechanism. She'd never thought that people would care if it were a mailbox or a real address.

41

"OK. So the address was a mailbox. I don't see the problem," Amy said.

"The address had an auto forward to another address. In *Africa*," Diane shouted again. "My dresses are on their way to the other side of the world, and I've got nothing but a bogus credit card. I want to know who these people are," she demanded.

Amy's mind whirled. She didn't have a clue.

"Ma'am, I'm very sorry. But I have no idea where the caller was. The other end of the connection is via the Internet. The caller could have been anywhere. I can't believe he ripped you off like that. Are you sure?" Amy asked.

"Of course I'm sure," Diane replied angrily. "I just got off the phone with the mailbox company. They gave me the address everything is forwarded to. It's somewhere in Uganda. My dresses were shipped out the day after they arrived there."

"Can you track them? Call the shipper?" Amy asked.

"They don't use FedEx or UPS," Diane lamented. "It's regular mail. It's not very fast, but it's totally untraceable. Once a package enters the mail system, particularly if it's leaving the country, there is no way to get it back," she sobbed, holding back tears. "We're a small company. Ten dresses will wipe out our profits for a couple of months. I can't take hits like that during the off-season."

Amy searched her mind, desperate for a solution. She had nothing.

"You can't trace the call?" Diane asked finally.

"No," Amy told her, having learned the technology during her orientation. "The callers come in over the Internet, so there's no number to trace like with a telephone call. They can be next door or around the world."

"I can't believe these people can just make free international calls," Diane said.

"As long as they're talking to a U.S. citizen, we have to put the call through," Amy explained. "And even if we could somehow trace the Internet connection, though I don't actually know if that's possible, the FCC forbids it. We cannot reveal anything about a caller."

"Even when they've committed a crime?" Diane demanded. "I'm out my dresses, but somewhere out there is a legitimate credit card holder trying to track down who got their card number and how."

Amy stammered her reply. "Yes, ma'am. The law makes no distinction. We cannot get involved, even if the technology was there to do so."

"Well, I can't believe this." Diane was no longer crying. There was a distinct sense of determination suddenly in her voice. "I'm not taking this lying down. Somebody has to do something about this. How can you sit there and help these people commit crimes?" she asked.

"Ma'am, we're not committing crimes," Amy replied. "We're just trying to help people talk to each other. Would you like to talk to my supervisor? She's got a lot more experience than I do and can answer your questions better than I can."

Amy was reaching back to open the door to the hallway when Diane started speaking again.

"Well, you just told me I couldn't talk to the person who ripped me off! A lot of help you are! I hope you realize what happens now!" she said.

Amy's eyes widened. Was Diane threatening her?

"The cost of my dresses has to go up to cover my losses," Diane said. "Honest, hard-working young girls and their families will have to pay more because people like you are helping criminals get away with theft!"

"Ms. Similton, I'm sorry for your loss, but I really don't see how I can—" Amy started. But Diane cut her off.

"Oh, just save it! It's never your fault, is it? It's always someone else. Society, education, the government! Always passing the blame! Well, I hope you're happy that some young bride won't be able to afford the dress she *really* wanted because interpreter 112 helped some African asshole rip off honest business owners! I hope they steal your credit card sometime—let you see what this feels like," Diane finished.

43

Amy was about to respond when the dial tone returned. Diane had hung up on her.

Amy pulled off the headset. She remembered the caller now. The black man. Since she couldn't hear him, she couldn't know if he'd had an accent. His sign language, what she could remember of it, appeared fine. Could he really have been in Africa? How would she know in the future?

She pushed back from the terminal and stepped out into the hallway. She tapped quietly on Kathy's door and leaned against the wall as she waited for her to finish. After a few minutes, Kathy opened the door.

"Hey, what's up? You OK?" Kathy asked.

"That call I just had," Amy said, "she was a bridal shop owner. A call I made a week or two ago was apparently fraudulent. The guy was using stolen credit cards."

"Oh, yeah," Kathy replied. "I've had a few of those. It really sucks when you realize halfway through the call that they're ripping someone off."

"You know it?" Amy asked, incredulous.

"Sure. After a while you recognize it. The story gets repeated, it's the same people but told a different way, or it's regionally focused, say Texas versus Georgia, with the accompanying accent. Happens every day."

"What are we doing about it?" Amy demanded.

Kathy shrugged. "Nothing, as far as I know."

"Why not?"

"What can we do?" Kathy asked. "We cannot interfere with the communication in any way. It's no different than any junk mail you get at home. You don't see the postal service trying to stop that."

"That doesn't make it right!" Amy exclaimed. "These guys are using VRS to rip people off! We have to do something!" she said.

"Hold on there, wild thing," Kathy said, holding up one hand. "You're relatively new here. This is an old idea. As my grandfather would say, 'It's the same old thing—just a different crowd doing it.' He's right. Scams are as old as humanity."

"But they're taking advantage of something set up for the Deaf community," Amy said.

"Look," Kathy said. "Maybe you're a little overly sensitive to it since your husband was deaf."

"What's that got to do with it?" Amy demanded, clearly agitated by the point.

"This is just a job. Don't take it so personally," Kathy said. "It will drive you nuts."

"They're taking advantage of the Deaf community," Amy repeated. "They see something they can exploit and they're taking something away from people who don't recognize the scam. We have to warn them!"

"Hey! No way, sweetie!" Kathy said. "You can't do that. All we do is relay the call," Kathy warned her.

Amy turned away, finished with the conversation. She understood Diane's frustration now. When the person you're speaking to doesn't want to help, doesn't appear to care about an issue that's important to you, it's infuriating. For Diane, it was her dress shop. For Amy, it was her husband's legacy. If someone had somehow used him to commit a crime, he would not have hesitated to kick a few butts to get the situation corrected. So, what would Jeff have done?

But the problem was, she knew she was not Jeff. She was Amy. She wasn't deaf. If she revealed the contents of a VRS call, she would be fired and subsequently blackballed by the very community she sought to assist. How could she correct this? There had to be a way to warn the Deaf community. There had to be a mechanism within FCC guidelines to account for this type of problem. She would research it, find what the regulations actually said, and figure out a way to prevent these types of calls from giving the Deaf community a bad name.

Dr. Brown had said to find a purpose. A purpose had found her.

SEERS PARKED in front of an attractive Tudor home. Two Georgetown patrol cars were already there, and police tape was draped around the centuries-old oak trees in the yard. He stepped from his vehicle and was waved over by Officer David Damato, who introduced him to the home owners.

"Detective! Over here. This is Chris and Sally Ellis."

Seers stuck out a hand. "It's a pleasure. Sorry to meet under these circumstances."

Sally Ellis was crying and dabbing her face with a tissue. Chris just looked mad. Real mad. Like he was going to rip someone's head off. Seers recognized someone much like himself.

The blowhards were never a concern for him. A guy blowing off steam, jumping up and down mad, was venting his frustrations the only way he knew how. Perhaps an indication of limited intelligence, but the blowhard at least offered the luxury of being predictable. The strong, silent types, however, were another story. You could never quite be sure what was going through their heads. Chris looked like he was ready to mow the neighborhood down with a machine gun. Seers chose to let him vent in private and took Damato aside.

"We'll be right with you folks, if you can just give us a second," he said, leading the officer away. He looked around the living room they'd just walked into. "What's up? I thought you said there was a burglary."

Everything seemed to be in place. Everything was fine in the room they'd just left. The house was immaculate.

"Yeah, that's right. It's not in here. They've got an in-law suite out back," Damato said. He motioned Chris and Sally to rejoin them. "Can we go out back?" he asked.

"This way," Chris said quietly.

He led Seers and Damato through the house to a back door and out across a small covered patio. A detached garage had been converted into living quarters, and Chris rapped strongly on the door. Seers wrinkled his brow.

"Rented?" he asked.

"No," Chris said firmly as the door slowly opened.

An older gentleman stood before them, perhaps in his early seventies. He was fit—not muscular, but clearly someone who'd been in good shape most of his life. His salt-and-pepper hair was thin and very short. He wore a blue button-down shirt and khaki pants with nary a wrinkle evident on either of them. It was obvious by the manner in which Chris and Sally quietly, almost reverently, approached the old gentleman that they felt tremendous concern for his well-being.

Chris took the man by the arm and made sure the door didn't strike him. Sally slipped between Seers and Damato, her face no longer flushed by crying, but still upset.

"Dad? It's Sally. These gentlemen want to see your apartment. Is that OK?"

Her father made a sound, though Seers couldn't tell if it was positive or negative. She motioned them inside.

It was a small place. Bigger than a studio, but still small. The main room contained only a two-person love seat, a chair, and a coffee table. Along one wall was a tall glass shelf full of photographs of Sally during various stages of life, concluding with pictures of her wedding. Standing next to her in one photo was a man in a military dress uniform.

Seers looked at the opposite wall. Numerous military photographs covered it, as did several medals and a framed photo of the man in younger years with President Reagan. Seers examined the photos closely.

"Yes, that's him," Sally said, reading his thoughts. "My father's been in poor health for some time. When he was diagnosed with Parkinson's he came to live with us."

Seers nodded. The residence, though smaller than the main house, was similarly immaculate.

"So, what was taken?" he asked.

"Two things," Sally replied. "A sword and one of my father's decorations."

Seers looked around. Decorations were sparse in the tiny space. "Did you say a sword?" he asked.

"It's called a Mameluke sword," Chris piped up. "It's the sword worn by . . ."

"The Marines," Seers finished. "Somebody took his sword? Where was it?"

"Here." Sally had moved around behind him. She pointed to an empty wooden shield with a hasp for holding a sword. An engraved plaque on the front read COLONEL FRANK STRATTON.

"What else?" Seers asked as he scribbled on a notepad.

"Didn't you say a religious artifact was gone, too?" Damato asked.

"No. It's a Navy Cross," Sally replied.

Seers's head spun around so fast, Sally nearly jumped back. She was holding an empty military shadow box. Seers noticed that the wall of photographs opposite the couch had an empty space the same size as the shadow box. An old brass nail protruded from the wall.

Seers squinted carefully at the other memorabilia. He read aloud from the framed citation that accompanied the shadow box.

"Awarded to Captain Frank Stratton for extraordinary heroism while serving in the 1st Battalion 8th Marines, 2nd Marine Division, on 23 October, 1983 . . ." Seers's throat tightened, cutting off the remainder of the sentence. The color drained from his face. Damato stared at him.

"You OK, Mike?" he asked.

"You were in Beirut," Seers croaked in a voice barely above a whisper.

"Yes, he was," Sally said quietly.

Seers kept reading. When the Marine Corps barracks was bombed in Beirut, Lebanon, then Captain Frank Stratton had rescued three Navy corpsmen pinned down by sniper fire while digging through the rubble for survivors. Stratton had rescued the medics, then circled the shattered remains of the barracks and killed the sniper before returning to assist with the wounded and dying.

Two hundred and forty-one American servicemen had died. When the recovery effort concluded several days after the attack, the medics nominated him for the Navy's second-highest honor.

"Nothing else. Only the sword and the cross?" Seers asked.

"Yes."

"No forced entry? Could it have been one of your kids? Maybe wanting a look at Granddaddy's stuff?"

"We don't have any children," Sally replied. "Nobody comes in here. Dad never has any guests, and there's really not room for anyone, as you can see. He comes into the house whenever there are visitors. But this is his space. He can live comfortably and privately, but we're nearby if he needs anything."

Seers looked around. A small kitchen was located in the corner, across the room from him, with a bathroom down a short hallway behind it. To his left he could see into a single bedroom on the other side of the wall. It was small but comfortable. All the retired marine needed, especially with family so close.

Seers frowned. This didn't make sense. There was nothing else worth stealing in the apartment. A turntable with some old Frank Sinatra albums sat next to a television that might be older than his own, which was saying something.

"Maid service?" Seers asked.

"We have a woman that comes in every other week," Sally explained.

"Trust her?"

"We've had her for years and there's never been a hint of anything like this. We've left cash and jewelry around. There are electronics and expensive toys in the house. Nothing's ever been touched. She's even house-sat for us when we've been on vacation. Never had a problem. Nothing."

Seers was stumped. The only things in the room of any worth were valuable just to the colonel and his family. Swords and armed forces decorations were easily obtained in military surplus stores or on dozens of Web sites on the Internet. Why would someone come take his memories? How did anyone even know the stuff was in here?

"The maid actually discovered the theft," Chris spoke again. "She cleans Pop's apartment when she does the house. She noticed the sword and medal missing."

"He didn't tell you? Was he not living here at the time?" Damato asked, motioning at Frank.

"He was here. But my father's faculties are not what they used to be," Sally said.

It occurred to Seers that Frank Stratton had not uttered another sound since Sally had asked permission to enter the apartment. He had simply sat down in his chair. He wasn't watching any of them. He was staring out into space.

"I explained to Mr. and Mrs. Ellis that there's not much to go on here," Damato said. "If nobody is in the apartment, there's not really much we can do."

"We can do something," Seers shot back, catching Damato off guard. "I'll look into it myself. Check out pawnshops and some of the military surplus after-markets. It might pop up on eBay, too. I'll make some inquiries. See if anyone's heard of any unusual military-oriented thefts."

"Thank you, Detective," Sally said.

Damato walked back to the front door of the apartment with the couple but realized Seers was no longer with him. Looking back, he could see Seers was in no hurry to rush off. Instead, he had walked back to where Frank Stratton was seated. Damato squinted at him. He'd never seen Seers like this. His movements were slow, deliberate, and precise.

Seers knelt next to the colonel's chair and leaned in close. Damato couldn't quite make out what Seers was saying.

"I will get that medal back," Seers said quietly. "I swear it."

He stood up, bid Chris and Sally good-bye with a promise to be in touch, and rushed out of the apartment. Damato yelled after him.

"What's your hurry?"

Seers didn't turn around when he replied.

"I've got to find this asshole."

AMY SAT in a middle row of the courtroom. The mahogany walls and marble floors looked like something from the television drama *Law and Order: Special Victims Unit*, which she enjoyed watching every week. She half expected to see actress Mariska Hargitay, playing Detective Olivia Benson, stride into the courtroom.

Amy admired Hargitay's character. Strong yet feminine. Not afraid to be a girly-girl, but quite capable of getting in a suspect's face or strong-arming a guy on the street when the situation called for it. She envied that kind of confidence.

The seats in front of the judge's bench filled with properly dressed attorneys and support staff. The bailiff appeared to her right and checked his watch, looking over the growing crowd in the gallery. Suddenly, someone was standing right next to her.

"Miss . . .Kellen. Is that right? From the Video Relay Service?"

Amy stood to greet Dan Banducheck. "Yes. That's right." She shook his hand warmly. "Nice to see you again."

"I'm surprised to see you here," Banducheck replied.

"Oh, I just wanted to try and help however I could," Amy stammered back, suddenly uncomfortable she'd come downtown.

"I'm sure he'd appreciate that," Banducheck said.

Amy was quiet for a moment. "*Is* there anything I can do?" she asked.

"Not that I can think of," Banducheck replied. "This should be just a formality. I can't imagine a compelling reason for keeping the animal alive."

"All rise!" the bailiff called.

Banducheck continued to the front of the courtroom, opened the half-door leading to the defense and prosecutor's tables, and sat down.

"The Honorable Charles H. Bridges presiding," the bailiff finished.

"Everyone please have a seat," Judge Bridges stated. "What's on the agenda today?"

His clerk stood up.

"Sir, you must determine the disposition of a dog owned by one Harold J. Kensington. Mr. Kensington was mauled to death by the animal two days ago."

"I see," the judge said as he examined the documentation his clerk handed him.

"Sir, the people believe the animal must be put down in the interest of public safety."

"I see," Bridges repeated. "We have a police report?"

"Yes, sir," the clerk replied.

"Is the investigating officer here?"

Mike Seers stepped out from an adjoining room where a number of uniformed officers were milling around waiting for their cases to be called up. "Right here, Your Honor," Seers replied.

"Good morning, Mike. Anything I should know here?" Judge Bridges asked.

"Good morning. No, sir, I believe you'll find the report pretty much spells it all out."

"So it appears. Any discussion?"

The district attorney spoke again. "Your honor, the people believe the violent nature of Mr. Kensington's death requires the animal be disposed of. We see no need for the county to maintain an animal that is a clear danger to the community."

"Any comment from the people?" Judge Bridges asked.

Amy marveled at how much it really looked like the courtroom dramas on television. There were very cordial relations among all the relevant parties. Everyone behaved themselves and generally agreed on all the major points. Odd how overly dramatic television tended to make the normal routines of everyday life.

"Your Honor, we suspect this was some sort of accident," the public defender replied, "possibly brought on by the victim himself."

Amy jumped from her seat and ran up to the front row immediately behind Dan.

"No, he didn't," she whispered too loudly. "He did nothing to provoke that dog!"

Banducheck turned around and discreetly motioned for her to remain quiet before leaning over to whisper to the district attorney.

"Your Honor. I think the record shows the victim took extraordinary care of this animal. He was well fed and cared for, and groomed regularly. We've no indication that suggests otherwise," the DA countered.

Mike Seers noticed Amy for the first time. He was surprised by her presence in the courtroom for what should be a straightforward session.

"So there was no witness to the attack?" Judge Bridges asked.

Seers looked at Amy, and Banducheck turned around briefly in his chair. Neither gave any outward indication she might know something, and they remained silent.

"Should I repeat the question?" Bridges asked when he saw the two men's actions.

"No, sir. No witnesses," Seers answered finally as Banducheck stood up to address the judge.

"Your Honor, I spent a good bit of time around the victim and the animal in question. I've no quarrel with calling this a tragic accident, but I'm compelled to tell you in the strongest language possible that Hal Kensington loved that dog."

Amy nodded from her perch in the front row.

"I see. I've no reason to doubt the veracity of your statement, and the people appear to agree that in the absence of a witness your testimony is the most relevant of anyone's here."

Banducheck sat back down.

"If you're so certain of the animal's temperament," Bridges continued, "there's no reason for me to be in a hurry to pass judgment and summary execution."

Banducheck's face crinkled in confusion. "I didn't mean to imply, sir, that . . ."

Bridges held up a hand.

"Just a minute. The animal can do no harm where he is. I'm inclined to leave him there until Mr. Kensington's family has the opportunity to express their views. They may want the animal and remove it from the area. It would therefore no longer be a threat to the community, and the local taxpayers would not be on the hook for any costs," the judge finished.

"But he's dangerous!" Amy said too loudly.

"Young lady! That's the second time you've interrupted my court," Bridges barked. "It will be the last. If you have anything to say for the record, come be recognized and say it where everyone can hear you!"

Amy sat back as her face and neck turned a deep shade of crimson.

"Do you have something to say?" Bridges continued. "This is your only opportunity."

Seers looked at Amy sympathetically, but remained quiet. Long experience had taught him not to interfere with an angry judge, especially on matters of protocol. They were all sticklers for it. Dan Banducheck stood up again.

"Your Honor, this young woman knew Hal Kensington as I did. As a fine man, a leader in the community, and a friend to everyone who knew him. I believe she's simply expressing the loss and frustration we're all feeling."

Bridges's face and tone softened. "Very well. Your sentiment is appreciated, but please don't interrupt again," Bridges instructed. Amy nodded her acknowledgment.

"Now then. As I was saying. I'm inclined to delay a decision until the next of kin has the opportunity to weigh in on this matter. Until such time as the family has done so, the animal will remain in quarantine at the Arlington animal shelter."

Bridges tapped his gavel to end the session.

Chapter Five

Amy stared at the bottle on the table. Her doctor had accommodated her with a prescription for sleeping pills. She hated taking medicine—even aspirin. Some people took prescriptions without thinking, but she'd never been particularly sickly as a child, so the quick-fix notion of popping a pill did not appeal to her. She was still trying to decide whether or not to take them. What if Celia woke up in the night and needed something?

Since sleep was obviously not in her immediate future, she sat down at her computer once again and began surfing a Deaf-related Web site that Kathy had phoned her about earlier in the evening. The language on the site was not nice.

Diane Similton either had a great deal of free time at her bridal shop, or she was enlisting the help of friends and family to post her unhappiness on every blog, Web site, and chat room they could find. They said the Deaf community was filled with phonies: a pit full of vipers looking to rip off the small American businessperson with fraudulent purchases that ultimately were beyond the jurisdiction of U.S. law enforcement. The postings were getting an enormous amount of strongly worded responses, most of them personal and rather hateful toward Similton and her bridal shop.

Amy watched silently as the chat room became increasingly hostile. She wished she could help, but didn't know what to do without risking her job by jumping into the conversation. She reminded herself once again that even if fraud was being conducted, federal law protected every call.

Mentally she was still struggling with the finality of it. Suddenly she saw a glimmer of hope. She couldn't be VRS interpreter Amy Kellen in the chat room, but if callers could be anonymous, why couldn't she do the same in a few chat rooms and Web sites? There was no reason to give her name and identity. Had she actually hit upon a way to help? She began to write.

"The majority of videophone calls are certainly legitimate," she wrote. *"To protect themselves online, companies can take a number of precautions, just as they do with other consumers."*

She smiled. This was perfect. She could respond to Similton's postings without giving up any protected information, and she was able to help the Deaf community. This was the best of both worlds. She clicked over to a Web site she'd visited earlier and posted similar suggestions for consumers and companies who might be concerned with using VRS for transactions they weren't sure were legitimate.

"Be wary of the use of multiple credit cards on a single transaction," she wrote. On another site she suggested *"getting the consumer's name and telephone number and calling them back to finalize the transaction."* After all, there was nothing illegal or untoward about that.

Exhilaration kept her writing for over an hour. It felt wonderful to make positive suggestions that might make a difference. With newfound pluck, she even made a few postings for other videophone interpreters on handling such problems, going so far as to suggest how they might lobby the FCC.

She felt good. She might actually get some sleep tonight. The phone rang and interrupted her train of thought. "Hello," she said.

"Hello, Ms. Kellen, it's Mike Seers. Did I wake you?"

"I wish."

"Not sleeping, huh?"

"No, but my doctor gave me a prescription. I'm just trying to decide whether or not to take it."

"I understand you dropped by the kennel."

Amy's elation was short-lived, and she was overtaken suddenly by a sense of guilt, like a child caught doing something they know is wrong.

"Yes. That was a mistake. I'm sorry."

"No need to apologize for it. I'm sorry you had a bad time."

"You talked to the kennel guy?"

"Yes. I think his name was Jim Skelton. He was concerned about you. Said you left in a hurry."

"I guess I did. I didn't even thank him."

"That's all right. I think he understood." He cleared his throat. "Listen, the reason I called is because some animal rights nut has convinced the judge to authorize Champ's release."

"He's *out?*" she asked.

"This guy specializes in mean dogs or some such nonsense. Kohler, I think is his name. Harold Kensington's son authorized it through his law firm. He's busy settling his father's affairs and wasn't available for court, so somebody came up with this. Anyway, they're taking him out first thing tomorrow morning."

"Do you think he can be rehabilitated?" Amy asked.

"I don't know. I didn't see what you saw. The question is, do *you* think he can be rehabilitated?" Seers asked.

Amy shut her eyes, trying to block out Kensington's call and the kennel visit. "I doubt it," she said finally.

"So do I. Anyway, I wanted you to know before you hear about it on the news. I think it's a bad idea, but there's nothing to do when a judge gets involved like that," he said.

"So, does this mean you're dropping the case?" she asked.

"Well," he hesitated, "there's not really much of a case. You have to understand—I've got a backlog of other crimes to work on. I've got a burglary case I'm trying to resolve that's going nowhere. There's not much I can do for Mr. Kensington. I'm sorry."

"That's all right. Thank you for calling, Detective."

"Sleep well, Amy."

She chased two of the prescription pills down with a glass of water.

THE HEADQUARTERS of the U.S. Secret Service was a concrete-and-glass fortress in downtown Washington, D.C. Inside, the furnishings were about as lavish as in a convent. Minimalism taken to the extreme—anything extraneous was set aside in the interest of clean surfaces and nominal upkeep. A museum to the austere.

Heath Rasco worked in Special Services, a training and operational support element available to the executive protection details or any Secret Service field office on a moment's notice. Specialists in forensics, behavioral science, advanced weapons, and a host of other unique disciplines that could be brought to bear anywhere in the country on short order were housed in a single department sharing a common infrastructure.

"You wanted to see me, sir?" Heath asked.

Special Services chief Walt Broomer was a slight man in his fifties, with a wisp of salty hair surrounding the smooth crown of his bald head. He was legendary in the service for his ability to sniff out funny money. For twenty-two years he'd held the record for seized cash by a single agent—over $400 million. Now Walt ran Special Services, assisting other (that is, *younger*) agents with whatever they needed during investigations. He liked it. It was solid law enforcement work, and he didn't get shot at or dragged out in the middle of the night anymore. It wasn't a bad job for a guy his age who had no interest in retiring.

"There's some chatter on the Internet we need to chase down. Got some folks upset," Walt said, barely looking up from the *Washington Post*.

It always amazed Walt how many bloggers would actually take the step of reporting something they'd seen online that they thought had the potential to develop into a really nasty situation in the real world. Most of the time it was a complete waste of resources. But it only took one ignored warning to cause a congressional inquiry, so better safe than sorry.

"Important people or not so important people?" Heath asked.

"Not so important right now, but let's not let it worm its way up the flagpole if we can help it," Walt replied, folding the paper. He picked up a Georgetown University coffee mug that was older than Heath and took a long sip. "Know what I mean?"

"Yes, I do," Heath said. "What am I looking for?"

"Don't look *for* anything. Just look *at* everything," Walt replied. He enjoyed talking with Heath. The guy was smart and motivated. Heath loved being a Secret Service agent as much as Walt did. He could see many similarities between them, which was no doubt the reason Harold Kensington had asked specifically for Heath to be assigned as a special assistant. Walt had been around long enough to recognize when a political figure had designs on promising young talent.

Kensington had had enough vision to imagine a hard of hearing guy as a field agent, and had made a convincing argument to Walt to take on Heath as his unofficial protégé to test the idea. Heath had promise, and Walt was determined to ensure he had a fair shot at a field agent job. Heath was hungry, determined. He had talent, there was no question about that. But the interoffice grumbling about a hard of hearing field agent meant Heath would have to be head and shoulders better than other candidates.

Walt hadn't been sure if or how Heath would rise to such a tall challenge, but he was certain it wouldn't happen at all unless he moved closer to the action. Heath had to work a security detail, even if it was just on the fringes at first. Phil Thompson had cleared that lane, and Harold Kensington's plan was put into place.

"Look *at* everything?" Heath repeated.

"It's like porn. You can't really describe what it is, but you know it when you see it," Walt replied, masking his delight at the outlandish comparison.

"Porn, huh? Sounds like quite an assignment," Heath observed.

"Don't get your hopes up. It's not *that* good," Walt assured him. "Fraud. Apparently a growing amount. Lots of chatter about it on some of the Deaf Web sites. I'd like you to take a look."

Heath scowled. Walt was one of the only senior leaders who had never made an issue of his hearing. Walt stared at him thoughtfully.

"Don't get the wrong idea," Walt continued after a moment. "You're getting this because you're the best qualified for the work, not for any other reason. You speak the language. You know the culture. If it makes you feel any better, it's not logged as a Deaf issue. It's fraud. CFF sent it our way since you know their methods. No different than assigning it to someone who speaks French or Arabic. But they don't have anyone with ASL skills to talk with people. Don't overanalyze it."

Heath's racing pulse slowed. The guys in Computer Fraud and Forensics, or CFF, had recommended him. He realized his face was flushed, embarrassed that Walt could so easily tell he'd jumped to conclusions on being assigned to the case.

"Roger that. I'll take a look," Heath said finally.

"They must think the world of you to let you work it after you left."

Heath only nodded, kicking himself because an expert in "tells" had virtually shouted his indignation at a guy who was on his side.

Walt handed him a piece of paper. At the top was a Web address with a link to two other Web sites. Fraud and Forensics had indeed looked at it and handed it off to Special Services. A very rare event.

CFF was loath to give up anything. They were the most insular group inside the Secret Service. Counterfeiting had been the original impetus for the agency. While protecting the president and foreign dignitaries garnered a lot of press coverage, there was a certain cadre of agents whose only interest, their passion—hell, for that matter their entire *life*—was finding funny money. For years, it was derisively called the Comedy Club—"where funny money comes home."

In the Internet age, funny money was all electronic. There were fewer people trying to manufacture paper money. Now it was all invisible bits of data floating across the world's telecommunications systems. Fraud and Forensics was the answer to that particular problem. The men and women who ran it were computer geeks of the highest order—pushing the narrow culture of the Comedy Club to a fringe technological extreme. Heath had earned his credibility in their rarefied world and maintained several friendships from his time there.

60

As much as he loved computer science, it was important to him that everyone see a deaf agent out on the front lines. He couldn't just be a computer specialist. He wanted to be a ground-pounder, in the field, working investigations and calling the shots. That meant moving on to another shop. Walt was only too happy to have him in Special Services.

"Thanks, Walt," Heath said finally, remembering his manners.

"Don't mention it," Walt replied, still smiling, pleased the younger man now fully understood the opportunity he was being given.

Heath returned to his office and looked more closely at the CFF document. Three concerned citizens had sent e-mails through the service's Web site describing a fraud issue that was being argued on a Deaf community chat room.

Heath read the exchanges. Yep. Looked like fraud to him. The wedding dress shop owner had learned an expensive lesson. Whoever had responded to her displayed a level of calm and concern that caught Heath's eye. She wasn't just defending the fraudulent transaction. She was, as Heath read it, defending her *part* in it. She hadn't admitted to participating in anything nefarious, but she was going overboard in her defense of what happened. It had to be personal. Psychoanalysis wasn't his area of expertise, but he knew the right person to ask about it.

He looked at the other two Web sites listed. Same log-on IDs as the other. Same type of outrage by the bridal shop owner. Same defense of the process by an anonymous hero of the faith. Her suggestions on how companies and individuals could stop, or at least slow down, future fraud seemed pretty sincere to him.

That's probably what had thrown off the CFF team. Until someone has had to use an interpreter to conduct the most rudimentary of conversations, he or she could never understand the level of trust that had to exist between the three parties speaking. The most intimate parts of a deaf person's life must be shared with a complete stranger in order for him or her to communicate with the hearing world.

When someone violates that trust to steal a bunch of dresses, well, it was going to cause an uproar.

An uproar was exactly what had happened. CFF didn't normally deal with anything like this. Fraud worked only when nobody knew about it. If this bridal shop owner was dropping blog grenades around cyberspace, the likelihood of it being a long-term problem was probably negligible. The Deaf community might not like it, but the uproar would help diminish the problem by making more people aware of it. The ability to continue the fraud would be short-lived. Maybe that was already the case. He could take a quick look and perhaps put the whole issue to bed right now.

Heath had anonymous Internet access left over from his time in CFF, accounts that did not reveal that he was on a U.S. government computer. If anyone took an interest in tracing him online they would, after five different nodal links, find themselves at the servers for the University of Tennessee at Chattanooga. It was one of several pass-throughs operated by the service to mask their Internet surfing. No sense telegraphing what they were looking into.

He logged on and found the original posting from a few days before. He then went through the replies. The exchange had created quite a bit of controversy that had, as he imagined it would, spread like wildfire throughout most of the online Deaf community. He captured all of it and ran the text through a computer program that plotted out links and relationships.

From the two original posters, nearly three thousand respondents had jumped in! That was insane. How many people did it take to argue about a single fraudulent purchase? As he scanned quickly through the history, however, it was clear that there was more than a single incident. A pattern was emerging.

People were citing other purchases using similar tactics of shipping to a private mailbox address, which then forwarded the package overseas. One word kept coming up over and over.—Africa.

Walt was right about one aspect. According to the statistical analysis, things were still heating up—not winding down, as Heath had hoped. The software analyzed the date and time stamp of the user's blog and chat room postings. Usually after a short burst of initial excitement, breaking news petered out in chat rooms and was overtaken by subsequent events. That hadn't happened. And the entries themselves were getting longer, with people dedicating more time to spelling out the problem. Not only was it not going away, it didn't even appear close to cresting yet. When a situation was melting away, the chat died down. This was still building. Three thousand responses in a couple of days! It hadn't yet reached a "tipping point," as the book on his nearby bookshelf was entitled.

Much of the most recent chatter was about an e-mail scam. Several users had received an e-mail from Africa promising cash for assistance.

"Oh, crap!" Heath said aloud. The African e-mail had popped up regularly every few months for several years. Hadn't everyone already gotten that damn thing by now? He went through the remaining chat room listings. The bridal shop owner had evidently thrown in the towel when the chatter turned to the African e-mail scam. Maybe she realized that making enemies in the Deaf world wasn't going to get her any new customers in the Charlotte area. In any event, she'd not been back on in two days.

She'd probably just needed a place to vent. She couldn't very well scream at customers or her employees, so the anonymity of an online chat room probably felt pretty safe. He guessed she'd been unprepared for the responses her simple Web chat had wrought. He joked to himself that she would likely "stick to her knitting" rather than try any more Internet assaults.

The original responder was a different matter. Heath saw the same ID at other sites within the Deaf community. New participants just getting word on the issue were quoting her now. She was getting a following. No name, though. Like many women on the Internet, she chose to keep her name private. He'd have to remember her online ID. See if it came up again anywhere. He wrote it on a Post-it note. JACK/3.

THE FOLLOWING morning, Amy woke up stretched out on her couch. Celia had gotten her up twice during the night, playing havoc with Amy's prescription-induced sleep. The second time, she decided to just stay downstairs and put Celia in her playpen. Then she crashed on the couch rather than go back up to bed.

Celia was playing quietly on the floor, having a tea party with her dolly and Mr. Pups, a stuffed dog Kathy had given her. Amy pulled the blanket up tighter. Maybe they'd just stay in all day. It was quiet, comfortable, just the two of them. What else did she need?

It had been a rough couple of weeks. This new job came with a downside she hadn't expected. Fraud. Death. It was very unsettling. She didn't like not being able to correct a wrong—particularly one that would be staring her in the face on a regular basis, if Kathy were to be believed. There had to be a better way.

She thought about Harold Kensington. She wished he were alive to ask. He'd know what to do. He was a very smart man. He was part of a small segment of the Deaf community—someone who had once been able to hear but now could not. It was much easier for her to relate to men like that. It had been one of the earliest and only stumbling blocks when she'd started dating Jeff.

He had been born deaf. He'd never listened to birds sing nor heard his mother's voice. At concerts, he *felt* the music. They'd met at a Styx reunion concert at Georgetown. He'd come over from Gallaudet. When he and his friend Chuck had started dancing to "The Grand Illusion," she'd naturally asked how he liked the song. Jeff had simply stared at her, transfixed.

She'd yelled at him over the band, not understanding why Jeff just looked at her and Chuck did all the talking. It took two more exchanges before she noticed Jeff's hand gestures. He was lip-reading, an exceptionally useful skill during a loud rock concert, and something he had grown up with during even the quietest of moments. Chuck recognized that his buddy was smitten. Not wanting to ruin his friend's night out, he'd carried the conversation as long as possible without revealing that Jeff couldn't hear her at all.

It wasn't that she was attracted by his deafness, but she was fascinated by how well he functioned in spite of it. Here was this deaf guy at a rock concert! What was he doing there? He knew the words to the songs, knew the guitar riffs and the occasional drum solos. After another fifteen minutes of back-and-forth banter between the three of them, Jeff had taken her by the hand and sung to her.

She smiled at the memory. The band was so loud; Jeff's hopelessly off-key lyrics were all but drowned out by lead singer Dennis DeYoung's throaty golden pipes. There was a spark. She'd been a Styx fan for years. DeYoung's voice overlaid Jeff's handsome young face, infectious smile, and gregarious personality. "Babe." That's what he'd sung to her. DeYoung had dedicated it to his wife, Suzanne, as he'd done the last six times she'd seen the band. But Jeff was singing it to Amy. She was smitten, too.

CELIA GOT up from her tea party and held out her arms for Amy to pick her up, dragging Mr. Pups along. Amy gave her a big hug, happy to have a permanent reminder of the agonizingly brief time with her husband.

"Hey, pumpkin," Amy whispered to her, "what do you want to do today?"

Celia's dark brown eyes looked back at her, but she remained silent. She could feel Jeff's presence whenever Celia did that. He'd learned to say more with his eyes than his voice could ever clearly say. Every now and again, she could see it in Celia as well.

"How about some apple juice?" Amy suggested. "You want some breakfast? How about a waffle?"

Celia nodded. Amy got up and walked toward the kitchen, tripping over the hallway threshold from the entry foyer to the kitchen. It took two heavy stomps before she caught herself on the wall to stop herself from falling all the way to the ground. How many more times was she going to do that?

She needed to fix that thing before she or Celia really got hurt. The new one was in the cabinet, where it had sat for a year now. But she didn't have it in her to replace it. Not today. Maybe tomorrow. Right now something else was on her mind.

Amy pulled the frozen waffles from the freezer and dropped two into the toaster. She would join Celia for breakfast. As the waffles toasted, she rapped her fingers against the countertop, plotting her next move. She wished Jeff were here.

He would know what to do; granted, he'd want to go kick in doors and slap someone around if they used the Deaf community to defraud an innocent business owner. He was every Deaf person's big brother. He watched out for them and fought for them, and they all loved him for it.

Since kicking in doors wasn't an option, she contemplated others as she poured apple juice for them both. She still couldn't think of any way to help Diane Similton. Nor could she think of a way to warn anyone during a call that it was a crime in progress. Surely there was a way out of this?

Her musings turned once more to Harold Kensington. Could someone have mistreated Champ? Could that be why he'd turned on his master? She couldn't imagine Kensington abusing him. Even on his call, Kensington had tried to reach down and pet Champ. Seemed like a solid relationship. Who else had access to the dog?

What about the groomer?

She put the apple juice container away and handed a glass to Celia. Could the groomer have mistreated Champ? Somehow gotten him angry, so angry he'd attacked Harold Kensington rather than have to return to the groomer? Thinking more about it, she wondered if she was onto something.

The dog had just come from the groomer's, but he hadn't looked very spiffy. He'd appeared unkempt, like his coat hadn't been brushed recently at all. What had the groomer actually done, then? She put down her juice.

She couldn't help Diane. She couldn't help Harold Kensington, either. But whereas someone far away who'd exploited VRS had ripped off Diane, Harold Kensington's dog groomer was local. He'd never called the groomer using a videophone. Not with Amy interpreting, anyway. Instead of a criminal using a Deaf community resource to commit a crime, had she found a criminal act committed *against* a deaf person—perhaps one that had actually cost a man his life?

As Amy carefully reconstructed the details of the call in her head, she nibbled absently on the waffle. Yes, she was sure. Champ looked rough, like he'd been out all night. He looked bigger than normal, though on the monitor that's not unusual. What do they say? The camera adds ten pounds? Maybe the same was true with dogs.

But she was sure about how shaggy and unruly he'd appeared. How could he have gotten that dirty, his coat so tangled, if he'd just come from the groomers? Perhaps the groomer was taking advantage of Kensington; deaf guy, big-time political player—may have figured he was too busy to monitor what was happening.

Amy nodded to herself. She could see that. If there were people who would exploit the videophone system to steal bridal dresses from overseas, then surely there were others who would stoop to take an older man's money without doing a good job on his dog. Incredibly, they had done just that to Harold Kensington, and somehow turned his happy companion into a crazed killing machine. But what to do about it now?

She juggled the facts methodically around in her mind. Since Kensington hadn't conducted any business with the groomer over his videophone screen, she was not obligated to any type of confidentiality. She didn't really know a whole lot, just suspected something was awry. What about the other interpreters? If they had worked with Kensington and his groomer, what then?

After a few moments of deliberation, she decided there wasn't a problem. There were other companies besides All Hands offering the same service. Not every interpreter is located near their caller—that was the problem with the African bridal-gown order. The caller could be literally anywhere. But Kensington's groomer was here in the area. If anyone else at All Hands knew anything about it, they hadn't said anything when Detective Seers started his investigation, so she presumed everyone else was in the dark, too.

She cleared the table with a new sense of purpose. Now she had defined her issue, characterized it. It was no longer some intangible idea. She could take action. She could sink her teeth into the problem. Diane Similton was a tougher nut to crack and would probably take a lot longer. She doubted she could do much more without some type of official help. She'd talk with Carol Burdick about it and find out what the best course of action was. Tackling Harold Kensington's rogue canine was much easier, more immediate.

Mariska Hargitay would be proud.

Amy reached over to tap a few keys on her laptop computer. After a quick online search, she found the address and phone number for the office of one Dell Kohler, canine rehabilitator. She dialed the number.

"Kohler and Kohler," a voice answered.

"May I speak with Dell Kohler, please?" Amy asked.

"He's not in at the moment. May I take a message?"

"I was calling about a dog I'm told he was going to rehabilitate. Mr. Harold Kensington's dog."

"May I inquire as to your interest?" the woman asked.

Amy hesitated. Did she really want to do this? She wasn't a very accomplished liar and knew she would feel terrible about doing so later. Better to simply misspeak than to lie. "I saw a piece in the paper about it, how Mr. Kohler was going to try and rehabilitate him. Is that a particularly violent breed?" Amy asked, trying to fudge her response.

"Oh no, ma'am. Not at all," the woman replied. "I'm Stephanie Kohler, Dell's wife. Shepherds are great dogs. He shouldn't have any trouble straightening him out. Dell's got a gift. It's like watching *The Horse Whisperer*," she joked.

Amy giggled with relief. She'd loved that movie, how Robert Redford's character was able to return a traumatized horse to his former self. Could the same be done for Champ? She wasn't sure.

"When would they start working?" Amy asked.

"Dell's already gone to pick him up. I think he was going to take him for a walk across the Georgetown campus since he'd been penned up for several days. He'll be back here before the end of the day, though. I can have him call you, if you like."

"Thank you. I'd appreciate that," Amy said, sharing her phone number with Stephanie.

Amy hung up and sat back. Should she wait for Dell to call? That didn't seem to be the most proactive way of getting to the bottom of things. Maybe she should go observe Kohler in action. Watch him evaluate Champ, see how they got along. She was more than a little surprised to learn he was taking Champ to walk in a very public area, remembering how the dog had lunged at her when she'd visited the kennel. She reasoned that an experienced dog handler would be able to take care of such problems.

She looked out the window. It was a beautiful morning. Why not go poke around a bit? See if she could find Dell Kohler and Champ walking around in the late-morning sun?

Chapter Six

GEORGETOWN UNIVERSITY was synonymous with the neighborhood that shared its name. Coexisting on a thin sliver of land along the Potomac River, the community and the school resembled an old married couple that finish each other's sentences—their futures and fortunes intimately entwined. Chic boutiques flanked antique dress shops. Authentic Irish pubs shared courtyards with fern bars. Beer bongs were as accessible as wine by the glass. The young and the old resided here side by side, with few nuclear families nearby.

Amy could easily pass for a graduate student, though pushing Celia in the stroller certainly didn't help her blend in. Fortunately, the object of her amateurish surveillance attempt was unaware of her interest.

Dell Kohler was a tall, gangly, middle-aged man, probably no more comfortable with standing out from the university crowd than she was. She'd spotted his van, with its prominent signage, parked south of M Street on her third circle through the neighborhood. It hadn't taken long to find Kohler walking Champ on a short leash up Wisconsin Avenue.

The pair had stopped and turned left on Q Street. The crowds were thinning. While Wisconsin held the majority of car and pedestrian traffic, heading up the hill toward the campus tended to weed out many of the commuters. The higher up the hill, the more likely someone was to be associated with the university in some way. It also made it more likely Kohler would notice the woman with the baby stroller following from across the street. Amy considered whether or not to continue at all.

A horn jolted her from her thoughts. The events occurring before her eyes appeared in slow motion—but in actuality took only a few seconds. A Honda sedan barreled around the corner from behind a Gap Kids store and swerved into oncoming traffic. Champ and Kohler were midway across the street. Both froze as the car raced toward them; its swerving motion made it impossible to know in which direction to run. Another horn blast filled the mid-afternoon peace. Kohler's head spun around and he dropped the leash.

The Honda slammed into Champ, hurling him across the street and off the alley wall of the Chico's store on the corner. The dog's impact on the ground sent a plume of dust into the air. He remained still. At the same time a Mustang convertible, trying to avoid the Honda's uncontrolled tear through the intersection, veered toward Dell Kohler. Dell looked frantically to the right and left—but never had time to move.

Kohler skidded over the hood only to be flung skyward by the slanted windshield. He paused briefly in the air over the convertible's soft top. The tortured scream of rubber on concrete produced a ghastly dark cloud that enveloped him as he fell to earth. A horrified scream from the driver's-side window pierced the midday air as the car lurched to a stop.

Amy pushed Celia up against a flowerbed and locked the stroller wheels to prevent it from rolling. The Honda disappeared down Q Street, accelerating all the way.

She quickly reached Champ, who lay in a broken heap. She hesitated momentarily, but then stepped forward to see if he was alive. His eyes were wide, his tongue grotesquely swollen and protruding from his mouth. Tufts of fur swirled around his body like tiny tumbleweeds.

Amy had no idea what to do. She'd seen people check for a pulse on a human in her television police dramas, but had no concept of how to do the same on a dog. She gingerly reached out to Champ's head, but there was nowhere she could pat to comfort him on the off chance he was alive. Her hand trembled above him, uncertain what to do.

A young clerk, no doubt a Georgetown student working a part-time job, screamed into the Chico's store.

71

"Somebody call an ambulance! And get a manager out here quick!" he said. Amy walked over to where he stood.

Blood pooled onto the street under Dell Kohler's head. Amy knelt down next to him and took his hand in hers.

"Tell my wife I love her," he whispered.

"Easy now. Just hold still," she said in a faltering voice. She heard a police car's siren already.

"Tell my girls . . . I'm very proud of them," Dell continued, grabbing Amy's blouse with a bloody fist and pulling her close. When he lifted his head, pieces of skull remained on the pavement, causing the crowd to gasp.

"Oh my God!" Amy cried. "Just lie quiet now. Don't panic, don't panic," she repeated, as much to herself as to Kohler. She turned back to the store. "Did anybody call an ambulance?"

Dell Kohler settled back, his face relaxed, his eyes fixed on her in a serene gaze. A rush of air pushed blood through his lips as his head fell to one side.

Kohler died there on the street, his last recollections of family spilled out to her ears alone. Amy took several deep breaths, fearing she might pass out. This couldn't be happening again, could it? It was bad enough to watch a man die on her monitor. Now a man was in physical contact with her as his life slipped away. His blood was literally on her hands, and she was similarly unable to assist him.

Had Jeff's passing been similar? Kohler at least had someone to hold his hand. Jeff had died alone, staring up into a lightning-streaked sky, his body not found for hours.

Had Jeff called her name as Kohler had his wife's? Did he tell the grass and the trees about his newborn daughter with his final breath? Amy laid Kohler's hand back down and stepped away as someone covered him with a jacket, a modicum of dignity to a death that, like Kensington's, made no sense. What in the world was going on?

And what of Champ? Amy stole another glance toward him while the crowd continued its group analysis of the events. She was struck by the difference between what she had seen on-screen and the pitiful, lifeless animal now laid out on the street. She was still trying to reconcile the differences when she noticed Celia staring silently at the unfolding drama.

Amy mentally reprimanded herself: what had she allowed her poor daughter to see? Had her sleuthing damaged her little girl in some way? But how could she have known what a devastating afternoon this would become? A dead man, a mutilated dog, and her mother soaked in blood. Was this Amy's penance for sticking her nose in someone's business?

Amy saw the Mustang's driver pass out in the middle of the intersection. Passersby surrounded her, but it was more than Amy could bear. She pulled Celia out of the stroller and hugged her tight—as much for her own comfort as for Celia's.

Mike Seers drove up to the police barricade and stepped out into a brilliantly sunny Georgetown afternoon. The sordid underbelly of the nation's capital had its downside, but on a day like this, it was hard to be cynical. Then again, dead people lying in the street were not the most uplifting way to interrupt his lunch. He gestured at the uniformed officer.

"OK. Walk me through it."

Officer Damato flipped open a report pad. "Pretty cut-and-dried. A graduate student from Georgetown swerved to miss the other car. Never had a chance."

"Was he alive when you got here?" Seers asked.

"If you want to call what he was 'alive,' then yes, but only briefly," Damato responded.

"Any witnesses?"

"Yeah, all pretty consistent. This student had nowhere to go. It was either a head-on collision or the guy. You know how narrow these streets are."

Seers looked around. "Yes, pretty narrow. What about the other vehicle?"

73

"Honda sedan. Brown or light tan, depending on whom you ask. Nobody saw the plates. Nothing on the driver."

Seers turned back to face him. "That's it?"

Damato nodded. "Witnesses said the sedan came screaming around the curve—made a last-minute correction to avoid the guy, hit the dog straight on—just kept on going."

"Not an animal lover, huh?"

"Famous dog, too. Or, I guess, *infamous* dog."

"How's that?"

"It's the German shepherd that killed that political consultant a few days ago."

Seers stared at him a moment, still making the connection in his mind. "Harold Kensington?" Seers asked.

"That's the one. You worked that case, didn't you?"

"I wouldn't call the case *working*. I don't have any strings to pull," Seers said. As he looked over Damato's list of witnesses and statements, a familiar name jumped off the page. "Then again, maybe I spoke too soon," Seers said.

"What?"

"What the hell is *she* doing here?"

At that moment Amy walked up behind him, pushing Celia in the stroller.

"Miss Kellen. I just can't seem to avoid you these days," Seers noted sarcastically.

"So it would seem, Detective."

"Would you like to tell me what you're doing here?" Seers asked.

"I was taking Celia for a walk," Amy replied.

"You live around here?" he asked.

"No, actually I'm parked down Wisconsin."

"So, you drove here to walk up a steeply inclined street? What? Abs workout?" he challenged.

Amy searched her shoes for a proper response, but had little luck.

"Miss Kellen, you are dangerously close to interfering with a police investigation. Is there something about the Kensington case you're not telling me?" Seers demanded.

"I can't tell you anything, Detective. I'm sorry," Amy replied.

"You can't just run around here playing Nancy Drew," Seers yelled. "Police investigations are not simple. They're not easy. And they're not for the general public! Stay away from this investigation unless you've got something to share on the record!"

Seers stomped off as Amy stood helplessly with Celia on the corner.

GOLF PARAPHERNALIA adorned every inch of the walls. It was a duffer's paradise in which dimpled balls, long white tees, and sun visors embodied the Holy Trinity. Amy recognized a few pieces of the memorabilia she'd given away after Jeff's death. She was glad someone was able to enjoy them.

She sat across the desk from Jeff's childhood friend Chuck Meyer. Chuck was a couple of years older than she and Jeff, having done a stint in the military before using the GI bill to attend Georgetown. She still couldn't get used to seeing him in a suit and tie. Back in the old days, every shirt Chuck wore had the sleeves cut off. He'd even bought a secondhand tuxedo jacket to wear to Jeff and Amy's wedding bash and then cut off the sleeves as a joke. He was a great guy and a good friend, especially over the past year. She handed him an envelope.

"I got this in the mail and I don't know what it is," she said.

Chuck accepted the envelope with one hand while the other skillfully scooped up a letter opener to meet it midstroke, effortlessly slicing it open.

"Let's see what we've got here," Chuck replied. He scanned a few lines. "It's just your escrow account. They're adjusting your mortgage payment."

"They're going to make me pay more for my house?" she demanded.

"Relax, it's going down, not up."

"So it's OK?"

"It's fine, Amy. You're just fine."

She was relieved. "Great! I thought something was wrong."

"Amy, I don't mind telling you you're doing very well financially."

She stared into her lap. "Jeff always handled all the financial stuff, you know. It's all new to me—I just worry."

"You don't need to worry. That's my job. And you don't need to moonlight. Your investment portfolio is growing nicely. Celia's college fund is taken care of, and refinancing the mortgage dropped your house payment a couple hundred a month. You're fine!"

She sat quietly, her expression still solemn, betraying her total feeling of inadequacy—as though she were failing Celia by not being more business savvy now that it was just the two of them. "Thanks, Chuck. You've always been a good friend."

"I love you, man, always have. Always will. Anything you need, you have only to ask."

"I know."

"Now, business aside. Where's my picture?" he only half-jokingly demanded.

Amy dug into her wallet and produced a picture of Celia she'd brought especially for "Uncle Chuck." He pinned it to the bulletin board behind him, near a college-era picture of himself, Amy, and Jeff on the fourteenth hole at Greenbriar.

"So, how are you doing?" Amy asked.

"Hey, I'm supposed to be asking you that, aren't I? After all, it's been a year," Chuck said.

"Yeah, a full year, all right."

"You OK?"

"I'm good. I just miss him."

"I know. Me, too."

Chuck looked back at the picture of the three of them and studied it thoughtfully.

"I hate to lose, but I can't complain about getting beat by someone who turned pro. Going on the tour. I can't imagine what that was like, even after hearing all of your stories. It's something the rest of us can only dream of."

Amy looked wistfully at the collectibles. "It was a short career," she noted.

"It takes a couple of years for a pro career to take off," Chuck pointed out.

"But only a couple of *seconds* for a lightning strike to end it! He knew better than to be out when . . ."

"Hey!" Chuck held up a hand to interrupt her, "just keep reminding yourself—the guy had everything he'd ever wanted: a loving wife and an adorable baby girl. Not much more a man can ask for."

"Growing old together would have been nice. Five years is not very long," Amy said pointedly.

He frowned at her, unable to think of a comforting reply to that thought. He switched subjects.

"Are you getting out at all? Maybe a night out with the girls? Happy to babysit, you know."

She smiled for the first time. "I know. Celia misses you."

"Maybe I should schedule an appointment with her," he said, grabbing a pen.

She spread out both arms in mock defeat. "I get the hint."

"It's good to see you smile again. I haven't seen that for a while."

AMY PULLED off the headset as she finished the call. She needed to stop by the ladies' room, but before she could sign off her computer, it routed another call. She could take one quick call, she thought, and put the headset back on.

"Good evening, All Hands VRS . . . oh, hello," she said.

Sammy Clark stared at her from the monitor. "Yeah," he signed, "number's coming through now."

Amy adjusted her microphone nervously as the call connected.

"Hello," a woman's voice said.

"This is interpreter number—"

"She knows it's me," Sammy interrupted.

"Oh, OK," Amy stammered. "Go ahead with your call."

"I'm on for tonight," Sammy signed.

"What time?"

"You can pick up the stuff around three. I don't want it overnight."

"You should get out of the residential stuff and go bigger. Commercial, the jewelry exchanges, some big-ticket items."

"Can't do that by myself."

"Put together a team. Make some real money."

"No, thanks," Sammy signed. "Stores and warehouses mean real security systems. Guards, electric fences, stuff like that. These yuppie pukes don't want to be bothered by all that. They just want to park their beemers and go about their silly little lives. It's easier than taking candy from a kid."

"If *you* are around a kid, it's got nothing to do with candy."

"Leave my Internet adventures out of this. Are you ready or not?" Sammy signed.

"Why don't you let me show you what a real woman can do?" the voice in Amy's headset asked demurely. "You'll never think about children the same way again."

Sammy Clark leered at Amy while she signed. "Don't flatter yourself. Just be ready to pick up the stuff. I'm tagging a couple of places tonight. Should have quite a selection."

"Maybe you should do this full-time."

"Naw. I make more money with my Internet-based business."

"I'd hardly call that a business."

"'Cause you didn't think of it. I gotta go to work."

He pulled a finger across his neck to indicate he wanted the call terminated, then started signing again. "I've got some more calls I want to make. No need to announce anything. She's expecting the call."

Amy's jaw tightened and she swallowed the words she longed to say. It infuriated her to assist Sammy in what she suspected was almost certainly illegal. She hoped to be rid of him, but now he had *more* calls to make! Gathering all the professionalism she could muster, she replied with the least amount of enthusiasm possible.

"Put the number through, please."

She saw the number on her computer, and the system dialed an area code several counties over. A woman answered the phone.

"Hello?"

"Hello, Suzanne?" Sammy signed.

"Yes."

"It's Rebecca Gahranz. You so kindly replied to my e-mail."

"Oh, yes, dear. How are you?" Suzanne replied. Amy thought she sounded rather elderly.

"I'm fine, thank you so much for asking," Sammy replied. "I'm just still struggling with getting over my husband's death."

"You poor dear," Suzanne replied.

Amy felt a stab in her stomach. What was Sammy up to? She really didn't need to hear a made-up story about his made-up husband's made-up death. He was working some sort of scam. What was it?

"Like I told you in my e-mail, Sarron was the president-elect of Nigeria. He would have made a fine head of state! He could have pulled the nation out of poverty, brought them democracy and capitalism. Nigeria could have been something. We were both educated in the United States. We know what our little nation could be. Africa could've pulled itself out of its self-destructive cycle and taken its place on the world stage," Sammy finished.

"It's just not right what they did. There's still been no investigation? What's that group called? Oh, I just can't remember things the way I used to. They investigate crimes internationally," Suzanne stammered.

"Do you mean the United Nations?" Sammy asked.

"No, no, no. They're international like that, but they're police officers."

A long pause as Suzanne struggled to recall.

"Interpol?" Sammy came up with finally.

"Yes! That's it! Interpol! Can't they do something about it?" she implored.

Amy's pulse raced. What was this sleazeball doing? At a minimum, he was lying to this poor woman about being an African politician's widow. What was he really up to?

"Unfortunately, no, Interpol doesn't do investigations of this type. This was a Nigerian military helicopter that crashed, so the international community considers it an accident. But I know my husband was murdered. I know it. But I'm all alone now. I've no one to protect me," Sammy said.

"You poor dear. What will you do now?" Suzanne asked.

"I'm rebuilding my husband's party from the ground up. We'll start a new campaign, and I'm going to finish the important work he started. Nigeria will become a sovereign nation again. I swear it."

"You sound so determined!" Suzanne gushed. "I admire you so much for what you're doing."

"Thank you for your comforting words. Only someone like you who has also lost a loved one can understand what I am going through right now. The goal of carrying on my dear husband's work is the only thing keeping me going these days. Sadly, however, I simply cannot do it alone," Sammy continued, opening a bag of Doritos as he signed.

It was bad enough having to lip-read when people were eating—to also have to read their hands when they were popping food into their mouths only made it harder. Amy couldn't decide which was more disgusting—the silently mouthed words escaping his lips or the half-chewed food they were passing through.

"We must secure a mandate from the people. Our inspiration comes from your American revolution! We will begin small, just as you did so many years ago, and build into a grassroots movement that no false government will be able to stop!"

80

Amy could almost hear Suzanne's heartbeat. It was obvious she had become totally caught up in the "dream" Sammy had placed before her.

"How exciting! What can I do to help?" Suzanne asked breathlessly.

Amy felt a knot in the pit of her stomach. Anger was surging up within her—she knew exactly what Sammy was up to now. She knew what was coming before Sammy's hands even left the jar of salsa wedged between his legs.

"We need money to support the cause," Amy relayed. "We've identified corrupt officials we can bribe to get a few things done for us. They think it is for humanitarian aid from the U.S. and Europe. In actuality it's opening doors for us that would never be opened otherwise. We're going to build an insurgency of our own to take down the militias that are tearing the country apart."

"Oh, that sounds dangerous," Suzanne said hesitantly.

Amy perked up. Maybe Suzanne would back off, not want to participate because she thought it would be dangerous.

"No, this will be a bloodless coup," Sammy said. He had done his homework and was more than ready for the old lady's objection to violence. He tweaked his dialogue to give it an air of excitement and intrigue; made it sound like the good guys were just outsmarting the bad guys with his sly explanation. "We're going to sneak our way in. Remember how the Colombian Army rescued those hostages by tricking the insurgents? We are going to do the same."

"Oh, I saw that on CNN! It was very impressive. You think you can do that?" Suzanne asked.

"Only with help from good, God-fearing people like you," Sammy replied. He'd finished the chips and was now working through a bag of popcorn. "If you can spare a few dollars, it will go a long way to helping us free our nation. We can become a partner of the U.S. in Africa. We can make the world a better place. Wouldn't you like to be part of that?"

"Of course! How much do you need?" Suzanne asked.

Amy fidgeted, brimming with indignation. Surely there was some way to stop this.

Sammy Clark had as much to do with Nigerian insurgents as he did with the near side of Mars.

She couldn't believe Sammy was using her like this. He was going to take this poor woman's money and buy more—what? More popcorn? More chips? Maybe some more kiddie porn. Wouldn't that be nice?

Amy's jaws were locked, her head pounding. Her profuse sweating created dark stains under her arms. This piece of trash was taking advantage of an old lady, and Amy was forced to help do the job! It was all too apparent he fully knew the legal constraints involved. His arrogant smirk was more than she could bear.

Think, Amy, think, she chided herself. Surely there was a way to turn him in. Exactly what was his crime? She racked her brain trying to think of something. Anything.

Could it be mail fraud? Probably not, since most of their communication had been through VRS. How about a wire transfer? No. Amy had done numerous wire transfers for people buying houses or cars, or simply moving money around from one account to another. She'd interpreted every type of personal business transaction in the world, but her understanding of the legal limitations was rather thin. She could not think of a thing to stop this process from taking place right now, nothing to help this poor woman discover that she was being scammed.

Sammy had perfect timing. He knew the exact moment had come to make his move.

"Can you send five thousand?" he asked finally. "That should be enough to bribe the Nigerian Bank of Regents to get us an account started, and we can launch our internal struggle. You are a great woman to stand with us on this," Sammy continued. "Our grateful nation will hold you high in our thoughts and prayers."

"Oh, I'm just glad I can help," Suzanne said. "I've got my check-book. I'm writing you a check for five thousand dollars. Where can I send it?"

"We've set up an address in the United States so you don't have to pay overseas postage," Sammy replied.

How nice, Amy thought to herself. Not forcing someone to spend the additional postage necessary to give their money away for no reason. Amy was bouncing around in her chair so much that she noticed Sammy's eyes moving up and down in synchronicity. She stopped bouncing and started kicking her feet around instead. Maybe if she made enough noise in the background, Suzanne wouldn't be able to hear the information needed to make out the check.

"It's in Charlotte, North Carolina. The address is. . ."

Sammy suddenly disappeared, replaced by a blue screen. Amy cocked her head to one side. She'd never seen this before. She tapped a few keys on the computer, but Sammy and all his conniving plans were gone. She looked under the desk to determine what had happened.

Her kicking had accidentally dislodged the Ethernet cable from the computer. Sammy's videophone call had been dropped. She was at fault, but what could she do? Suzanne was still on the phone. Amy simply hung up.

"Can you hear me now?" she asked sarcastically, mimicking the popular cell phone ad. "Good. I just saved you five grand."

She felt bad for dropping the call, but at least Suzanne would keep her money. It gave Amy some satisfaction to realize Suzanne didn't have the videophone call-in number to call Sammy back. In fact, Suzanne was not even aware that a Video Relay Service was being used. Sammy had been quite cunning, using Amy's interpreting to make it appear to be a woman who was calling rather than a man. Suzanne would likely not have spoken to a man at all. But a woman claiming to be a widow, angry that her husband had been murdered, spreading democracy in Africa, trying to better herself and her country by partnering with the United States? Who wouldn't like that?

Amy's frustration took over and she kicked the computer again, this time on purpose. So many members of the Deaf community had lived in relative isolation because they had been unable to participate in the hearing world. Now the technology existed to converse with anyone over the phone, even another deaf person, and scum like Sammy Clark exploited the service to rip off old ladies. She was incensed, almost overcome with disgust and anger.

Calm down, she thought. *Deal with the question "What can I actually do about this?"* Kicking computer cables out was hardly a permanent solution, and it's not like she could advocate that other interpreters have the same sorts of accidents on a regular basis. Carol Burdick would never stand for it. Somehow there had to be another way to push back against people like Sammy Clark.

She was determined to figure out what it was.

Chapter Seven

SEERS PUT the report down. He'd already read it three times, and it still wasn't sinking in. It was impossible to concentrate on other investigations. He couldn't get his mind off Frank Stratton's Navy Cross. He was a marine. But there was more to it than that. Stratton was an officer who'd put his life at risk for enlisted guys. Those Navy medics and the majority of the Beirut casualties were low-rank grunts. Many of them were just kids. But that hadn't factored into Frank Stratton's decision that day in 1983. Seers respected the hell out of that. He would need some help on this one, but he didn't want the aggravation he would have to endure to get it.

"I'll make it worth your while," Seers said aloud.

Earlier, he'd tried and failed to con Ryan Richter into doing him a favor. Richter was a young officer, the techno-wizard brain trust for the Second District Metropolitan Police Department. Seers wanted him to get on the Internet and check out some of the more nefarious sites where military materials were routinely swapped, sold, or bartered for other stolen booty.

Ryan knew these sites intimately. Being the technology guy meant a lot of time behind a computer screen, but as a member of the SWAT team, he also got to go out on the more interesting criminal investigations. Seers had always thought the kid had the perfect job for someone his age. Long periods of time playing on the computer punctuated regularly by running out of the building to the SWAT team van. As the technical surveillance officer, Ryan had a huge assortment of high-end electronics for snooping on bad guys.

"What do you have in mind?" Richter asked.

Seers pondered just how much it would take to motivate Richter to tackle this job for him. "I'll take you on my next surveillance assignment," Seers offered.

"Boring!" Richter shouted. "What else you got?"

Seers thought for a moment. "How about meeting some of the candidates? I can probably get you backstage with someone for a photo op. Get them all and you're guaranteed to give your parents a picture of you with the next president."

"Nope. I'm apolitical," Richter said.

Seers had known all along the carrot to dangle before him; he just hated offering it. The guys would call for his head for this.

"Fine. Do this for me and I'll take you to poker night," he said.

"Really? You mean it?" Richter replied, as excited as a child bribed with a trip to the zoo.

"Yes, damn it, I promise. Can you just look, please?" Seers asked.

"I'm on it."

Ryan practically floated to his computer terminal and sat down. Seers could hear the young man typing—a Billy Joel–style virtuoso on a different breed of keyboard. He shook his head. If Stratton's sword and cross were anywhere in cyberspace, Richter would find it. Seers picked up his phone and dialed a downtown extension.

"Good afternoon, FBI. May I help you?" a voice asked.

"Glenn Carver, please," Seers said.

"Thank you. Just a moment."

Seers waited. After a couple of seconds, a gruff voice spoke.

"Military Affairs."

"Glenn! Mike Seers. How's business?"

"Don't ask! I've not had a day off since they made it a felony," Carver replied.

The Medal of Honor had long been the only military decoration protected by federal law. The Stolen Valor Act had extended similar protection to other decorations and made it illegal to wear or falsely claim to have received the nation's highest awards for military service.

Glenn Carver was the FBI's point man on the issue, taking considerable pleasure in locking people up for impersonating legitimate honorees. Unfortunately, business was brisk.

"Listen. What's the market value for a Navy Cross?" Seers asked.

"Market value?" Carver repeated.

"What's it worth? How much can you get for it?"

"You'd have to be pretty stupid to wear one nowadays. Every medal's legitimate recipients are on the Internet. Anyone can look them up and dime out a fake pretty quick. Happens every day."

Seers thought about this for a moment. Why would someone go to so much trouble to steal Frank Stratton's medal?

"How about this," Seers continued. "The sword. A Marine Corps sword. Gotta be some value there."

"Not much, really. Either someone's really desperate or they stole something they didn't know had little real monetary value," Carver said. "What are you chasing down?"

"Retired Marine colonel. Someone got into his apartment and took his sword and a Navy Cross. He's legit. I saw the citation. I can't get a bead on *who*, because I can't figure out *why*."

"Nothing else taken?"

"Nada. No forced entry. No kids in the family. No other visitors. The man himself isn't much help. He's in poor health. Getting older. Parkinson's. Some other problems. You know what I mean."

"Yeah, I do," Carver said quietly. "Sorry, Mike. I've got nothing. You might check the pawnshops. My guess is whoever got them probably had trouble unloading them. We've gotten too good at prosecuting anyone claiming a medal they didn't earn. And there are not too many places you can go anymore carrying a sword. I'm afraid I'm not much help."

"It's OK. Thanks for your time, Glenn. I've got one of our guys doing the online thing right now. Maybe he'll come up with something."

"I can probably help you with a replacement if you want to go that route," Glenn offered.

Replacing someone's medal didn't sit well with Seers. If it was lost or damaged, sure, he understood that. But getting the government to replace it would be time-consuming and take a mountain of paperwork. Replicas would be faster and could be picked up right downtown at street vendors, but he could never do that, either. Frank Stratton deserved a real medal. More to the point, he deserved his own damned medal back. He'd earned it.

"No, thanks, but I'll keep the offer in mind. If anything with the name Stratton crosses your desk, can you give me a shout?" Seers asked.

"You got it," Carver replied. "Listen, there are some groups that can help the family out with the Parkinson's problem. Some good guys, ex-military, too. I've gotten to know some of the leadership over the years. I'll e-mail you their names and phone numbers."

"I'd appreciate that. Thanks," Seers answered.

There was a short silence on the other end of the phone.

"This one's pissed you off," Carver noted finally.

"Am I that transparent?" Seers asked.

"I'd be disappointed if you weren't. Wish I could be there when you catch the son of a bitch."

HEATH WALKED down the fourth floor hallway at Secret Service headquarters and poked his head into office 431.

"Is this a good time?" he asked.

Cheryl Corely looked up from a file on her desk.

"Hey there! Sure, come on in," she replied. "You never come see me anymore," she cooed.

Heath shrugged. "Sorry. You know the rules. No fraternizing."

"Spoilsport!" she teased.

They enjoyed a healthy flirtation, both comfortable in the fact that it would never go anywhere. The service strictly forbade intra-staff relationships. The few times it had occurred, one party was always transferred and the other forced to leave the service completely for other parts of the U.S. government. Word had gotten around, and nobody else was foolish enough to break the simple rule: don't fish from the company dock.

Heath dropped into a chair across from her desk. "Same old thing?" he asked.

"Yes and no," she replied. "Yes it's the same Nigeria e-mail we've seen a thousand times for the past few years."

"And?"

"Well, Lagos, Nigeria, may not be the most glorious spot on earth, but they aren't stupid, either. They know we have virtually no way to reach out to them and, even if we did, we have no leverage to stop this type of activity," she said.

The Secret Service had recently closed the Nigeria field office due to the increasing violence in the country. Insurgents attacking oil fields and refineries were increasing their strikes in the major cities to include American government and business interests. It was simply too dangerous.

"So it's a free-for-all now, huh?" Heath asked.

"More or less. I did a semantics analysis, and it's the same thing we've seen in the past. Not a real threat to anyone. English is their second language. Whoever is writing is simply in it for the money and suckering enough people to make it worthwhile. Apparently they figured out how to tweak it specifically to address what the U.S. media is covering on events in Nigeria. It'll die down again after making the rounds and be dormant for a while. Then they'll figure out another unique tweak based on the story of the day, and we'll see the whole thing all over again," she said.

"Great," Heath replied. "So there's nothing to be done."

"Not really," she said. "Too bad, too. I took the semantics analysis and did a quick and dirty remote psychological profile."

Cheryl had majored in psychology at Georgetown. That's where she and Heath had met, when a sorority sister fixed them up on a blind date.

"Remote profile?" Heath asked.

"The bureau isn't the only agency that profiles bad guys they don't have access to," Cheryl noted. "I've got the advantage of these e-mails. Lots of good fodder to filter through, get a picture of the guy, or gal, sending it."

"Which is it, gal or guy?" Heath asked.

"Can't say. Since they're not using their primary language and altering it for a target audience, it's nearly impossible to determine the original author's gender."

"But you can tell other things?" he asked.

"I can tell their preferences, or at least a close approximation of them," Cheryl replied. "You remember taking the MBTI when you applied to the service?"

Heath loved the ins and outs of how Cheryl could dissect, analyze, and profile people and their circumstances without them even being aware of it.

The Myers-Briggs Type Indicator, or MBTI, was the most widely used psychological instrument in the world. Unlike similar tools, it had been used successfully overseas in non-English-speaking countries and was therefore helpful in solving crimes that had an international perspective.

MBTI categorized people into sixteen distinct subsets based on their preferences. What was a person's orientation in the world? Were they an introvert or an extrovert? How did they perceive information? By sensory gathering or via intuition? How did they make decisions? Were they a thinker or a feeler? Finally, which of these did they generally prefer—taking in information or making decisions? Did they like to judge or perceive?

After determining which of the categories a person fell into, it was possible to determine what preferences he or she might have. MBTI was not a good instrument for predicting action—or, for the Secret Service's interests—specific *behavior*. But it did offer a powerful starting point when looking for certain types of personalities who might threaten a president or other government official. Knowing what a potential bad guy preferred gave the service a starting point.

"Sure," Heath replied.

Cheryl pulled the file from a nearby credenza. "Your author is most likely an ISTP. That's an introvert, sensor, thinker, and perceiver."

"I vaguely remember the different categories. What can you tell me about the person?" Heath asked.

"You're dealing with an impulsive type. An egalitarian, someone loyal to his perceived 'brothers' and leery of authority. ISTPs are insubordinate. They don't break rules and regulations so much as simply ignore them. He is, however, a master with a weapon, a real virtuoso with whatever he chooses," she said.

"Sounds like the perfect insurgent," Heath said.

"I doubt it," Cheryl cautioned. "Insurgents are temperamental. This guy's not like that. His weapon of choice is a computer. ISTPs work on impulse, not on a schedule. He would avoid any type of hierarchy or authority. To others he'd seem like a loner. His companionship is only through that weapon—in this case, a computer. But he's not a conversationalist. Nowadays we might label someone like that as dyslexic or learning disabled, which is complete crap. They're simply bored. Normal education tactics won't work on them. They learn at their own pace and in their own way."

"A fun bunch," Heath noted wryly.

"Fortunately, like many bullies, they're not difficult to defeat if you know how," Cheryl said. "These guys aren't good strategists. They're great fighters, though. You'll see a lot of this type on SWAT teams or in Special Operations. But they have to lead from the front. They're sort of glory hounds. They want the credit. Patton and Rommel were both probably this type, good at utilizing what limited resources they had available to exploit an enemy."

"Like a naïve bleeding heart American who gets a note from overseas promising big bucks for helping out with this minor banking transaction."

"Exactly," Cheryl finished, closing the file. "They want no obligations or confining duties. They just want to be left alone to bask in what they've managed to pull over on the rest of the world."

"Terrific," Heath said.

"I can probably do a FIRO-B for you if you think it's worthwhile," Cheryl offered.

Heath thought for a moment. To what end? What could he possibly do with Cheryl's work once she finished? There was no longer a Secret Service office in Lagos, so it wasn't like someone could simply stump out a few hours of shoe leather if he asked. Not that they would have done it anyway. Nigeria was one of the last few countries churning out high-quality counterfeit dollars. The agents who had just left the country had active investigations going on that would now either fall by the wayside or be conducted out of another nation.

Given the recent spike in violence, the likelihood of flying someone into Nigeria to chase down an e-mail's author was very low. There was nothing he could do with this. The case may as well be closed. Other than tell American consumers to ignore and delete the e-mails, there wasn't much to do.

"No, don't waste your time," Heath told her. "I'll tell Walt it's just a variation on what we've seen before. Maybe instead of trying to stop the writer from sending them we can reach out to his target audience more. Get the word out that another variation is making the rounds."

"That's a good idea. Be proactive."

"Exactly."

"If I can help in any way, let me know," Cheryl said.

"I will. And thank you. This is way more than I expected. I may share a few of your points with the community."

Heath was getting an idea. Walt might not like it—but then again, he just might. He looked at her thoughtfully, wondering if there were any legal obstacles to this.

"What?" Cheryl asked.

"Well, since we know this guy's preferences, what if his e-mail was inundated with spam? Suppose people started giving him false information about their contact info, banking records, that sort of thing? You said if he's making money he'll keep doing it."

"Right."

"What if he's no longer making money? What if it becomes such an inconvenient pain in the ass he can't get to the legitimate victims who might actually give him money, because all of these others are now in the way?" he smiled.

"You're bad," Cheryl said.

"What? That's not a crime. Imagine if thousands of people started responding to this crap, but rather than give their real bank information they just provided random numbers? As long as they use the correct number of digits for routing and account numbers, the guy would have no idea what's real and what's BS until he tried them. The banks, even in Nigeria, would have to notice. They'd get tired of him taking up their time. He'd have to move on. Eventually he'd get sick of spending all that wasted time and money with nothing to show for it!" Heath replied.

"Not exactly Eliot Ness, but not bad!" Cheryl said.

Heath flashed a wickedly satisfied smile and gave himself a mental *attaboy* as he bounced out the door to Walt's office.

AMY LEANED back against the soft wicker of the rocking lounge chair. She loved Hilton Head, the gentle sea breeze, and the smell of the low country. She recalled how she and Jeff had always relaxed for a few minutes over iced teas before the back nine on practice rounds. The Sea Pines Resort was hands down her favorite part of the professional tour.

One year they went a few days early to attend the annual Blessing of the Fleet in nearby Beaufort, South Carolina. Every year, commercial shrimping vessels received a blessing from the church in a festival that continued to grow in popularity. Amy had never heard of a shrimp burger before, but quickly moved it to the top of her tour food preferences. She could smell the marsh on the patio of the Shrimp Shack right now.

"So—how are things since our last visit?" a voice asked, interrupting the pleasant memory.

Amy's eyes opened. She could still see the horizontal stripes of the Harbor Town Lighthouse, but the framed lithograph couldn't hold a candle to the real thing. Why Dr. Brown had ever chosen to leave that area escaped her.

"OK, I guess," she answered finally.

"Friends and family still helping?"

"Yes," she replied.

"Are you getting out?"

"Kathy and I go out for drinks every now and again. She's pissed at me for not going out the other night."

"Ah. The anniversary?" he asked.

"Yes," she answered in a hoarse whisper.

"Probably would have been a good idea. What did you do?"

"I took Celia to his grave and talked about him."

"I thought you talked about him every night."

"I do—but I thought it was important to go to his grave."

"Important for you or for her?"

"Touché."

"Who else are you going out with?" he asked.

"Do I need more than one?"

"A man. Are you seeing anyone?"

"No."

"Don't you want to?"

"What? Bring home a guy from a bar? It's bad enough Celia wanders the house at night looking for her dad. All I need is for her to find some strange man in the house instead. You'll have both of us in here, and the guy would run for the hills if a little girl he'd never seen before walked up and called him Daddy."

"So she's not just crying out?"

"No. She gets up and walks around. She was just coming into my room."

"What is she doing now?" he asked.

94

"She wanders throughout the house. Guest room, bathrooms, I even found her in the kitchen one night. I'm terrified she'll fall down the stairs and hurt herself."

"Not unusual for a child her age to sleepwalk after the loss of a parent."

"Sometimes I feel like joining her."

"Do you?"

"No, of course not," she replied irritably. "I just put her back to bed."

"Why would you want to join her? Are you sad?"

"It's not just sadness. I'm, I'm . . ."

"What? Say it!"

"I'm angry! I'm angry, damn it!" she said forcefully.

"What are you angry about?"

"He left me!"

"You're mad at Jeff for dying?"

"Yes," Amy cried. "I'm a derelict wife."

"You're not a derelict wife. Frankly, I was concerned you hadn't gotten angry earlier. It's one of the major milestones in the grief process," he said.

"See! I can't even grieve right!"

He cast a sarcastic glare at her. "So why aren't you seeing anyone?"

"You mean dating?"

"Yes! Don't make me pull teeth."

"I'm too screwed up to be attracted to anyone, not that they'd be attracted to me right now, either."

"So you've not had a physical relationship since . . ."

"No, Dr. Brown, I've not had sex in over a year."

"Does that bother you?"

"Not as much as talking about it, no."

He couldn't suppress his smile. "Points for honesty. So you're telling me that in a year you've not met anyone even remotely interesting?"

Amy hesitated before answering. "Well, no. I met a guy recently."

"Tell me about him."

"He's a Secret Service agent."

"Are you going to see him again?"

"I didn't really see him to begin with. We met professionally."

"Why not meet him personally as well?"

"I don't think it's a good idea. He's deaf."

Brown stopped scribbling on his notepad and glared at her. "I could write a book on the irony of your last statement," he said. His deadpan response caught her off guard.

"What? Why?" Amy asked.

"The stereotyping, discrimination, and host of psychological prejudices you just succinctly stated."

"Me?"

He put his pen down and leaned toward her. "Have a drink with him. Do it as a favor to me. Just one drink. I promise it won't kill you."

Chapter Eight

A MY TURNED off the television. There was nothing good on, and she wasn't paying attention anyway. She had too many things on her mind.

Dr. Brown wanted her to date. Mike Seers wanted her to mind her own business. Sammy Clark wanted her to help him steal. Nobody cared about what *she* wanted! Of course that begged the question: *What did she want?*

A normal life, but she'd given up on normal. Her life had been anything but normal for way too long. Jeff. Hal Kensington. Dell Kohler. Even Champ. Too much death. It was overwhelming. None of it made any sense. She'd never even had a chance to figure out the story on Champ. She'd hit a brick wall on that front. She couldn't do anything now that he was dead.

What about the groomer? She'd concentrated so much on Champ she'd never chased down the groomer. She remembered the name of the shop from the newspaper article the day Kensington died: Pawfect Grooming Services. She'd never determined whether the groomer was ripping Kensington off. Granted, her only source of evidence was gone, but maybe there were other things she could find out. Perhaps she could prevent the same thing from happening to someone else.

Amy fired up her laptop and logged onto the Internet. Pawfect had a good Web site; lots of photos of dogs and testimonials from satisfied customers. She clicked on Favorites and then on Angie's List.

Amy loved this site and had recently subscribed to the magazine as well. She'd used the service to find a plumber, a flower shop, and a mechanic, and was extremely satisfied with the recommendations she'd gotten. Angie's List was also very popular in Deaf circles because it included companies and service providers that were either proficient in American Sign Language or had ready access to someone who could interpret.

Amy clicked through a few screens and noted several reviews of Pawfect. They glowed: "Best dog groomer in the Washington area, hands down"; "Exemplary service"; "Nicest guy on earth and a hell of a dog enthusiast." Additional comments went on and on in the same vein. They didn't support her theory of Kensington being ripped off. She wondered if these comments could be put-up jobs, planted by people friendly with the groomer or placed by the groomer himself. She should look elsewhere.

Amy checked on the Greater Washington Better Business Bureau Web site. Clicking through the vast database, she found numerous dog and cat groomers. The huge number of well-paid Washington residents, from diplomatic staff to senior career government types, apparently included in their numbers quite a few dog lovers. They were willing to spend extraordinary amounts on their fur-covered family members. There were four doggie treat stores in Alexandria alone. It was crazy!

But the BBB had listings for everyone. Amy found many negative statements and more than one legal action against groomers, kennel operators, so-called pet spas, and even a couple of pedigree fertility clinics for maintaining blue-blooded genealogies. Pawfect was listed there as well, but there wasn't a single negative word about it. There were several positive statements of record, though none as effusive as what she'd seen on the Web site. This guy's clients really loved him.

Maybe she should drop by and take a look at the place firsthand. See what it felt like inside. But Amy didn't have a dog. Chasing Celia was more than enough of a workout. How would she explain loitering around a grooming business without a dog? Maybe she could ask if the owner knew of anyone wanting to get rid of an animal. She looked at Celia playing on the floor.

She'd need a child-friendly dog, of course, she would explain. Something big enough, but not too big. Something she could care for without it completely taking over her life. She would seek the groomer's counsel because she would need his services. She wouldn't have time to properly care for a dog with work and her daughter and everything else in her life. Seeking his advice—well, it just made good sense.

"Want to go for a ride, pumpkin?" she asked Celia, who jumped from the floor into her mother's arms.

Twenty minutes later, Amy pulled up in front of Pawfect Grooming Services. It was very quiet. There were no cars in the small parking lot outside and the interior of the shop was dark. Amy got out of the car and looked around nervously. It wasn't a bad part of Arlington, but it wouldn't win awards for neighborhood of the year, either. What really bothered her was that she couldn't see anyone at all.

Amy put a movie into the vehicle's DVD player to occupy Celia and adjusted the sound since the car was now stopped. She left Celia inside but didn't lock the door. This made her uncomfortable, but she didn't want to risk being locked out in this neighborhood with Celia strapped inside.

"I'll be right over there, baby," Amy said. She left the window cracked but closed the door. She made another furtive glance in both directions before approaching the front door.

Two large UPS delivery boxes were stacked on the front stoop. Nobody had been in here recently. She looked at the date on one box. Could it really have been there for three days? She heard barking inside but no movement. She banged on the door several times before noticing the doorbell. She pushed the button and saw several blue lights flicker inside. She pushed the button again. The lamps momentarily lit again before returning to darkness.

Several sticky notes were affixed to the doorjamb. The company phone number was prominently stenciled on the front door and Amy called it, wondering if someone was in the back of the shop. The call was picked up by an answering machine that indicated that the message recorder was full and couldn't accept additional calls.

Weird. There was no one here. The front stoop contained packages and notes, and nobody answered the phone. What to make of this? Should she call the police? That would only mean another visit from Detective Seers. She really didn't want a repeat of their previous conversation. She'd nearly broken down and told him what she'd seen. She was just so frazzled when Seers berated her. No wonder people falsely confessed during interrogations. She couldn't imagine what it would be like at police headquarters.

No, calling the police was out. Seers might actually consider charging her with something. She needed another option. But what?

The shop's proprietor was listed as "BJ," along with a cell phone number. Amy dialed the number and got another voice-mail system that similarly said it was full and could not take additional calls. Amy hung up the phone, listening to Celia's annoyance at Marlin's overbearing nature in *Finding Nemo*. Nobody here, nobody on the phone, no way of knowing when anyone would be here.

Where was this BJ?

By the time she drove them home, it was dark and Celia had fallen asleep. She tucked the little girl into bed and decided to retire early herself. Too much running around with no results to show for it. A good time to simply turn in.

Amy left a few windows open upstairs so the cool fall air could move through the house. After the sultry D.C. summer, it was nice to let a few early whiffs of autumn creep into their lives. She slept better with the windows cracked a bit; air-conditioning had never really appealed to her.

Tonight was perfect, barely a hint of fall but nonetheless there. She slept soundly and deeply, never hearing the movement in the hallway. She didn't roll over, didn't stretch out on her back, and had no reason to suspect anything was amiss. It was the first decent sleep she'd had since Harold Kensington died. She was calmly, blissfully dreaming—until the screaming began.

Amy rocketed out of bed, her feet flailing wildly against the thin sheet still draped around her. Her eyes took several seconds to adjust to the ambient light, giving her heart plenty of time to race up to a hundred beats a minute. Her pupils dilated as adrenaline poured into her bloodstream. Screams. In the house. Outside her bedroom.

Amy flung open the door, unprepared for the scene before her. Celia lay on the ground, eyes squeezed shut, her entire face bathed in crimson. Her tiny fists were rubbing her eyes raw, and her hair was coated in blood. From where she lay her legs were straddling the hallway table leg on the corner. A corner with a pronounced bloodstain.

"Oh my God!" Amy yelled as she swept Celia into her arms. She carried her into the master bedroom to wipe her daughter's face with the comforter. Celia screamed even louder. Amy fumbled with the phone to dial 911.

"Emergency services—can I help you?" a man's voice asked.

"It's my daughter," Amy cried. "She's hurt. She's bleeding. Send an ambulance, please!"

The emergency dispatcher confirmed her address and told Amy he would stay on the line with her until the ambulance arrived.

"Can you open the door for them? Do you need assistance?" he asked.

"I'll try," Amy replied. "I'm alone in here and I'm trying to stop the bleeding."

"Hold on. Let me get a nurse on the line," he said.

"Good evening. What's your emergency?" a woman asked after a minor eternity.

"My name is Amy Kellen." She struggled to control her emotions. "My daughter Celia is three. She walked into a hallway table and caught the corner. She's bleeding."

"Did she hit the corner directly or did she fall on it?" the nurse asked.

"From what I can tell, she hit it straight on," Amy replied.

Celia continued screaming. The comforter was dripping blood. Amy stood up to take Celia to the bathroom.

"Hang on. I'm moving us to the bathroom."

She put the phone on the vanity and flipped the light on. Celia's cries went up an octave and Amy immediately flipped the light back off.

"What happened?" the nurse yelled from the handset.

"She freaked out when I turned the light on," Amy replied. "What does that mean? Does she have a concussion?" she cried.

"That doesn't automatically mean a concussion," the nurse replied. "She could be scared, she could be light sensitive, it could be several things. Is there enough light for you to see where the wound is?"

Amy peered closely at her daughter. "It's somewhere in her hair, I think. She's all bloodied and matted. Oh my God!" Amy sobbed.

"Ma'am!" the nurse yelled. "You can do that later. Right now I need you to check out your daughter. Can you tell if she hit her eyes? Is there any apparent damage there?"

"Not that I can see, but she's got them squeezed shut. Should I try to force them open to check?" Amy asked.

"Absolutely not!" the nurse said. "If you don't see anything let's assume they're not damaged. Concentrate on her mouth. She's crying, so there's no immediate airway blockage, but do you see anything there? Any teeth missing? Any blood in her mouth? Did she bite her tongue?"

"No, not that I can see," Amy replied, sticking her face all the way into Celia's.

"Do you see a wound in her hairline area?" the nurse asked.

"I can't see it, but there's so much blood," Amy said, her voice cracking again.

"Ignore it," the nurse said unflappably. "Head wounds are notorious bleeders. Apply direct pressure, but don't overdo it. Just enough to keep her from bleeding too much. You say she hit a hallway table?"

"Yes," Amy replied.

"Is she normally up this late?" the nurse asked.

"She wasn't up," Amy said. "She went to bed at eight. She's been sleepwalking recently. But she's never walked into anything before."

There was a pause on the phone. Amy couldn't hear anything and thought the line had somehow disconnected. "Are you still there?" she asked.

"Recently divorced?" the nurse asked.

"No. My husband died about a year ago," Amy replied. "Why?"

A siren announced the arrival of the ambulance to the front of her house. Amy stood up, still cradling Celia in her arms.

"Sounds like the guys are there. I'll see you when you arrive," the nurse said.

Amy hung up the phone and raced down the stairs to unlock the front door. An EMT burst in carrying an enormous first aid kit, followed by a second medic pulling a wheeled gurney. She tried laying Celia on the couch, but she kicked and screamed too much.

"Ma'am, why don't you just sit down and hold her?" the EMT said. "My name is Rob. Let me ask you a few questions as we work."

Rob inquired about any allergies Celia had to medications, about her general health, and about the last time she'd eaten. Amy didn't care that she was clad in little more than a sheer nightgown, but once they lifted a calmed Celia onto the gurney, the night air pouring in from the open front door felt cool against the blood-soaked fabric. She self-consciously looked down, more horrified by her daughter's loss of blood than by any modesty.

"Ma'am, why don't you pull on some clothes while we get her stabilized in the truck?" Rob said.

Amy looked at them both, two strangers walking out into the night with her daughter. She didn't have the first idea of who they were or where they were taking her.

"We won't leave without you," Rob said reassuringly, aware of what was racing through her mind. "It will take us a few minutes. Go do what you need to do, and don't forget your keys."

Amy raced through her bedroom and peeled her nightgown off. She pulled on a T-shirt and sweatpants, then grabbed her purse and stepped into a pair of shoes. In a few seconds she'd locked the front door and was sitting by Celia's side as the ambulance pulled away.

Four minutes later they arrived at Georgetown University Hospital's emergency room. A team of physicians awaited them and carefully lifted Celia from the rear of the vehicle. Amy walked in and was immediately directed to the admitting office to complete the requisite paperwork. A few minutes later, she was back by Celia's side as doctors examined her.

"Amy?" a voice behind her asked.

Amy turned to find a young Hispanic nurse standing to one side.

"Yes," Amy replied.

"I'm Carlene. We spoke on the phone," she said, extending her hand.

Amy stared at her for several seconds, trying to process the information. "You're the nurse," she said finally. Carlene smiled. "Oh my God, thank you so much." Amy moved past the hand and hugged Carlene like a linebacker.

"You're very welcome," she replied. "Do we see any real problems here?" Carlene asked the medical team.

Both physicians and the trauma nurse looked to each other in silent coordination before shaking their heads in agreement. Celia would be fine.

"I don't think this will even warrant stitches," one said. "We'll have to shave a little area of hair away, but I think a butterfly bandage will more than suffice."

He returned to his work, the brief interruption of speaking with his patient's mother apparently now out of the way, allowing him to concentrate on more important matters.

Amy's knees weakened at the news that her daughter's injury was less traumatic than she'd first thought. Carlene noticed Amy's unsteadiness and reached out to grab her arm.

"We'll be outside," Carlene said to the medical team as she moved Amy through the double doors of the surgical suite to a couch in the waiting area. She sat Amy down and offered her a bottle of water.

"No, thank you," Amy said, still shaking. "I kind of lost my balance there for a second."

"Happens all the time," Carlene said. "We got interrupted on the phone."

"We did?" Amy replied, trying to recall at what point Rob and the ambulance team had arrived.

"You said your husband died around a year ago?" Carlene asked.

"Yes. An accident," Amy said, still regaining her composure.

"I'm very sorry to hear that," Carlene said. "That's got to be very tough, trying to raise a little girl on your own."

Amy allowed a nervous, exhausted, exasperated laugh as she teared up. "Yeah, that's something of an understatement."

"How long has she been sleepwalking?" Carlene asked.

"That's a fairly new thing," Amy said.

"Have there been other 'things'?" Carlene asked.

"She was just crying out for her father," Amy said. "It's been more pronounced lately."

"What's changed?" Carlene asked.

"I had to switch careers to take care of her," Amy said. "Jeff was the primary caregiver before he died. We're still getting the hang of it."

"It will definitely be an adjustment for you both. Sounds like you know that."

"I heard it from someone who knows a few things about this," Amy said guardedly.

"Bereavement therapist?" Carlene asked.

Amy's gaze fell to the floor.

"That's nothing to be ashamed of," Carlene said. "It's not like they offer classes on how to live without your spouse when you get married."

Amy nodded. "Yeah," she managed to croak as her throat tightened. She refused to cry in front of Carlene.

"I'm not trying to upset you," Carlene said. "But I want to make sure you discuss this with your therapist."

"Why?" Amy asked.

"Sleepwalking after the death of a parent is not unusual," Carlene says. "What I'm concerned about is that she must have been moving pretty fast."

"What do you mean?" Amy asked.

"Most children who sleepwalk go slow. They're not in a real hurry. They may be looking for something, like a recently lost parent, for instance, but they're not rushing around. Most sleepwalking takes place at home, where the child knows the location of most objects. Like a blind person who has memorized the location of everything in their home, kids don't normally collide into stuff when they sleepwalk."

"So what happened tonight?" Amy asked.

"She might not have been walking. She might have been running," Carlene said.

"But why?"

"I don't know. She might have been running *to* something, or maybe *away* from something. She might have gotten scared. Bad dreams are not unheard-of with sleepwalkers. If she's upset about her father's death, she might have gotten scared and was trying to find him when she hit the corner of the table."

Amy was lost in an incredible feeling of loneliness. Picturing Celia running past her bedroom, hitting the hallway table on her way to the stairs and out of the house. How was she supposed to deal with this? Celia hadn't come to Amy's bedroom when she was scared, running from some midnight bogeyman.

Amy winced at the realization that Celia was trying to find Jeff, who, a year after his death, was still her foremost parent. There had hardly been time to grieve over him. Amy had been thrust immediately into the position of accepting a new job—a new career, actually. She recognized she had somehow not met Celia's needs in adjusting to all the changes. Any three-year-old is a handful, but Amy was not able to explain the concept of death to Celia. She'd struggled with telling her that Daddy would never come home—that he was gone, forever.

How would Celia not feel she was somehow at fault? How could Amy convince her, when she wasn't convinced of it herself? But Celia was not to blame. If anyone was responsible for Jeff's death, it was not his daughter—it was his wife. She was the reason he'd gone to the driving range that night.

Amy buried her face in her hands and slumped over sobbing into Carlene's lap.

Chapter Nine

AMY PICKED up her cappuccino and walked into the DeafCoffee meeting. She did a double take when Heath Rasco waved at her from a nearby table.

"Hi," Amy said. "What are you doing here?"

"Oh, I volunteered to talk about some of the stuff the Secret Service does besides protect the president. Explain some of our sneaky techniques," Heath replied.

"Hey, that's great!"

Heath smiled, pleased that Amy was happy to see him. "Well, I guess I'd better start," he stammered, suddenly nervous.

"Are you going to talk about what you showed us?" Amy asked.

"No. This is something different, another one of our dastardly methods."

Heath was introduced to the crowd. He began signing and speaking to the twenty-five attendees about something called elicitation.

"Now, when I say elicitation, I don't want you confusing it with *solicitation*," he warned.

Laughter rippled through the crowd; people made the ASL gesture for clapping by holding their arms up and wiggling their hands. Amy smiled.

"That's all I need, is someone calling my boss tomorrow saying, 'The Secret Service told me to hire a hooker.'"

More laughter. Heath was apparently accustomed to speaking in front of groups.

"Elicitation is a means of coaxing someone to say or do something without their conscious knowledge that they are being manipulated. It's used all the time by car salesmen, lawyers, and other disreputable members of society," he continued.

Amy watched him, his relaxed way of communicating with the group, and suddenly found she was considering Dr. Brown's advice. Maybe she should have a drink with him. What could it hurt? He was around her age. Attractive. He didn't have a wedding band on, but that didn't mean he wasn't married or seeing someone. Surely an attractive federal agent had a girlfriend?

Girlfriend? Her thoughts shocked her. Was she really concerned about whether or not he had a girlfriend? With all the challenges in her life right now, she didn't need to worry if Secret Service Special Agent Heath Rasco had a girlfriend. Still, he *was* cute. Maybe it might come up in conversation over that drink.

"Now, speaking of disreputable," Heath said, "there are people out there who will take advantage of you. The good news is, you, we, are not actually being discriminated against because of our hearing problems. People with perfectly good hearing are getting the same e-mails, chat room conversations, and snail mail that we are. What's brought it to the attention of the Secret Service is the use of Video Relay Services."

Amy leaned forward. Could Heath be working on this issue? She didn't even know the Secret Service was aware of it, much less that they were trying to respond.

"Capture rate is what I think is getting this some additional attention. Unfortunately, this is all guesswork. We don't have any real numbers about how many of these solicitations go out, much less how many get routed, intentionally or otherwise, to members of the Deaf community. What we do know is that the people doing this are using video relay to reach out specifically to you. We wanted everyone to be aware that this is going on, aware that it's totally fraudulent, and aware that there is something that can be done about it."

Numerous people in the crowd nodded and clapped. Even some of the other Starbucks customers who were not deaf were milling around trying to listen. Heath signed and spoke aloud to reach all the members of his audience.

"Please understand this—the interpreters working in video relay cannot do anything about it! Work with me here, folks. They can do *nothing*. The people trying to take your money certainly understand this. It's not just the Nigerian e-mail scam anymore. These guys have figured out lots of new tricks and will use the video relay system to contact you. They're getting your information from MySpace accounts, LinkedIn, and a thousand other Web sites covering any area of interest you care to name. It's not only Deaf sites—your information is moved, shared, and copied by the firms you do business with just as it is in the hearing world."

Amy looked around the room. Everyone was paying rapt attention. She didn't know why the Secret Service had gotten involved, but she wished everyone who used VRS could be sitting here. Too bad nobody had thought to videotape it. It would be a good YouTube video to share with the community.

"Your VRS calls are not covered under the National Do Not Call List. You *can* receive commercial pitches this way. I know you don't like it. Neither do I. But right now, at this time, there is no way around it. I suggest every one of you contact your congressional representative. It's an election year, so they should actually be paying attention. This issue affects their constituents, all of you, and they should hear from you. This can be solved, but it has to be done by lawmakers. They only take action when enough people *force* them to do so. Tell your government officials to give VRS the same 'do not call' protection as the phones in the hearing world. We'll all be safer consumers as a result."

Heath answered a few questions, then rejoined Amy at the table.

"Wow! You're a pro!" she exclaimed, accidentally revealing more admiration than she'd intended.

"No, not at all. The last thing I want to do is talk in front of a crowd. I'm a watcher, not a talker."

"Well, I thought it was great," she gushed.

Heath smiled, his confidence bolstered by the compliment. "Thank you. I appreciate that."

They fumbled for a follow-up topic.

"Seems like a nice crowd," Heath offered. "Do you come here much?"

"No," Amy replied. "This is my first one, actually."

"Don't get out much, huh? That's too bad."

"I have to work around babysitter schedules. I've got a toddler at home," Amy said.

"Really? Wow! That's got to be tough."

OK, I'm new at this, she thought, and I just lost him. No guy wants a single mom—they think we're all out looking for new husbands. Of course, that might not be entirely untrue in her case.

Husband?! Where did that come from? She couldn't even get through a thunderstorm without thinking of Jeff. Besides, why would anyone be interested in her? She mentally ticked off the issues: she was in therapy, had a toddler patrolling the house looking for her dead father, and was fumbling awkwardly through a career change. Hardly on any guy's list of most attractive qualities in a woman.

"Yes," she said after finally regaining a modicum of composure. "She is three, but still very much in the terrible twos stage. Quite a handful."

"I can imagine. But I decided never to grow out of that phase. My mom still gives me treats to shut me up."

Amy was so lost in her thoughts it took a moment for her to catch up with the joke. Maybe she hadn't lost him after all.

"It has its moments, trying to do it all by myself. But I'm managing."

"What's her name?" Heath asked.

"Celia."

"Her father's not around?"

Amy swallowed hard, unprepared for the question. "He passed away last year," she replied softly.

"I'm sorry. I didn't mean to pry," Heath replied.

"It's OK. I've got to get used to talking about it sometime."

"You don't have to right now, though."

He touched her on the arm. Normally she would jump if a man she didn't know touched her without warning. But she didn't. She knew instinctively that this was a supportive touch, nothing more. It had no sexual connotations, no "get her in the sack later" undertone. Not only was she not offended, she was quite taken by it. He was genuinely trying to put her at ease. She could really fall for a guy with the instinct to know when she needed a boost like that. What did it mean?

Was he simply being kind to someone who had experienced a loss, but had no interest in her as an attractive, possibly available, woman—or just the opposite? She recognized she had just "turned a corner" in the bereavement process. She had to admit she was interested in him.

She only nodded appreciatively, not wanting to reveal anything more.

"Well, I guess I should probably get back to work. I'm on government time."

"You know what they say about all work and no play," Amy offered, trying to lighten the mood.

"Yeah, well, *they* probably don't have to protect a presidential candidate. He doesn't know what play is, at least until after the election."

"How's Thompson's campaign going?" she asked.

"You tell me! Are you sufficiently motivated to vote for him?"

Amy rolled her eyes and shrugged for additional emphasis. "Eh!" she said playfully. "Hard to say."

"Then I'd guess he's got more work do to." He paused. "'Course, that will be more difficult now without Hal Kensington."

Amy's playful smile faded. "He was a really nice man."

"Yes, he was."

She looked up. "You knew him?"

Heath nodded. "Pretty well, actually. He and Mr. Thompson have been working the details of the campaign for some time now. I don't think, however, everyone in the party agreed with their views."

"Well, that's why there's more than one candidate," Amy observed. "I think some of the leadership had issues with Hal's overarching strategy. It took him forever to con Thompson into it, but now that he's gone I'm guessing it won't go as planned."

"No, probably not," Amy agreed.

"I'd imagine you probably heard a lot of that in his conversations with higher-ups like Chris Billings. No love lost between those two."

Amy opened her mouth to speak . . . but stopped. She squinted at Heath darkly. "Are you trying to elicit me?" she asked.

Heath's confusion delayed his answer. "What? No, I . . ."

"You of all people would know those conversations are private," she said loudly. Several Starbucks employees turned toward them.

"I'm only partially deaf! No need to yell," Heath said, motioning for her to lower her voice. Amy stood up as she built a full head of steam.

"I can't believe you'd try something like that!" she yelled.

"I'm only trying to have a conversation with you," he replied, looking around at the growing number of people looking their way, "a private one."

"Forget it, buster! It's bad enough that D.C. flatfoot was busting my chops! Now I've got you doing it, too!"

Amy stormed out of Starbucks as the rest of the store glared at a bewildered and embarrassed Heath Rasco.

"THIS IS the 'Damato case' you were working on?" Heath growled under his breath at Seers.

"Hey, I'm tired of getting my teeth kicked in around here. Any advantage helps," Seers whispered back.

"How did I come to this?" Heath asked ruefully.

Seers and Heath were seated with several other men around a dining room table. Officer Damato was there, as was Sergeant Williams and his boss, SWAT team captain Bill Hall. To their right, Ryan Richter was explaining the game of poker to Heath.

That in and of itself would have been fine, if Richter had been winning. Instead, he'd had to buy in twice already, adding forty dollars to the twenty it had cost them all to start the evening three hours earlier. Richter was paying so much attention to teaching Heath that he hadn't noticed the other officers ganging up on him to slowly and imperceptibly bleed his chips away.

Seers did his part, and pulled a few chips from the other players as well. He was having a bang-up night.

"What the hell is up with you, Seers?" Sergeant Williams asked. "You've won four out of the last six hands."

"Somebody pat this guy down," Damato said. "He's got to be cheating."

"Now, now. Don't you boys get all worked up. I'm giving you a chance to win your money back!" Seers said, laughing.

Damato shuffled and dealt out another hand as Seers puffed on a cigar and stacked his chips. "Everyone ante up," Damato called.

Around the table, chips flew into a pile in the center.

"Bill?" Damato eyed the man to his left.

"I'll take one," the SWAT team captain said.

Seers looked around, surprised at how well Heath's techniques had created a reversal of fortune in his play. Heath was the best poker teacher he never had.

"So, what new toys are you guys playing with now?" Seers asked, knowing SWAT guys loved talking about guns. "Any new steel?"

"Don't I wish?" Damato said. Hall gave him a dirty look.

"SWAT is more than shooting, Detective," Captain Hall replied coolly. "It's tactics, too. That's what the *T* in SWAT stands for, by the way. Tactics."

"OK," Seers replied, unaware he'd touched on a sore subject. "So, what new *tactics* are you guys employing?" He wished he had suggested something less prickly, like maybe politics or religion.

"Chris Billings made an issue out of police methods recently," Damato explained. "Apparently being a party chairman makes you an expert in urban conflict. He says SWAT teams should embrace nonlethal methods whenever possible."

"Sounds like a good way to get a bunch of cops killed, unless the bad guys are also only going to employ nonlethal rounds," Seers grunted. He had little patience for people giving military or law enforcement advice when they'd not served in a uniform since their high school band years.

"Don't have much choice anymore," Damato said. "Now everyone asks, 'Why didn't you use sticky foam on him?' 'Why didn't you try negotiating him out?' Christ! It's like everyone wants to do your job until the shooting actually starts. Then it's 'Oh, please save us!'"

"One thing's for sure," Captain Hall said. "We can no longer afford a 'kill-or-be-killed' mentality out there. Everybody and their brother has a cell phone camera. Many of them are itching to show a cop using excessive force. Even if the suspect was holding a school hostage and it's a clean shoot, they still disparage the cop that takes him out, and we'll get no support from the powers that be. Count on it. It's bullshit, it's political, and there's nothing we can do other than accept it."

Williams snorted. "'Risk of collateral damage' is the preeminent factor we have to consider now. Apparently the hostage is no longer a priority. Clearly the cops at risk aren't," he slammed down his cards to fold his hand. Damato dropped out, looking disgusted.

The topic didn't have the desired effect of distracting his competitors, as Seers had hoped. He decided to cut bait on the subject and change to something safe as quickly as possible.

"So, are you going to ask that Kellen woman out or what?" Seers asked.

Heath didn't realize Seers was talking to him. "What's that?" Heath asked, caught off guard by the question.

"You're both single. You certainly seemed to be getting some stares at that VRS office the other day. You might even say you speak her language!" Seers laughed to himself.

"Is she hot?" Damato asked.

"I'm not sure this is the time or the place, Detective," Heath said. Seers glared back at him, trying to "tell" Heath he wanted help distracting the players. Damato dealt cards around the table again. Seers barely looked at his hand as he watched everyone's eyes.

"So, Captain, what do you think about upping the bet on this one, huh?" Seers asked.

"Back off, Seers! You can't keep your luck up all night," Hall said.

The detective's cell phone rang. "Seers," he answered gruffly.

"There's a call for you," the police dispatcher reported.

Seers took the cigar from his mouth. "From who?" he asked.

"An Amy Kellen. Do you know her?"

"Yeah. Why, what's up?" Seers asked.

"She'd like you to drop by."

"I'm kind of busy right now. Can you take a message and I'll call her back?"

"She said it was important. Wanted to see you in person right away."

Seers folded his cards and moved off to a corner. He dialed the number the dispatcher had given him.

"Hello?" Amy answered nervously.

"Amy? It's Mike Seers. Are you all right?" he asked quietly.

"Um. I don't know. I got kind of spooked."

"Why? What spooked you?"

"I heard noises outside. Somebody going through my garbage cans or something."

"Have you gotten any sleep?" Seers asked pointedly.

"Some. I'm still kind of punchy, though."

"I should think so. I'm sure what you heard was just a vagrant going through your trash looking for something to eat."

"I don't know. Maybe. I was just thinking about that burglary case you mentioned. It's been in the paper a few times, too," Amy replied.

Seers looked back at the table. Ryan was swearing like a sailor. Having run out of money, he was now going in the hole, offering himself as a marker—a week's free slave labor if someone loaned him the chips to stay in the game. Heath was raking chips toward himself, apparently having just scored a big hand. If anyone was going to clean up tonight, it was likely him.

"Tell you what," Seers said into the phone, "I'm not far away. Why don't I come by your place and check it out? Would that make you feel better?"

Amy's relief was palpable. "That would be great! Thank you!"

"All right. I'll see you in a few minutes."

MIKE SEERS walked up the sidewalk to Amy Kellen's townhouse. She opened the front door before he had a chance to knock.

"Hi, Amy," Seers began. "Any more noises?"

"No. But please come in," she said.

"Thank you."

"Can I get you anything?" Amy asked.

"No, that's OK," Seers responded. He tripped over the threshold between the living room and the kitchen, catching himself on the doorframe before he fell completely to the ground.

"I'm so sorry! I should have warned you about that!" she cried.

"Wow! You might want to get that fixed!" Seers said. The sudden brush with disaster had kick-started his adrenaline, and he broke into a mild sweat.

"My husband was going to fix it," Amy said, "but he never . . . I even have the new one to install, I just . . ." she trailed off.

"It's OK, I'm fine," he said, realizing her late husband's unfinished chore was a long-festering issue for her. He looked around the kitchen. "Have you ever been robbed, the house broken into, that sort of thing?" he asked, changing the subject.

"No," Amy replied. "But with those burglaries in the neighborhood lately, and being alone here with Celia . . ." she looked down at the floor. "Maybe I'm just paranoid."

"Not a problem to have a look around for you. Do you have an alarm system?"

117

"No, but I've been thinking about it."

"Do you have a gun?"

She hesitated.

"It's OK if you do, you know. They're not illegal."

She walked a few steps and reached into a cabinet above the refrigerator.

"It's not even mine. It was Jeff's. I don't even know what kind of gun it is."

Seers's attempt at a subject change had failed miserably again and he felt as bad about reminding her of Jeff a second time as he had the first time. How much could one poor young woman take?

"It's a revolver," he said, opening the breech. "An older model 38. But it's in good shape. More than enough for home protection."

He returned it to her, and she placed it back on its high perch. He eyed the cabinet.

"Above the fridge? Don't you want it closer to the bedroom? Just in case?"

"I don't want it anywhere my daughter could reach," Amy replied.

"Ah—good point." He walked farther into the kitchen for one last try at changing the tenor of the conversation. "Beautiful place you've got here."

"Thank you. It's still pretty baby intensive."

"Yeah, well, that's to be expected. She's young?"

Amy broke into a smile. "She's almost three. Quite a pistol in her own right," Amy laughed.

Seers played along. "Cute, very cute. I'm going to use that!"

Amy turned toward a baby monitor on the counter nearby. Celia was standing in her crib, signing.

"Hey! Look at that! She does sign language, too?" he asked.

"Oh yes! Sign language is very good for babies. They can sign long before they can speak."

"No kidding!"

"Keeps them from screaming all the time because they can't communicate."

"So she can, really, *talk* to you?" he asked.

Amy moved closer to the screen. "Absolutely. It's a real boon to a peaceful house."

"What's she saying there?" Seers asked, pointing to the screen.

"She says her *dolly* needs a drink of water."

"Her dolly, huh? That's really something! How big, um, how much vocabulary does she have? I mean, is she talking in complete sentences?"

"No, not really. She's pretty limited still in what she can . . ."

"I meant talking, well, you know what I meant," he interrupted, afraid he'd misspoken.

"I know what you meant," she smiled, relaxing for the first time since he'd arrived. "She's got a pretty limited vocabulary, and it's difficult sometimes to read her tiny little signs."

"You mean she does it differently than you?"

"Of course. Don't you speak differently from your parents?"

"So how do you learn every possible caller's individual style?" he asked.

"We don't. That's one of the challenges. We have to adjust on the fly. We're trying to mimic the dynamics of a phone call—it's not easy."

"I'll bet."

"That's why we're called interpreters, not translators. It's two very different skill sets."

Seers paused. "I've never really thought about that. How so?"

"Translators convert the words of one written language into another written language. Sign language interpreters convey the context of a spoken conversation into a visual language."

"So it's harder?"

"Much. We don't simply change the letters and words into hand gestures. There are all sorts of specialized movements to convey emotion and attitude."

"Really?" Seers asked.

"Then you've got accents, which can get really hairy."

"Accents? In sign language? You're kidding!"

"Not at all. Any characteristic of the spoken word exists in the sign language. We just have to interpret it correctly and communicate it to the other party."

"That's really something. I ..."

His pager interrupted him. He looked at the number and scowled. "Sorry," he said. "The watch captain. Excuse me a moment." He pulled out his police radio. "Good evening, Captain."

"Seers!" the radio barked. "Have you gone home yet?"

"No, sir."

"Are you sober?"

Seers rolled his eyes. "Yes, sir. What's up?"

"Drop the cards and get to 4212 Copeland. There's been another robbery."

"Yes, sir." He turned to Amy. "I think you're OK tonight. Apparently my bad guys have hit someone else. I've got to go."

"Thank you for stopping by. I feel kind of silly about calling."

"Not at all. That's what I'm here for. Now, if you'll excuse me, I'm in for a long one. Good night!"

COPELAND COURT was an expensive alcove of multimillion-dollar homes on the bluffs above the Potomac River outside Georgetown. The views, particularly during autumn, were especially spectacular. It was one of the reasons for living in the neighborhood. Which is why a multi-home robbery was so stunning to everyone involved. Not only were people robbed, their homes violated—it had been done to multiple houses on the same street, and nobody had seen a thing.

Seers walked into 4212, where Officer Smith was coordinating the investigation.

"Detective, what are you doing here? I thought it was poker night."

"It *was!*" Seers deadpanned.

"Sorry. Captain called you, huh?"

"Yeah. Same MO as the others?"

"A hair different this time. Mainly jewelry, a little cash."

"How do they always know to hit when nobody's home?"

A slim black woman in her thirties spoke with an officer on the other side of the room. She was fashionably dressed and holding a toddler, while two young boys milled around at her feet, nervously watching the policemen trolling through the house. Smith waved her over.

"Ma'am, this is Detective Seers. He's been working on the burglary cases in this area."

"Very sorry you've had trouble tonight. Nothing of value missing so far, then?"

"I'm not so worried about missing cash or jewelry. But they broke into my husband's office and it looks like they concentrated more on that than on the rest of the house."

"He works from home?" Seers asked.

"Sometimes. He's a psychiatrist. His briefcase was taken. The files he had here are strewn all over the place."

"Anything missing?" Smith asked.

"Not that I've noticed. But he would need to look to be sure."

"Can we speak with your husband?" Seers asked.

"He's out of town. He's giving a behavioral science lecture at Johns Hopkins. I've called his cell and left a message. I'm sure he'll rush back as soon as he can."

Seers handed her his business card. "He can call me at his convenience. What was your name again, ma'am?"

"Cherie Brown. My husband's name is Dr. Reggie Brown."

Chapter Ten

HEATH LEANED back in his office chair. The online chatter was overwhelming. A woman's grandmother had received an e-mail from Africa that appeared to her to be a scam, so she had posted it on her Web site. Her grandmother was in a lather because the phone line had gone dead in the middle of the call. She'd not been able to complete her donation. The granddaughter suspected it was a scam targeting the deaf. Had anyone else seen anything like this?

Heath clicked on the attachment. A *grandmother*? It was bad enough people had to protect their children from online predators. Now they had to watch over their parents as well? How had he gotten stuck with this thing?

He let out a loud sigh. He was having trouble holding on to Walt Broomer's opinion that this was a legit assignment. He'd left CFF, but was still doing the same kind of work. He felt doubly pigeonholed, still doing CFF and somewhat constrained to the Deaf community. This would never make him a field agent.

Bending over a keyboard all day was *not* how he wanted to spend his career. Maybe it was time to look elsewhere, perhaps in the private sector. Surely there were some good corporate or protective detail jobs out there. He had a security clearance that would give him a leg up in seeking employment with government contractors. Perhaps that's what he'd do. Punch out of government service, since the powers that be wanted to keep him where he least wanted to be.

But he wanted so badly to be a field agent on a protective detail. He was conflicted. This whole CFF project, valid as it might be, seemed like a step backward. He enjoyed the work he'd done for field offices around the country. His name was getting out there. People were calling and asking for his input. Maybe he should just suck it up, get the CFF case concluded, and keep pressing on. Maybe he was making it a bigger deal than it needed to be. After all, it was just an e-mail scam.

The document opened on the screen. It was very different from the previous versions. It was even dated. None of the others were. This was dated two days ago. Cheryl was right, apparently it was not lost on the criminals of Lagos that a presidential election was under way here. They did keep innovating based on what was going on domestically. This scam centered on a woman claiming to be the widow of a slain presidential candidate. It was at least original. He placed the note on a flash drive and moved it over to his Secret Service terminal.

He sent it to Cheryl via e-mail, hoping she'd look over a second unknown e-mail for him. Her previous analysis might have been a bit off. The writer might be an introvert, but he was apparently a real opportunist, too.

Heath called Cheryl and offered to buy lunch, since she'd be helping him a second time on something that most likely would not end with an arrest. As before, he just hoped he could use the information to better prepare the Deaf community and maybe dissuade others who were thinking of doing something similar. He hoped it would also help him close the case to Walt's satisfaction.

After lunch, Heath bid Cheryl good-bye in the elevator and returned to his office. He was behind on some other work that had been well under way before Walt had asked him to spend so many hours on the Internet. He was helping Phil Thompson's advance team with some behavioral metrics. Good, solid assistance to a field office. The best way to eventually join a field office was to make as many friends as he could around the country. It would be harder to turn him down if he was a known entity, someone who'd helped them out a couple of times, and not just another Beltway bandit doing a rotation out in the world. Now was as good a time as any to bang out what the guys needed.

Three hours later, he felt like he had a good enough package to send to the team in the Richmond field office. Thompson was scheduled to visit there in a week. Unfortunately, a very disturbed young man had just been released from a halfway house in the area.

The local Secret Service office would pay him a visit and remind him that the conditions of his release forbade him from going anywhere near a presidential contender. Heath figured his brief would help the local agents grab the guy if he was foolish enough to show up at Thompson's rally after he'd been warned.

There was an e-mail from Cheryl asking him to call her. He'd left her only a few hours before. What could she need? He dialed her extension.

"What's up, wild woman?" he asked.

"Leave it to you to take the most uninteresting scam in the world and make it your front and center concern," she said.

"How's that?"

"The attachment you sent me? Totally different than the others. Couldn't be more different."

"How's that?" Heath asked.

"The other note had a purpose—financial gain. The goal with this new one is different. It's manipulation."

"So it's not a copycat?" Heath asked to make sure he understood.

"Not at all," Cheryl said. "With the Nigerian guy the purpose was money. With this guy, the whole thing is a setup to compel telephone contact."

"For what purpose?" Heath asked, leaning forward in his chair. "What could he possibly do from Nigeria?"

"Well, there's your first problem. This guy's not Nigerian. He's not even African."

"The e-mail has a South African address," Heath said.

"And you have how many overseas e-mail addresses?" Cheryl asked.

She had him there. E-mail from U.S. law enforcement agencies such as the Secret Service made a lot of people nervous. Especially overseas. Heath had a roster of dummy accounts to pick from to mask his government status.

"So that's not just a change in origination to throw people off? I mean, Africa, Nigeria, whatever. Does it really matter?" Heath asked.

"I've got this guy pegged as American as you and I. English is his primary language. I'd guess East Coast. Probably in his forties or fifties, but I can't say for sure."

"You can tell that from a single e-mail?" he asked, astonished at how her department could detect what passed right by the average person.

"I wouldn't testify to it, no, but the grammar is pretty evident. This is not an exact science, but it's got teeth now that the whole Joe Klein matter is resolved," she said.

"Joe Klein? Why does that name ring a bell?" Heath asked.

"Remember *Primary Colors* a few years back?" Cheryl asked.

Heath closed his eyes. That book might actually be on his bookshelf at home. Hadn't someone given him a copy as a gift? He wasn't much of a reader anymore. Didn't have the time.

"Yeah, I think so," he stammered.

"Don't hurt yourself," Cheryl teased. "It was a satire on Bill Clinton's 1992 presidential campaign written by an anonymous author."

Heath remembered it now. The *Washington Post*, the *New York Times*, the White House, everyone in the country had tried to figure out who Anonymous was. The novel so closely paralleled what had occurred in Clinton's campaign that it had to have been written by someone on the inside—or at least someone with access to the inside.

"Yeah, I remember it now. That English professor from Vassar figured out it was some reporter," Heath recalled.

"Joe Klein," Cheryl said emphatically. "Klein vehemently denied it, called the professor all sorts of names in the press. Don Foster's his name. Nice guy."

"He called out Ted Kaczynski as the Unabomber, right?" Heath asked.

"That's him. He also ID'd the author of the Lewinsky–Tripp talking points," Cheryl said. "He's got some bona fides. Anyway, he really turned the issue of textual authentication into a science. He doesn't try to figure out the author's identity or psychological profile, only the authenticity of a particular document."

"OK. So what's the use to us?" Heath asked.

"I could use the same methods to search the Internet and see if there's anything out there that's similar to how this is written," Cheryl replied.

"And additional documents . . ." Heath started.

". . . give me the material necessary to come up with a psychological profile you can use for targeting," Cheryl finished.

"I can't ask you to do that. This isn't going anywhere. You've got real work to do—this will take up too much time," Heath said.

"We'll call it a training opportunity," Cheryl said. "Does that make it more palatable for you?"

Heath noticed the edge in her voice. "What is it?" he asked.

"You don't seem very interested in chasing this down," Cheryl observed.

"It's my job. I'm very interested in my job," Heath replied.

"Ease up, buster! I knew you before you had the job, remember? I've seen you when you're geared up. You're not, not on this project anyway. Something's got you distracted. Since I doubt there's a serious threat against Phil Thompson right now, it's got to be something with you. I suspect it's got to do with this case."

"It's hardly a case. That's why I don't want to waste any more time on it," Heath said defensively.

"Sure it is. It's a crime. It's being perpetrated against American citizens. It falls directly in our lane. That's not the problem."

"Don't say it," Heath warned.

"You don't like it because it's a Deaf issue," Cheryl said.

Silence. Neither said a word. Neither of them breathed. For a moment Heath thought she might have put him on hold, until the chair squeaked on her end of the line. She was still there.

"That's not fair," he said finally.

"It's fair and it's honest," she said quietly. She pushed the point.

126

"You've always been overly sensitive about it. You think you got this assignment because you've got a hearing problem and not because you're a good investigator," she said.

Heath sat there fuming. Who was she to make such an accusation? A few dates back in college and a psychology degree didn't make her Sigmund Freud and his mother all rolled into one.

"We aren't dating anymore, tough guy. The silent treatment doesn't work on me," Cheryl said after another thirty seconds of awkward silence.

"I'm trying to think of something to say that's not offensive, rude, or unprofessional," he replied.

"Taking you that long, is it?"

"Yep!"

"Look, I'm not trying to pick a fight. I'm just saying if this were aimed at any other segment of society you'd be out in front. It's only because it's the Deaf community you're afraid of it. Sorry. Wrong word. You're not *afraid* of it. You just want to avoid it," she quickly corrected.

"Can't you understand why?" he asked a little loudly, startling a secretary walking by his office.

"Yes, I can," Cheryl said. "But remember they are part of the constituency we serve. I know how hard you're working to become a field agent. But that doesn't mean you leave the Deaf community behind you. They need your support, your understanding of their world, and your legally sanctioned protective oversight when someone takes advantage of them. The badge is meant to serve them as well as any hearing American."

Heath's jaw tightened. All ten toes had definitely been stepped on. Walt had assured him this was a legit assignment. Perhaps he needed to do a bit of soul-searching. Was there something Cheryl could do? That damned Nigerian e-mail crap had been circulating around the Internet for nearly a decade. What the hell could he possibly do about someone customizing it for the Deaf community?

Probably nothing. But Cheryl's bigger point was obvious. He wouldn't know what he could do until he tried. He was so busy trying to get out of it, to work on what he perceived as more *legitimate* projects, like Phil Thompson's protective detail, that he was willing to let it slide. Ouch! So much for being equal.

"If it's not too much trouble," he said quietly into the handset, "I'd appreciate it if you could profile the author of that e-mail for me."

"I'd be delighted to offer any assistance I can," Cheryl replied with an equally measured touch of friendly, juvenile cynicism.

SEERS SAT at his desk. Behind him was a large computer printout showing a Social Network Analysis of all the burglary victims—none of whom were linked together in any discernible way. They were a variety of ages, races, and socioeconomic backgrounds.

There were blue-collar line workers and professionals. Some were single parents, and others had an entire tribe under one roof. He couldn't see anything they had in common—other than the fact that they'd all been victims of a burglar who, thus far, was outsmarting law enforcement. It really pissed him off.

The television in the corner featured a Chris Billings commentary on a fundamental change in the way Washington, D.C., was run, so it would no longer be a joke on late-night comedy shows. He declared that the murder rate shouldn't be astronomical in the nation's capital—where the laws are made for the rest of the country. Billings promised that no matter which candidate won the nomination, his party would return to its core values and restore law and order.

Officer Damato walked up to Seers's desk.

"Hey, Mike," he said.

"Yeah," Seers answered, still staring up at the large computer printout.

"Man, don't ever bring another fed to poker night again."

"Why's that?"

"That guy killed us!"

Seers spun around in his chair to face Damato. "Rasco? He barely knew how to play!"

"He mopped up the place!"

"You're kidding!"

"That dude walked out with over three hundred bucks!"

Seers turned his head so Damato wouldn't see his grin. Apparently, Heath had figured out another application of his "tells" methodology. Good for him.

"Got it," Seers said, turning back. "No more feds."

His phone rang, and he snatched it up before it finished.

"Seers."

"Detective? This is the Operations Center. There's a call you might have an interest in."

"OK. Let's have it."

"Go ahead, ma'am," the dispatcher said.

"This is Detective Seers. Can I help you?"

"Yes, Detective. My name is Marian Wells. I'm trying to take Hansel to the groomer's, but I've not been able to reach him."

"Hansel, ma'am?"

"Yes, Hansel, my poodle. I took Gretel to the groomer's last week, but I've not been able to get hold of him. Brent Jordan is his name. He owns Pawfect Grooming Services."

"Have you tried calling or stopping by? Maybe they've been quite busy. I know we're quite busy here, ma'am."

"Just a moment, Detective. I may be an old lady, but I'm quite aware of my faculties. I've called and left several messages that were not returned. Very unusual. I also went by the shop, and he's not opened it in several days. Also very unusual. He did a wonderful job with Gretel, and I always take Hansel exactly a week later. I'm afraid something's happened to him."

Seers rolled his eyes skyward. *What does this have to do with me?*

"Ma'am, we can try to call out there if you like and see if we have any better luck. Do you have a number for him?"

"Of course. But Brent is deaf, so you have to use a TDD line or go through one of those Video Relay Services."

Seers's eyes rolled back down. "What's that, ma'am?"

"Such a nice young man, though. Built that business up from nothing. I've been going there for years."

"Do you know how to use sign language, ma'am?" Seers asked.

"No, but I don't really need to with Brent. He knows what I like and he's very good at reading lips. I always make sure I brush my teeth thoroughly and apply fresh lipstick when I go there. We also texted each other quite a bit—he showed me how! Technology is such a wonderful thing! Such a nice young man."

"I'm sure he is, ma'am. Listen, I'm going to see if someone at a VRS facility can help us out, and I'll call you back."

"Thank you so much, Detective."

"Can I get your number, please?"

Seers wrote it down and scribbled a note to himself. A phone elsewhere in the squad room rang, and Damato picked it up.

"Seers!" Damato yelled. "Secret Service on three."

"Ms. Wells, I've got another call I must take. I'll let you know as soon as we find out anything." He switched lines. "Seers."

"Thanks for abandoning me last night," Heath Rasco said.

"What are you complaining about? From what I hear, you stole them blind."

"It did help soften the sting of being left behind. Fun game. I'm going to pay you back by giving you a slave for a week. Drive you around, pick up your laundry, that sort of thing."

"Really?" Seers asked.

"I'd love to run that kid Ryan around as my personal manservant. But I can't get him cleared to trail me through our offices for a week. Boss would never allow it. So you've got your very own concierge for seven days with my compliments. Don't say I never gave you anything."

"That all you're calling for?" Seers asked.

"Actually, no. One piece of official business. I just went through the reports for the night Harold Kensington died. Turns out our guy on duty that afternoon made a note that the fellow who delivered Champ was not the regular groomer."

"So?"

"The agent said this guy was a real cretin. When asked where the groomer was, the guy acted like he couldn't hear."

"So?" Seers said cautiously. "A few of these groomer guys are deaf."

"Deaf, sure, but not rude. It's a business, not a privilege. Kensington had used this place for years."

"This groomer named Brent Jordan by any chance?"

"Yeah, that's him. How'd you know?"

"Hansel's mama just called in a missing persons on him."

"*Who's what* called in a report?" Heath asked.

"Doesn't matter. Said she's left him several messages but didn't get a response."

"Those messages on a landline, a cell phone, or something else?" Heath asked.

"What do you mean, *something else?*" Seers asked.

"Just find out," Heath said.

Seers frowned. "I'll find a judge and have the tech guys get started."

SEERS AND Heath drove up in an unmarked police vehicle and parked on the street in front of a modest home in Arlington, Virginia. Ryan sat in the backseat checking his equipment.

"This is it. These are the same GPS coordinates," Ryan said.

"And this is a phone that's not a phone?" Seers asked.

"It's called a Sidekick, Detective. It's a PDA, a personal digital assistant, like my Blackberry. Think of it as a cell phone, laptop computer, camera, and text messenger all in one," Ryan responded.

"They're very popular in the Deaf community," Heath said.

"Why?"

"It's a perfect nonverbal communications device," Heath said.

"Why?" Seers asked again.

"The problem with sign language is it's public. Anyone watching nearby can see the conversation. Sidekicks let you text-message privately."

"Why would anyone want that? I thought sign language was the great link for including the deaf into society?" Seers asked.

"Sure, integrate them. But it doesn't mean they want everyone knowing their business by watching their sign language exchange. Text messaging offers some privacy. It's how deaf people whisper—nobody else can see or hear it," Heath said.

Seers eyed the For Sale sign in the front yard.

"So, what do you think? Want to call for an appointment? Get the tour?" he asked.

"No. I don't like the neighborhood," Heath replied. "Bad element around here."

The two walked up to the door and peered into the house. Empty. Working their way around back, they quietly walked up to a detached two-car garage. The outside light was on.

"Think the garage door is open? We could turn the light out for them," Seers offered.

Heath tried the door. Locked. Seers pulled on the big roll-up door. A noxious smell hit them both full in the face. Richter, who was shadowing them several feet away, scrunched up his face.

"Whew! What the heck is that?" Ryan asked.

Both men pointed back to the street. "Go back to the car and call for backup," Seers instructed.

The back of a Honda Accord was visible under the half-raised roll-up door.

"What kind of car did you say hit the dog?" Heath asked.

"A brown four-door Honda," Seers replied, trying to wave away the stench. "I don't see anything on the floor. You want to do the honors?"

Heath pulled out a handkerchief and opened the driver's side door to pull the lever for the trunk. It popped open. Inside was a large black tarp crammed into every available bit of space. Seers used a pocketknife to carefully slit open the tarp to reveal a young man's face. His eyes were frozen open in death.

"Brent Jordan, I presume?" Heath asked.

A barking dog distracted Heath from the noxious task at hand. He walked around behind the garage.

"Detective, do you have a minute?" he called back.

Seers walked out to the corner of the garage.

"Does he look familiar?" Heath asked.

Tethered on a long chain, looking hungry and tired, was a white-faced German shepherd.

Two hours later, forensics personnel had scoured the entire property—the house, the garage, and the backyard. The realtor was called, the neighbors interviewed; even the utilities records were pulled. It was a full-court press on a small, nondescript house.

A tow truck took away the Honda after the forensics team had finished sweeping the interior and trunk. Fingerprints, DNA, fibers, any and all potential evidence was removed, sealed, and shipped back to the crime lab before the vehicle left the premises.

Seers called a K-9 officer to the scene to provide the necessary expertise in handling an unknown animal. Heath was looking forward to having an experienced handler answer a couple of questions. But since this was the first time the officer had ever seen the animal, he couldn't provide much more than cursory answers.

Heath and Seers walked away as the K-9 officer finished his write-up on the investigation.

"You think *this* could be Champ?" Seers asked.

"I don't know. But why is the guy who was supposed to deliver him dead in the back of the car that killed an exact look-alike?" Heath asked.

"According to the realtor, nobody is supposed to be anywhere near this house. It's being pulled off the market—apparently they've leased it as a corporate residence for a couple of egghead types. A frat house for the corridor," Seers said.

The Dulles Technology Corridor was home to numerous small technology start-ups as well as the lobbying offices for many of the larger West Coast firms.

"We need to know if this is really Champ before we get too far into this."

"Kensington had no family here. The only person who saw him on a regular basis did it through a monitor," Heath pointed out. "And she's kind of mad at me."

"I'll give her a call," Seers said.

Jim Skelton led a dog along a narrow sliver of grass at the Arlington animal shelter as Heath and Seers chatted nearby. Heath had Champ on a leash when Amy walked up. Seers shook her hand.

"Hi, Amy, thank you for coming, especially on such short notice," he said.

"It's not a problem. I don't really understand what you are asking. You think this is Champ?" she asked.

"Well, we're hoping you could tell us for sure. You're the only other person who saw him regularly," Seers replied.

Amy was nervous. The dog jumped up and down at the end of the leash, which agitated both of them.

"He certainly seems to have recovered quickly," Heath said, as he dug his heels in to hold the dog in place.

"Recovered from what?" Amy asked.

"He was tied up behind a house in Arlington. We think he's been like that for a few days," Seers replied.

"Since Mr. Kensington died?" she asked.

The dog barked incessantly, straining on the leash, pulling away. Amy was jumpy being so close to him.

"Maybe. We don't actually know. That's why we called you," Seers said.

"I'm really not comfortable with this," Amy said.

"You said in your statement the dog was unkempt, yet he'd just been delivered that morning from the kennel," Seers said.

"Can't you just talk to the groomer?" Amy asked.

Seers and Heath exchanged glances. "We're not getting much . . . cooperation from the groomer right now," Seers said finally.

The dog struggled to get away from Heath.

"He looks like Champ. Right weight and all that. I just don't know for sure," Amy said.

The leash snapped and the dog succeeded in escaping from Heath's control. He leaped at Amy, hitting her square in the chest. She fell to the ground, with the dog standing over her.

Amy screamed.

But to her astonishment, he didn't attack. Instead, he was licking her face and neck as his tail wagged furiously. Amy kicked and squirmed as she fought back laughter. "Agh! Stop! Help! I'm ticklish! Please get him off me!" she cried.

Heath tried to pull him up, but the animal was too powerful. He shook with excitement. Amy made a few quick signs, and he immediately sat down.

"What the . . . he knows sign language?" Seers blurted out.

"I saw Mr. Kensington use a couple of special signs with him. Signs that were just between the two of them."

"Huh!" Seers replied.

"What?" Heath asked.

"Nothing."

"Don't *nothing* me. What?" Heath repeated.

"It's nothing. It's just that we had something similar in sniper school," Seers replied.

"You were a sniper?" Amy asked.

"I was a marine," Seers replied. "Best snipers in the world. They work in pairs—a spotter and a shooter. The spotter watches the target and clears obstacles for the shooter. The shooter concentrates on pulling the trigger and taking out the target."

"Wow. And they use signs?" Amy asked.

"Each pair uses a special language known only to them," Seers replied. "I've never really thought about it that way before. Interesting."

"Their own language?" Heath asked.

"Well, yeah. Every marine learns the basic hand signals, but sniper training is competitive. You had to communicate even if you couldn't see, like in complete darkness or underwater. Had to be by feel as well as sight. We had hand signals for hold . . ."

He pressed his thumb against his first two fingers.

"Clear," holding one thumb up.

"And take the shot," forming a pistol with his thumb and forefinger.

Heath nodded. "We use hand gestures, too, though ours are synched with American Sign Language to prevent miscommunication. It's simply the first letter for each word—stop, clear, fire, and hold. He single-hand-signed each letter as he spoke.

Seers turned to Heath. "I'll be damned. Working together all this time and speaking different languages."

Amy sat on the ground beside Champ, petting him on the head. "That's why misinterpretation is such a problem. Nobody realizes something's gone wrong until after it's too late!" she said.

She stood back up with the two men.

"So if this is Champ," she said, as she dusted herself off, "where did the other dog come from?"

"We're trying to get to the bottom of it as fast as we can," Seers said.

Heath waved for Jim Skelton to come over and offered him Champ's now broken leash.

"Can you take him, please?" he asked. "I don't care if Mother Nature herself shows up and wants to take him home. Nobody goes near him without authorization from the Secret Service."

"What's going on?" Jim asked.

"We're not sure. Until we are, I want this animal here and under your supervision," Heath replied. He scribbled on the back of a business card and handed it to Jim. "Cell phone is on the back. Got it?"

Jim looked at the card and took Champ into the kennel.

"Can we offer you a ride home?" Seers said to Amy.

"Oh, that's OK. I took the Metro over here."

"The least we can do is give you a ride back to your car," Seers said.

"OK."

Seers drove with Amy in the passenger seat and Heath in the back. Heath's Blackberry beeped and vibrated.

Seers peered at him through the car's rearview mirror. "Jeesh! Does everyone in the Deaf community have one of those damn things?" he asked.

"Technology has opened up whole new worlds for the deaf, Detective. It evened the playing field for people who had largely been left out," Amy said.

Heath texted on the Blackberry. "My boss. Now what?" He fiddled with a few buttons. "Sorry."

"No problem," Seers replied. He looked at Amy. "Do you have one as well?"

"No. I've just got a regular cell phone."

"They've leveled the playing field for the disabled, but you don't have one?"

"I wouldn't call the Deaf community *disabled*," Amy replied.

"No offense," Seers said into the mirror.

Heath didn't look up from the Blackberry. "None taken," he said.

"Being deaf today isn't like it was a few years ago. It's a language barrier—nothing more. There are plenty of people in the United States who don't speak English. Nobody considers them handicapped," she said.

"I see your point," Seers replied. "What are they, then?"

"We're a cultural minority," Heath said as he put away the Blackberry.

137

"You're serious? That's your definition?" Seers asked.

Heath nodded. "It's not sexy, but yeah, it's accurate. There are lots of cultural minorities, Detective. You should know that. You're in one of them," Heath said.

"I am?" Seers asked.

"A marine, you said?"

"That's right."

"Being a marine isn't a cultural minority?" Heath asked.

"I never thought of it that way."

"If you were in a bar wearing a Marine Corps T-shirt and I took a swing at you, what would happen?"

Seers nodded. "Every jarhead in the joint would pile on."

"Really?" Amy asked.

"Without hesitation. Without question," Seers assured her.

"You're bound together. A brotherhood," Heath said.

"Yep. Pick on one and the rest pile on," Seers replied as they pulled into the parking lot at All Hands VRS.

Chapter Eleven

Seers looked at the Brent Jordan crime scene report. DNA analysis would take a couple of weeks. The fibers removed from the vehicle included dog hair from numerous animals. It would take several more weeks for that analysis to come back. The fingerprint results were ready now, however.

There were two distinct pairs found in the car. Those in the back-seat, based on their size, appeared to be from children. No surprise there—the car was traced back to a Sally Reid, mother of three, whose car was stolen from a downtown parking structure six days earlier. The prints in the front seat were another matter.

Technicians found two sets of prints in the front. They'd sent the results off to the crime lab IT department to see if they matched any known dirtbags. All he could do now was wait. But Seers didn't feel like sitting around. What he needed was a better timeline. When did Brent Jordan die? How long had the Honda been in that garage? He couldn't speed up the forensics data, but he could work on the timeline. But for that he needed Ryan Richter.

Ryan finally sauntered in fifteen minutes later. "So can you break it for me?" Seers asked.

Ryan flopped down at his workbench slurping a milkshake. He didn't reply at first as he theatrically removed the tiny screws from the back of Brent Jordan's Sidekick. He shook his head.

"You doubt me. That's troubling," Ryan said with false annoyance. "I told you I could do it. Stop breathing down my neck."

"Hey, what's the matter? You lose a bet or something?" Seers asked sarcastically.

He watched the young man work. After a few minutes Ryan had the plastic external case removed and was attaching a couple of wires to his laptop computer. He tapped a key, and moments later Brent Jordan's text message record log was on Ryan's computer.

"Hang on a sec," Ryan said as he flipped a button on the bench top. A thirty-two-inch computer monitor next to Seers popped on. "That should help out those old eyes of yours."

Seers glared at him, but was obliged to put his glasses on. He watched the cursor fly around the screen. "So, what's the story here?"

"First things first, Detective," Richter replied. He pulled out a flash drive and dumped the contents of the Sidekick's memory onto the drive. He handed it to Seers and repeated the action with a second drive. "Hold onto that in case anything goes caflooey," Ryan said.

"If that was supposed to be a confidence builder, it wasn't," Seers replied.

"Just being careful. I'm going to make this thing dance on the head of a pin. Don't want data manipulation to be a court issue later," Ryan said.

"The man's dead. What are you worried about?" Seers asked.

"Dead men tell no tales," Ryan said, "but their electronics speak volumes. Let's start with where he's been."

Ryan clicked and tapped his way through the PDA device's GPS records. "This is everywhere it traveled the twenty-four hours prior to his death."

Seers watched as the computer plotted the data from the device. With a small clock running in one corner of the screen, the computer overlaid a consecutive series of stick tracks moving around the Georgetown area.

"Keep in mind this is the PDA. It may not reflect everywhere Mr. Jordan had been, because people leave these things at home, in the car, you name it," Ryan cautioned. "But it will at least give you a starting point."

Seers flipped open a notebook. "If I give you locations, can you drop them onto that map so I'll know where he is in relation?"

"Sure," Ryan replied. "Do you want a timeline for the entire route?" He tapped more keys, and numbers appeared all over the screen. The top and bottom of every hour showed up along the stick route the Sidekick had taken.

"Yeah, that's great. Nice idea."

Seers read aloud a few addresses. Jordan's house. His grooming shop. His parents' address. The empty house where his body was found. With each address added, a red pushpin appeared on the map.

"So, he'd been there for around three and a half days when we pulled up," Seers observed.

Ryan looked over the impromptu analysis. The PDA had arrived at the house at 10:42 p.m. three days earlier.

"Yep. That's about right. Probably used cover of darkness to pull the car in," Ryan suggested.

Seers leaned back. After ten o'clock at night was a smart time to dump the car and body. Late enough to be dark and early enough that the sound of a car doesn't pull everyone to their windows. Folks are either engrossed in television or brushing their teeth before bed. In either case, nobody heard a car pulling into an empty house's driveway. Very smart.

"Print that," Seers said gruffly. Silently he admired both the technology and Ryan's abilities. He might be more than just a little bit useful after all. "What else you got?"

"Let's see," Ryan said, closing the map overlay and returning to the PDA's main internal menu. "How about some text messages? Surely there's something in here."

He pulled up the queue of incoming and outgoing messages for Brent Jordan's last day.

There were numerous personal messages from friends. Three from his mother and one from his dad. He had exchanged messages with someone about attending DeafCoffee, made a haircut appointment for the following week, and e-mailed his travel agent about his vacation plans next month.

"Doesn't look like a guy ready to die yet, does it?" Seers asked pointedly. People always seemed to get cut down during the best parts of their lives.

"Well, look at this, Detective," Ryan interrupted Seers's melancholy moment. He returned his attention to the screen.

"What?" Seers asked irritably.

"A message from Harold Kensington! 'Can you pick up Champ? He stinks like hell—not sure what he got into. Will leave back door unlocked if I'm not here when you come by,'" Ryan read aloud. "Leave the back door unlocked? Isn't this guy under Secret Service protection?"

"No, not really. He could leave his back door unlocked if he wanted. Wouldn't recommend it, though."

"No kidding," Ryan snorted. "I don't like to leave anything unlocked. Too many nut jobs out there."

Seers thought about Frank Stratton. His door was locked—and still he got ripped off. It wasn't fair. The good guys get taken advantage of. He had to figure out a way to track down the sword and the medal. Ryan's Internet searching, while interesting, had yielded exactly nothing. And a database search through the criminal records was similarly a dead end. Seers couldn't shake the feeling in his gut that this was not some random event. Something was going on, and it irritated the hell out of him that he hadn't figured it out yet.

"Say, I could also crack Harold Kensington's PDA," Ryan suggested.

"What's that?" Seers replied, only half listening.

"We could look into Kensington's device. Maybe it would shed some light on what was happening with him."

Seers thought about it. It would be simple enough to ask a judge. But what would they gain? Kensington certainly couldn't be texting his dog. They knew what had happened. Was there any reason to invade Kensington's privacy? He thought about it for a moment, then picked up the phone and dialed.

"U.S. Secret Service," a voice answered.

"Heath Rasco, please," Seers said.

"Rasco."

"It's Mike Seers. Hey, listen, I'm wondering if there's anything to be gained in going through Harold Kensington's PDA. You guys were talking about how invaluable they are in linking the Deaf community to the hearing world. I'm thinking there may be something there, a string to pull on," Seers said.

"To what end?" Heath replied. "We know what happened. I don't think the service would endorse this. As a matter of fact, our agents sent text messages to Kensington's PDA— things that shouldn't be in the public domain," Heath said.

"Smells like political cover-up to me," Seers noted. "You sure you're not trying to mask any indiscreet liaisons he might have had?"

"Speculate all you want. We're in the protection business. But sorry to disappoint you. As far as I know, politics was the only mistress he'd had since his wife died."

"Had to ask," Seers said.

"But as far as the PDA is concerned, texting is invaluable for us, especially in getting someone as long-winded as Kensington to stay on schedule. Much easier to move vehicles into place, cordon off streets, and generally keep everyone away when we take a protectee out," Heath said. "There's going to be operational stuff on there the higher-ups are not going to want to let out. They might even move to seize it."

Seers thought for a moment. The last thing he wanted was another reason for the media to be all over the department. "Someone could view this as a political thing, couldn't they? Think we're trying to hurt or help Phil Thompson's campaign."

"Good point," Heath said. "Once you've got it downloaded, the whole thing becomes part of the public record, gets shared around the other agencies and all. Yeah, I'm sure there's some stuff about his campaign strategy in there. It's probably not the complete plan, but I'll bet there are some useful tidbits."

Seers shook his head. No way, no how. He didn't want any part of it. He regretted even calling about it.

"Do me a favor and make my life easier, would you?" Seers asked. "Put an interoffice memo out tomorrow requesting Kensington's PDA be destroyed. Put it through internal security channels so there's no public disclosure. I'd rather not have the damn thing around here, now that you've brought it up."

"Sure," Heath said. "The funeral is tomorrow. I can say we suddenly thought it might be a security issue. No sweat."

"Thanks," Seers replied. "Are you going to the funeral?"

"Yes. I'm riding with Phil Thompson's family. I'm on the advance team, not the security detail, but I'll ride back with him to work on some other stuff. I'll mention to him that we're destroying the device, just so he knows."

"Thanks," Seers said again.

THE ENTRANCE to Arlington National Cemetery reflects the solemn debt owed to those who've served their country. It's the nation's last chance to acknowledge citizens who've served her interests. Stone columns, granite slabs, and marble floors denote an air of reverence, especially during funeral services.

Harold Kensington's funeral was conducted at St. Augustine Catholic Church near Dupont Circle. Afterward, there was a long procession through downtown Washington, D.C., taking an obvious detour in front of the White House, before turning left to cross Arlington Memorial Bridge over the Potomac River.

Amy was not surprised to see the many politicians in the crowd. Hal Kensington had been a longtime Washington insider and had helped many a political rookie get their footing in the corridors of power. Senators Rebecca Mehaffey, Wendy Powell, and Carol Loeffler, all of whom owed their early political victories to Kensington's guiding hand, were in attendance together.

White House chief of staff Darrell Wolfe was there, as was House speaker Stephen Clark. Several senior staffers from the State Department, the Pentagon, and the National Intelligence Council were also present—people Amy had seen often on television. There were others she'd also seen, but whose histories were somewhat less storied. She could only recall a few names. Even then it was only first names. The short guy with the comb-over was Anthony. She'd helped him sort out a mortgage recently despite his bankruptcy filing three years ago. Two rows over was Sylvia, who was clinging tightly to her husband, but who had also been having an affair with a coworker for nearly five years. Behind them was Dustin, a real klutz with women who tended to go on a lot of *first* dates only, poor guy. As she scanned the crowd, she recognized more faces from the local Deaf community.

On the periphery of the graveside service, Amy saw a flurry of activity. Phil Thompson and his wife had arrived with a small Secret Service detail. Heath Rasco was with him. Amy turned away.

"Amy," a voice behind her called quietly.

She turned. Dan Banducheck was seated behind her.

"Mr. Banducheck. Good to see you again," she said.

"Please call me Dan. It was good of you to come. You didn't need to."

"I felt like I should. I was there with him. If only I could have done something."

"Nonsense," he replied quietly. "There was nothing anyone could do. I'm sorry you had to see something so horrific."

"Thank you. So am I."

"What have you been doing with yourself?" Banducheck asked.

Amy stole a quick glance at Heath again. "Oh, trying to get my life in order."

Banducheck noticed the quick flick of her eyes. He squinted at Heath in the early afternoon sunshine. "Do I know him?" he asked. "He looks familiar."

"His name is Heath Rasco. He's a Secret Service agent who came to All Hands the day Mr. Kensington . . . well . . . you know . . ." her voice trailed off.

"Oh yes. He was coming in as I was leaving. Why would the Secret Service be involved?"

"Heath's partially deaf. I guess they thought he'd be useful to the investigation."

Dan nodded. "Was he?"

"There wasn't much of one. I was hoping to pick up a few pointers from him but it didn't work out."

"Pointers? For what?"

"Oh, I was trying to figure out a few things. Something about Mr. Kensington's death just didn't sit well with me. I can't put my finger on it."

"What exactly do you suspect?" Banducheck asked.

"I think someone took advantage of him," Amy said. "I think someone used him."

Banducheck chuckled. "Hal was pretty smart. He knew how to take care of himself."

"Something about Champ," Amy said. "He really looked ragged that day. How could any groomer allow him to look like that?" she asked.

"Hal had been busy. Maybe he hadn't had time to walk him often enough and keep up with all the feeding and maintenance," Banducheck said.

"All the more reason he would have needed the groomer and the kennel," Amy countered. "He would need more assistance from those folks, not less. With the campaign heating up, the late nights, all the travel. He had to have known he couldn't take care of Champ properly. I think the groomer might have been ripping him off."

"Really?" Banducheck asked. He was intrigued by her suddenly aggressive tone. "What do you suggest we do about that?"

"Well, that's the thing," Amy said ruefully. "I don't know what to do. It's just a theory. I was hoping Heath could help me with it."

"You told him what you saw?" Banducheck asked.

"No! He just told me a few of the techniques they use on investigations and stuff. I figured it couldn't hurt for the only witness to at least try to understand what happened."

Banducheck leaned back in his chair. "How's that working out?" There was a pause before she answered. "Not too well. I'm going to have to do it on my own."

"You sound determined."

"I am," she said, her voice noticeably stronger. "This is something I'm committed to solving. I want to know what was going on with this dog and why the groomer brought him back looking like hell on wheels. Mr. Kensington barely even saw him before Champ attacked. I have to know why."

Her determination was unmistakable. She was going to get to the bottom of it, no matter the cost.

"Well, again, I think it's wonderful you came out today," he said.

"Nice to see you, too," Amy responded.

They sat in silence while the graveside service concluded. Several people walked up and spoke to Kensington's children next to the coffin. Amy stood to leave. She preferred to not be present when the casket was lowered into the ground. As she walked to her car, Heath broke from the security detail and approached her.

"Listen," he said, "about the other day. I don't want you to think I was trying anything funny. I wasn't."

"I know, I know. I overreacted. I've been doing that a lot lately," Amy said.

"Well, you've probably earned it."

"I don't know about that. I'm just tired, and irritable, and tired some more."

"You've had a rough couple of weeks."

She looked back as the last of Harold Kensington's well-wishers left the family to grieve in private.

"Not as rough as some people," she noted.

"Yeah, I know what you mean," Heath said. The Secret Service detail was loading into their vehicles with Phil Thompson's family.

147

"Listen, I've got to go. I hope you feel better soon," he said as he walked off.

Amy wistfully watched him leave.

"Me too," she whispered.

"THIS IS complete bullshit!"

Chuck wasn't mincing words. He never had been one to pull punches back in college. Amy had never seen him this upset.

"What do you expect me to do about it?" Amy asked. "All I do is interpret the call."

"You have to understand—some of my clients are not sophisticated when it comes to handling their money. That's what they have me for," he replied. "I'm trying to figure out why someone would write a check like that to a complete stranger."

"Walk me through it again," Amy said.

Chuck started from the beginning. His client had received an e-mail from someone in Nigeria. There was some money available in a bank account. Eighteen million U.S. dollars. The owner of the account had allegedly died. Without a formal next of kin or power of attorney, the money was available to anyone who wanted to make a claim on it. For a small fee, the e-mail writer would represent Chuck's client to obtain the money, but he had to pay the fee up front. Taxes or some such nonsense. He'd wired five thousand dollars to a bank in the Cayman Islands.

Chuck's client had never said a thing about it. It was only after Chuck had conducted a quarterly review of bank records that he'd seen the entry on the statement and inquired.

"Not to worry," his client had said when Chuck called him. He was sure he'd be hearing from the firm who'd contacted him. He'd called them and spoken directly with the firm's managing partner—using All Hands VRS.

"I didn't handle the call," Amy said definitively. "But I can tell you that it wouldn't surprise me if it came through the shop. As long as one of the callers is in the U.S., we'll place the call."

"They ripped this guy off!" Chuck yelled. "You guys can't stop someone from making a call that you know is fraudulent?"

"No. We can't! And don't yell at me!" Amy insisted.

"I'm not yelling," Chuck yelled before catching himself. "You know this scam. It's as old as the hills. But my client is elderly and not Internet savvy. He'd never been exposed to something like this. He's on a fixed income. He thought this would really set him up long term. Instead, it's costing him big-time!"

"I know. I don't like it any more than you do," Amy replied.

"I even called the Secret Service," Chuck said. "I spoke to some guy in their local office, said he was working on something similar already. Somebody from the Deaf community had raised it. He was checking into it."

Amy's ears perked up. "His name Rasco by any chance?" she asked.

"Yeah. That's him. Heath Rasco. You know him? He pretty squared away?" Chuck asked.

"Yeah, he's pretty sharp," Amy said.

Chuck's expression radically changed. "Well, well! What's this?" he asked, suddenly smiling.

"What?"

"Don't *what* me like we're talking about the weather. I asked if he was squared away—you got all dreamy-eyed and said he was pretty sharp. You've been holding out."

"Whatever."

"You're still holding out! Come on! Give it! How do you know a Secret Service agent?" Chuck insisted.

"I'm the one who raised the issue." Amy picked her words carefully. "I had someone make a fraudulent call through me. I didn't like it."

"So you . . .?"

"So I started posting information on some of the consumer Web sites and chat rooms."

"I've never seen your name on any sites, Deaf or otherwise."

She hesitated. "I used Jeff's old log-on."

Chuck nodded but said nothing.

"It's not what you think. I just like using his because nobody knows it's a woman."

"They think you're Jeff," he said.

"No. His log-on was a name, but it wasn't his name. Well, not *just* his," she said.

"What do you mean?" Chuck asked.

"He created an account for the family. JACK/3—Jeff, Amy, and Celia Kellen, the three of us. He thought it was cool to let family and friends keep up with us on the tour. Something we could do together traveling, staying in hotels and all. Make an adventure out of it that people could participate in."

Chuck was thoughtful for a moment. "That sounds like him," he said quietly. "So how did the Secret Service come into the picture?"

"I'd met Agent Rasco due to some other . . ." she hesitated, not wanting to relive the entire incident again, "business. He was nice. We've chatted a few times. He spoke at DeafCoffee last week."

"So you finally went to a meeting," Chuck said.

Amy's face had lit up while talking about Heath, but now it darkened again.

"Hey! What happened?" Chuck asked. "You suddenly have a dark cloud over your head."

Amy blinked a few times. She was very uncomfortable. Chuck had been Jeff's best friend. Jeff had called him the brother he'd always wanted. Growing up as an only child who was deaf, he'd been incredibly lonely. Kids shied away from him. He talked funny and couldn't communicate well. It was a hard way to grow up. Then Jeff met this gregarious baseball player who didn't hesitate to jump into a fight when others picked on him.

Amy realized that bond was still there. Chuck still considered Jeff his closest friend a year after his death. She didn't like how it made her feel to be sitting there talking about another guy.

"You're too quiet," Chuck observed. "That usually means you're thinking about Jeff. Let me guess. You don't want me to know you're interested in another guy."

"I'm not sure I'm interested in him."

"Is he attractive?"

Amy remained silent.

"That means yes," Chuck said. "If he was a train wreck you wouldn't have wavered."

"You're not very nice," Amy said accusingly. "This is hard."

"Amy. I know Jeff is gone. It's been a year and I've had to adjust, too. I realize you'll find someone else, and that's OK. He was my best friend, and nobody will take his place. But that doesn't mean I expect you to simply sit around forever and not look for someone else. You're young, you're beautiful, and you're going to make another guy extremely happy."

Amy was taken aback. She'd still not had that conversation with herself, much less with anyone else. *Someone else.* Someone besides Jeff. She had never articulated the idea, even during some of the longer, lonelier nights. She'd had a few of those lately, even without Celia's midnight running around.

Celia. That reminded her of something.

"Hey, not that I'm not enjoying your analysis of my limited social life, but you just reminded me of something I wanted to ask you."

"Quit changing the subject," Chuck said.

"I'm serious. I'm happy to tell you about Heath, but let me ask you about something first. I'm thinking about spending a little money, and want to know what you think."

"What?"

"I'm thinking about getting an alarm system for the house."

"Why? Have you had troubles with someone trying to break in? I notice there's been a rash of burglaries recently."

Amy thought briefly of Mike Seers, but decided not to bring that up to Chuck. That would only bring on more questions she could not answer.

"No. It's Celia, actually. She insists on getting up and walking around at night half asleep. I want to install an alarm system to wake me up in case she leaves the house."

"I think I'd reconsider that."

"Why?" she asks.

"The police charge you for false alarms. If they come out every time she opens a door, it's going to cost you a fortune."

"Great," Amy grumbled.

"I do have a suggestion that would fix the situation for you, however."

"What's that?"

"Can I see your cell phone?" Chuck asked.

She handed it to him.

"You've got a camera phone. You can download a program called PhoneSpy from the Internet. It turns your cell phone into a miniature motion sensor and alarm."

"No way," Amy replied.

"It's pretty impressive. I've got it on mine. I can load it for you if you like."

"Sure," Amy nodded.

Chuck fiddled with the phone, connecting it to his computer and pulling up the program to download to Amy's phone. He talked as he worked. "OK. What do you want it to do? Text, beep, or call you if something happens? Do you have a phone by the bed?"

"Yes."

"I can set it to call the home line and wake you up."

He finished and handed it back.

"That's so cool. Thanks!" Amy said.

Chuck collected the papers on his desk and cleared things away.

"Are we finished here, so I can berate you some more about this Secret Service guy you chose to keep hidden from me?" Chuck asked.

"I was just trying to 'keep the secret,'" Amy joked.

"Full disclosure from now on," Chuck said. "I want to know what his intentions are with you."

Amy was relieved by Chuck's reaction. She enjoyed the playfulness of their conversation. She'd not laughed much recently, and she missed the headier times of the past.

"I'll have him come in and meet you and ma before the high school dance," she joked. "I promise I'll be in by ten."

"*Nine*," Chuck countered. "And the handcuffs stay with me. Don't get any kinky ideas!"

THEY WERE seated at his conference room table rather than in the rockers. It was the most relaxed she could ever recall being in Dr. Brown's office. Very collegiate, not the typical patient/therapist dynamic of the past year. She was accustomed to sharing the nuances of her life with him now and was almost eager to get started.

"I'm sorry I had to change our regularly scheduled time," Dr. Brown began. "Thanks for being flexible."

"No problem," Amy replied. "Is everything all right?"

"My office at home was broken into, and some materials were damaged or stolen. Quite a mess to clean up."

"You were burglarized?" Amy asked. "I've been reading about the break-ins in the newspaper."

"Yes. My filing cabinets were all tipped over and my briefcase taken. Even the webbing on my rocking chairs was slashed, if you can believe that."

"Why would someone break into your office?" Amy asked.

"Sad state of affairs, isn't it? But enough about my problems. Let's get on with Amy. My notes are somewhat incomplete. Kate's having difficulty getting everyone's files back in order. But you attended Harold Kensington's funeral, you said."

"That's right."

"Your first funeral since Jeff's?" he asked.

"Yes."

153

"How'd it go?"

"OK. Just reminded me, I guess."

"I'm sure. How'd you handle it?"

"I did OK. I feel guilty I didn't think more about Jeff."

"Why?"

"Because it was a funeral. And because that guy was there."

"The Secret Service agent?" He looked up from his notes.

"Yes."

"So you two hooked up? That's great!"

"No, it's not great, and no, we didn't hook up. In fact, we had a fight earlier in the week."

"What did you fight about?"

"I felt like he was interrogating me."

"Why would he do that?" Brown asked, leaning in closer.

"I don't know. I don't know who to trust anymore."

"I see. We're going to revisit that later, but I had something else I wanted to talk about first. How's Celia?"

"God!" Amy looked to the ceiling. "She's killing me!"

"Does she trust you?"

"What kind of question is that?"

"A real one. What's the answer?"

"I assume so."

"You don't know for sure?"

"Why wouldn't she trust me?" Amy asked.

"Does it make sense that Celia might have been unusually close to her father given the unique circumstances of your work life at that time?"

"Yes. I suppose so."

"My question is, what are *your* feelings toward *her*?"

"I love my daughter," Amy insisted.

"I have no doubt that you do. But how do you relate to her?" Brown asked.

"I don't understand what you mean," Amy replied defensively.

"What would you do, right now, if you didn't have Celia? Would you stay in your current profession or go back to your former one?"

Amy sat back for a moment, unsure how to even get her mind around the question. After an uncomfortably long pause, she looked back at him.

"I would go back."

"Do you resent Celia for interfering with that original plan?"

"No! Of course not!"

"Are you sure Celia's interruption of your career plan isn't more important to you?"

Amy's lip quivered. "You think that's why she's calling out for Jeff at night?"

"I think you've got to accept that that part of your life is over. A tough transition for anyone. No more appearances. No screaming fans."

"We never had any of that," Amy replied.

"I know. I'm wondering if that's part of the problem. Walking away from all that would be tough. Never quite getting ahold of the brass ring could make it tougher," he said, looking at her intently. "Golf has come a long way in the last few years. It's mainstream now. Lots of potential for big-money endorsements. Surely you thought about it."

Amy's head sank. Of course she'd thought about it. She and Jeff had spent many nights planning out their future. While they both loved the sport, they knew they'd be crazy not to take advantage of the opportunity while they could. The travel, the contacts they'd make, the business opportunities that would unfold in front of them. There were going to be multitudes of options—until that fateful overcast night when he'd gone out simply to hit a bucket of balls. Then everything went out the window.

"What do I have to do?" Amy asked quietly.

"You have to work on your trust issues. I don't think bereavement, at least in the classic sense, is your real issue."

155

"Then what is?"

"Celia must trust that you'll be there for her no matter what. Give it some time. Eventually, when she's frightened she'll call out for no one but you."

Chapter Twelve

THE FOLLOWING day, as Amy tried to get back into the swing of things at All Hands, a call came in on her line.

"Thank you for calling All Hands VRS. How can I help you?" she asked.

The monitor suddenly filled with a man's chest and stomach that backed up until they sat down in a chair. Her face fell. It was Sammy Clark.

Crap, she thought to herself, *why do I always seem to get him?*

"Number is coming through now," he said tersely.

Amy tapped a key to initiate the call.

"Haven't seen you in a while. Been out?" Sammy asked.

"I took a couple of days off," she replied curtly.

"Vacation?"

"No."

"Out sick?"

"Something like that," she said. A busy signal rang in her headset. "Your call destination is busy. Do you want to try again later?"

"No, can you try it again, please? They're expecting me," he replied.

"Just a moment."

The busy signal was back.

"The line's still busy. I'll need to move on to another customer if we cannot connect."

"Can you try again one more time, please? It's very important," Sammy pleaded.

Amy pressed the button again. Her last call with him had gotten to her so badly, she couldn't resist—no matter what the code of

157

conduct said, no matter what company policy outlined or what the FCC dictated, she had to ask.

"What's so important?"

"What?" Sammy replied.

"The call. What's so important about it that you have to make it right now?" she repeated.

Sammy looked down at the floor to his left. Amy stopped short.

"Oh, uh, it's business. I own my own company," he signed. "It's called Sprngiefeld Data Systems."

Amy hesitated. *Sprngiefeld* Data Systems? What kind of name was that? Did he mean *Springfield* Data Systems? How does someone get the name of his own firm so wrong? Deaf people rarely misspell their personal information. Their name, address, e-mail addresses, and certainly the company they own should roll across their fingers effortlessly. Maybe it had a unique spelling. Rather than ask him and endure any more conversation than necessary, she Googled it on the computer while they waited for the phone call to connect.

Google came back before the busy signal did. She clicked on a link to the local Washington, D.C. *Business Journal.* Springfield Data Systems no longer existed. Datamine Corporation in San Francisco had purchased Springfield Data Systems. Their local office had shut down two months ago.

She thought about his downward eye movement to the left before he answered the question. Was he lying? Why in the world would he lie about owning a firm? Why would he even care to talk to her?

"The line is still busy," she said as she looked at her computer screen. "Are you sure you want to keep trying?"

"Yes, please. Just give it another try."

Amy nodded as she skimmed the article. Parat Mikel, a self-made millionaire from Pakistan who'd started and sold three previous firms, owned Springfield Data Systems. He resided in Bethesda, Maryland.

"Do you like this kind of work?" Sammy asked, interrupting her train of thought.

"Yes, most days," Amy replied absently.

"Pretty exciting?"

"No, not really. I like the calm, quiet life."

Sammy nodded.

Parat had three small children and had already started another new firm. He reportedly loved the IT business and hoped to similarly sell this firm in a few years to make yet another sizable contribution to the Georgetown University Hospital, where he had donated a total of five million dollars in the course of building and selling his other firms. Georgetown had saved his second son's life when he was born premature, and Parat had become a very public advocate of the hospital's Pediatrics Department.

Sammy was lying! Why would he do that? Was he also lying to others about Springfield? Could he be trying to rip someone off by pretending to own the company? Amy thought about Michael's Bridal and how much a fraudulent VRS call had cost them. What had Diane Similton said? Two or three months' operating profit from a single sham phone call?

Amy turned to the monitor where Sammy was waiting. What had Heath said the day Harold Kensington died? He and Detective Seers chase different types of bad guys. He tried to force them to make mistakes they weren't prepared for. Maybe she should try that.

Sammy obviously had a crafty story put together. He was prepared to talk about Springfield, though perhaps not practiced at spelling it. She needed to ask about something totally unrelated and see how he reacted. If she could force him into something he was not ready for, she might stop these fraudulent phone calls.

"Is it a family business?" Amy asked.

Sammy took several seconds to respond. "Why . . . yes. It is. Why?"

"I read somewhere that Springfield does a lot with Georgetown Hospital. Does someone in the family have a serious illness?" she asked pointedly.

"Yes," Sammy answered halfheartedly.

"Who?"

"My brother. He's sick."

Amy's eyes narrowed. "I'm sorry to hear that. How many brothers and sisters do you have?" she asked.

Sammy looked down and left. It was as though a neon sign flashed before her eyes: Lie, lie, lie!

"Three—two brothers and a sister."

She no longer noticed the busy signal repeating in her ears. He was lying. The miserable son of a bitch was lying! He clearly wanted to talk with her and was lying his head off. He didn't have two brothers and a sister, nor was his brother sick. He was running a scam. But now what should she do?

She needed Kathy. She needed someone with more experience. Someone who knew the laws on video relay better than she did. Amy was still so new she wasn't quite sure what to do. She looked around the desk. Where was the All Hands operating manual? Surely there was something in there for this type of thing.

Sammy raised an eyebrow at her. "Something wrong?" he asked.

Amy didn't bother looking at him when she signed her response. "Everything's fine. Just a moment."

She pulled out drawers and emptied the overhead cabinet onto the desk. Phone books. Computer manuals. Office supplies. Where was that silly operating manual? She glanced back at the monitor. Sammy had moved much closer to his videophone. He peered into the camera as if it allowed him to take a better look at her. It was very disconcerting.

"Your call cannot be completed right now," she said as she turned toward the frosted-glass hallway door. Maybe she could yell down the hall for Kathy. "Are you sure you don't want to try your call again later?" she signed. Her eyes switched back and forth between the monitor and the door.

"What are you looking at?" Sammy asked.

"N—nothing," Amy fumbled as she glanced to her right.

"Is someone else there?" Sammy asked.

"No. I'm alone. I'm just . . ."

"These calls are supposed to be private!" Sammy's hands slapped against each other. But it was the shout that made her jump. Her hands leaped to her face, stunned at his sudden outburst.

"They are. I was just . . ." she stammered.

"You stupid bitch!" Sammy yelled.

The videophone went dead.

"HEATH!" a woman's voice yelled.

Heath Rasco turned from his car and looked across the parking lot. He thought he was alone in leaving so late. He'd spent two hours going through Phil Thompson's latest campaign trail changes, trying to figure out how the field offices would ever get their logistics in order. Chris Billings was putting all the candidates through the wringer trying to maximize their press coverage. But what's good for the candidates is murder for the Secret Service agents assigned to protect them.

Cheryl Corely ran toward him from the outside door of the building. She held a wad of papers in one hand and waved frantically with the other.

"Heath! Hey, you've got to see this!" she called.

She was breathing heavily when she reached the car. Sweat had beaded up on her forehead, and she wiped it with her free hand.

"Hey, slow down there!" Heath cautioned. "What's up? Did I forget something? Did the Richmond office call?" he asked. He'd been putting in long hours. Had he left something undone somewhere?

"No, none of that," Cheryl said dismissively, with a wave. "I found something you should see."

"What's that?" he asked.

"Your new e-mail scammer? He's been posting a lot of material out there."

Heath remembered how she'd berated him about letting a Deaf community issue fall by the wayside. He hated admitting to himself she'd been right.

161

"You found him?" he asked.

"Don't act so surprised," she said. "I told you I'd look. Some of the spiders the IT guys have put together are pretty impressive."

Spiders were small pieces of software that crawled around Web sites looking for particular pieces of data someone was tracking or researching. Just as Google searched for keywords, spiders looked for entire documents or pictures or any other large data source. They were an impressive bit of technology that had only recently entered common use in law enforcement.

"What did you find?"

"Lots of postings on Deaf community Web sites. But that's not important," Cheryl said.

"It's not? All the hell you gave me about supporting the Deaf community, and now it's suddenly not important?" he retorted.

"It's important. But this guy's not just randomly surfing. He's cyber stalking," she replied.

Heath frowned. "OK, walk me through this. You found him multiple times, yes?"

"Yes, but *only* on Deaf community Web sites."

"So?"

"So on every one of them he only talked to one person."

"This same person was on all these sites?" he asked.

"Yes! I looked at the time and date stamps. He followed her. But more importantly, he was running a denied address system not much different from ours." She handed him a printout.

"These log-on IDs are different," he said. "I see that she stays the same, but there must be half a dozen other user names here. How do you know they're all him?"

"The language is highly correlated," she said.

Heath nodded his head with a doubtful look on his face.

"What? Just because I've got a psychology degree I don't know statistics? Get over it," Cheryl said. "I ran the numbers, and the variables between these documents are superficial. The underlying language is essentially unchanged. He tried to change his syntax so he appeared different, but that would never fool a good mathematical model. It's one guy with six user names!" she said.

He knew better than to argue. Regression models were extremely powerful and good for teasing out patterns in large amounts of data. eHarmony.com was making a fortune using regressions to match up single people online. Amazon.com used them to analyze customers' purchases to recommend similar books, music, and videos they might like.

Heath was now fully engrossed in Cheryl's documents. Page after page of her attempted tracing to the source was unsuccessful. This guy knew computer science very well. He apparently also knew a lot about computer security.

"So, what's he after? What's his game? Is this a lovers' quarrel gone bad?" he asked.

"No, not even close. I get the impression they've never met. She posts something and he responds. It's just mushroomed. There's no indication they know each other in the real world, but they both seem to know the Deaf community. It's the strangest thing I've ever seen. It's like he was bullying her around to see how she'd react."

Heath reread the content of the chat room exchanges and other documentation. This guy was no Prince Charming. Cheryl was right—it was like he was going out of his way to provoke her, to get a rise out of her.

"He's definitely a real jerk," Heath said. "What can we do about it?"

"We better figure out something," Cheryl said. "This guy's MO is totally different from the Nigerian thing."

"How's that?" Heath asked.

"This guy's an ENTP. How about that?" Cheryl asked, pleased with her diagnosis.

"OK, he's an ENTP. So he has two characteristics different from the original guy. What's the big deal?" Heath said.

"It *is* a big deal," Cheryl replied. "He is not two characteristics different. It doesn't work that way. Each characteristic plays off the others in individually complex ways. ENTPs get their energy from the outer world of people and events. They're highly adaptable, ingenious problem solvers, and actually enjoy a good argument. They tend to focus several steps ahead of everyone else. They want freedom of action."

"So what?" Heath asked.

"So this guy's no wallflower. He's the real deal."

Heath frowned. This was taking a strange turn. "You're on. I'm listening. Convince me," he said. He leaned against the car and folded his arms.

"This guy's profile is different from that other lowlife. He's in a class by himself. I've never seen an exchange like this that wasn't designed to attack a specific person," Cheryl replied.

"Meaning what?" Heath asked.

"Meaning even if this was copied to everyone in Washington it was only intended for *one* person. The recipient may not even realize he or she's been targeted. But the sender was after a *specific* person. Everyone else copied was just window dressing to provide cover for the finale."

"Finale?"

"This guy wants to show the world how smart he is. Anytime someone says 'It can't be done,' this guy takes that as a personal challenge that he answers with a 'Watch this.' He's a dangerous improviser. Quick on his feet. Very good at figuring out intricate verbalizations of individuals. People like this are good with language. The guy that can flawlessly switch among five or even six different languages without thinking about it. You've met the type."

Indeed he had. Heath could think of a half dozen Secret Service agents in the building with that same skill set.

"But this guy is a lethal genius at debate. Types like this like to one-up the person they're competing with. They can quickly adapt to a competitor's shifting positions. They love to outwit the system and, unlike your Nigerian writer, they *exploit* the rules to get what they want rather than simply *ignore* them."

"Has he made any threats?" he asked.

"No, but he doesn't need to. That's the really weird thing. He's always on different IDs. I'm sure she's unaware it's the same guy talking to her all the time. While they both seem to know the Deaf community, I don't think either of them are deaf themselves."

"How's that?" Heath said.

"She knows it, but she's, I don't know—distant, for lack of a better word. She's impassioned but not passionate. Do you know what I mean? She's defending something she feels strongly about, but it's not her."

"And him?"

"He's trying too hard. Something about the way he writes, the attitude just erupts from the screen. Do you remember those *National Geographic* specials about tigers in Africa you saw as a kid?" Cheryl asks.

"Uh, yeah," Heath said, not following the analogy.

"Tigers know about gazelles. They know about zebras. They know about a lot of animals. But everything they know is from a predatory standpoint. They know how to take them down, their weaknesses and their vulnerabilities. That's the sum total of the tiger's knowledge, because it's the only reason it has any interest in them."

Heath realized this probably didn't fall into Secret Service jurisdiction. Not yet, anyway.

"You still with me?" Cheryl asked.

"Yes. I was just thinking," Heath replied. "I'm even less certain than before what to do with this, if there's anything I can do at all."

"Just understand this," Cheryl said. "This is a guy who will abreact to any kind of humiliation. He can't handle being fooled or hoodwinked. He'll lose his cool."

"Great," Heath said. He stared up at the poured-concrete ceiling. How the hell was he supposed to chase down someone like this? He didn't know the perpetrator, who hadn't committed any crime. He didn't know the prey, who was as yet not a victim. He couldn't investigate a crime that hadn't happened and might actually never occur. "So what's my take-away here?" he asked.

"This is an engineer of relationships. A master manipulator. Imagine a two-bit, backwoods evangelist with the best education and training possible. He's polished and professional, but at the end of the day it's about controlling the kill. Just like a tiger."

"That's not much to work with," Heath said.

"Hey! Focus!" Cheryl replied. "It gives you something to look *for*. An area to concentrate on. This is a politically savvy person. Someone who can employ his debate tactics to the disadvantage of others. You can't play that game with him."

Heath was taken aback. Something to look *for*? Wasn't that just the opposite of Walt telling him to look *at* everything? Or was that how he and Cheryl had gotten to this point? Looking *at* everything pointed them toward this one guy they should be looking *for*. It was strange the way investigations sometimes wandered around aimlessly before suddenly and dramatically drilling in on a single discrete fact. What would that mean here?

"You think he'd be violent?" he asked.

"If humiliated? If pushed? Yes, he'd be a handful. His over-reliance on improvisation means he'd be unprepared. He would overextend the brinkmanship and put everyone around him at risk against a worthy adversary," she said.

"So why is he manipulating this one person?" Heath asked.

"I don't know. But I hope to God they never meet."

Chapter Thirteen

Amy got Celia ready for bed and tucked her in. She removed her makeup and washed her face in the master bathroom. The phone rang as soon as she walked downstairs to the living room. She saw the caller ID on the handset.

"Hello."

"Hey, woman, it's me," Kathy Maynard said.

Amy sat on the couch and reached for her glass of wine as they caught up on the latest interoffice gossip. With Amy having so little social life, Kathy apparently wanted her to live vicariously through some of their office mates.

Amy heard a noise outside. She stood up and placed the wine glass on the coffee table. She walked to the window as Kathy continued talking.

"Hang on a sec," Amy interrupted.

"What's going on?" Kathy asked.

"I thought I heard something outside. I'm going to check it out while I've got you on the line."

Amy walked out and down the sidewalk to the street. Several people idled by, either jogging or walking dogs. A typical night in Georgetown. Seeing nothing, she returned to the couch to chat with Kathy.

After hanging up, Amy poured another glass of wine and watched a little reality television she'd recorded weeks ago. It was nice to just sit and relax. Celia was asleep, and Amy was finally getting used to being in the house. The creaks and groans of any home are unique, and she'd come to recognize and even welcome some of the more familiar ones.

The hum of the refrigerator, the buzz of the fluorescent light in the kitchen, even the drone of the dryer was comforting. The dryer! She had clothes in the washer that needed to be tossed in. She set the wine glass down and walked out to the laundry room. She removed the load from the dryer, dumped the washer load in, and started up the machine.

She returned to the living room with a laundry basket, folding towels and washcloths without much thought as she watched TV. She was on her fourth towel when she heard it.

A crack outside.

Amy spun around toward the window and stalked over to peer outside. She saw nothing in the darkness. She walked back to the coffee table and picked up the phone to dial the police. What would she say this time? She'd heard *another* noise? What had Chuck said about false alarm calls? The police undoubtedly had a similar charge for scared-mom calls. She put the phone down, picked it back up, and then put it back down again.

"Get a grip," she muttered to herself.

She finished the towels and turned off the television. With the stack of laundry balanced in the basket, she climbed the stairs to the bathroom. She returned to check the door locks and killed the remaining lights. She was ready to call it a night.

Back upstairs, she took the cell phone off the dresser and pulled up the PhoneSpy program Chuck had installed. She set the phone on the hallway table outside her room. Any movement by Celia would trigger a call to the house line on Amy's nightstand. A perfect and free alarm system. All of the table's corners were now wrapped in foam rubber. Celia could run straight into them and suffer no ill effects.

The house was quiet and dark. The joggers and dog walkers outside had melted away. Cloud cover had returned and obscured the glow of a quarter moon. Amy's clock read 2:42 a.m.

Ring!

The ringing telephone startled her awake. "Hello! Hello?" she babbled into the receiver. There was no answer. "Hello. Is anyone there?" she asked. She looked at the caller ID. It was her cell phone calling.

Celia!

Amy jumped out of bed. Still groggy from being awakened from deep REM sleep, she stumbled to the entrance of her room.

"Celia!" she called out softly. "Where are you, baby?"

She walked into the darkened hallway, still trying to clear the cobwebs from her mind. Celia's door was open.

"Celia?"

She stepped into her daughter's room and froze. Celia was sleeping comfortably. She didn't appear to be awake or to have even been awake. The door moved behind her slightly as the air-conditioning cycled off. She breathed a quiet sigh of relief.

"Stupid door," she muttered.

She backed gingerly out of the room and pulled the door shut. She walked down the hallway and reset the cell phone program. As she sat the phone back on the table, movement behind her reflected in the screen. She turned around.

"Mommy didn't mean to wake you up, sweetheart, I . . ."

Two strong hands reached out and pushed her into the master bedroom. Amy struggled to break free. When the assailant removed one hand to close the door, she thrust an elbow up into his chin to break his grip.

"Get out!" she shouted.

The stunned intruder staggered, catching himself against a dresser to regain his composure. He closed the door slowly, eyeing her from inside a black hooded sweater and a stocking over his face. He tackled her onto the bed.

Amy struggled, kicking and flailing against him. As soon as her hands and feet touched the bed, she crab-crawled over the pillow and braced one foot at the top of the headboard before pushing off with the other. They both spilled onto the floor.

She refused to be raped in her own bed.

She was on her back, unable to make solid contact as she lay on her assailant's chest. She pushed off from the bed to put as much distance between it and her as she could. The pair momentarily broke apart as the assailant got back on his feet. She leaped up first and faced him.

He tackled her again, barreling them both into the closet door. The shattering door mirror showered them in glass. The sound of crushed glass under his heavy boots punctuated their heavy breathing. She could think of only one thing.

Stay on your feet!

He couldn't rape her standing up.

She crouched to get a better center of gravity. College foot drills suddenly flooded her mind. What had her coaches told her? Imperceptible shifts in weight can have dramatic effect? The combined benefits of several improvements have a compounding effect on performance—force multipliers, they'd called it. Something like that. Each made an impact on its own, but when combined, they could make all the difference in the world.

She backed away slowly until she reached the bedroom wall. Dead end.

The contact with the mirror had propelled them back toward the bed, so she sidestepped along the wall back to the closet.

Stay on your feet!

Her eyes searched the room for anything to use as a weapon. The bedside lamp was her best option, but it was across the room. Right next to the bed.

No way. What else was there?

It's my *bedroom*, she thought. I live in it, clean it, and sleep in it. Nobody over three feet tall has set foot in this damn room in over a year! How can there not be something to use as a weapon? Her breathing was the only sound she heard above the pounding staccato of her heart racing. Her eyes darted around the room. Surely there was a weapon somewhere, just out of sight?

Jeff's fraternity beer stein! Thick. Solid. Heavy. But most of what was on top of the dresser now lay on the darkened floor around her feet. Amy glanced quickly to the floor. A momentary flash of lightning illuminated the room but provided no insight into potential arsenal choices.

He chose her moment of inattention to rush headlong at her again. They slid down the wall and crashed through the closet doors into the black interior. Amy reached out to steady herself, grabbing a handful of hair and hood that twisted into a tight ball in her fist.

He screamed and slapped her hand away.

The crash had awakened Celia. Her cries echoed down the hallway as they wrestled around. Hangers and belts flew everywhere. Shirts and slacks draped their heads. He released his hold on her to rip a blouse from his face. Then he pulled her close as he pushed deeper into the closet.

"Want to know what I'm going to do?" he asked.

Amy swallowed back the vomit that bubbled up into the back of her throat. She knew that voice. When he ripped the mask off, the pale glimmer of a corner nightlight revealed Sammy Clark's maniacal grin.

"You!" she hissed. "What are you doing in my house?"

"A job!" he replied and threw both arms around her.

She tried to sidestep around him, but the momentum spun them both deeper into the closet. He had her in some type of bear hug. She felt his arms tighten around her. She tried for the light of the hallway, but his weight was grounded and it pulled her back inside the closet as he squeezed ever tighter. He was trying to smother her.

Her arms flailed behind him, alternately pounding his back and reaching out into the darkness. Air slipped through her lips. This wouldn't take long. At least it wouldn't be painful. She was on her feet, but completely outmuscled.

In the fog of waning consciousness, her right hand touched something. A smooth rod. Cool but not cold. Hard but flexible. Recognition pierced the stupor of impending suffocation. She knew this object. Knew it well. They had been through a lot together, and once again it was about to change her life.

With her left hand she grabbed a handful of Sammy's hair and jerked him to the right. At the same time she pushed off with both feet to propel them toward the bed.

Ironic. She *had* to go toward the bed. Let him assume whatever he wanted.

He didn't resist as she danced a few steps to spin them around until she was walking backward. She had to wait. Another step or two. Couldn't be hasty. Timing was important. *Let him think I'm giving in,* she told herself. She pulled him toward the bed.

She estimated it to be slightly less than ten feet from the closet to the footboard. She was good at estimating distance. It had been her gift. Ten feet, with a slight roll to the left. More than enough room. She pulled his head toward her chest and ignored his abhorrent breath.

Another step. The bed couldn't be more than two feet behind her now. She relaxed her grip and allowed the rod to slide through her right hand until she felt rubber. Then, with the effortless advantage of a decade of professional instruction, she flicked her wrist as she'd done thousands of times.

Callaway's i-brid design was the latest addition to the firm's Big Bertha line of irons for women. TaylorMade had some good carbon fiber shafts for their irons, too, but Callaway had an unusually crisp snap. Easy to manage, simple to aim, not a lot of chance flexing as the head came around. It had a lower center of gravity and was easy to control under any conditions. Amy had always liked that. Control. She'd missed that over the past year or so.

Capping the six-ounce carbon fiber shaft was an 8.5-degree right-hand-faced club head weighing less than two hundred grams. A featherweight. But Amy could accelerate it to ninety miles an hour. Like the game itself, it wasn't just the speed of the club. Angle was important, too. If she didn't deliver the club head precisely, it didn't transfer all the pent-up energy from the flex of the shaft.

Not that this would be a problem today.

The impact shattered Sammy's left ankle. His eyes bugged out. His mouth opened grotesquely as he inhaled the room's air supply. He shifted weight off the destroyed appendage and released his hold on her.

She slowly withdrew a single step, until her calves lightly brushed the comforter she'd earlier shoved to the end of the bed. She took her time. "Don't rush it," her coaches had always said—the setup is often the make-or-break element for the shot.

She stared into Sammy's freakishly dilated eyes as gravity pulled the club to the floor. Her left hand met with her right in a seamless interlacing of fingers over an exact point, following a pattern learned long ago. She didn't bother to look down. She didn't need to.

It was called muscle memory. Years of training and repetition gave professional athletes an edge in that they no longer had to think about certain movements. It was a shortcut to executing the strategy that played out in their heads. It's why Michael Jordan was unbeatable on a basketball court but couldn't swing a baseball bat to save his life. Muscle memory. Get into the proper position and allow nature to take over.

The competitive instincts that had been dormant for the past year raced back with a vengeance. The six-iron was a key weapon in her arsenal. The intermediate-range shots were a competitive advantage she'd been lucky to claim as her own. She typically shaved a stroke every three holes through superior management of her mid-range game. In that arena, her six-iron had been a natural extension of her arm. Nobody could touch her. That was precisely how she felt right now—*don't touch me!*

With her eyes locked on Sammy, the six-iron climbed counterclockwise up her right side. She paused for a half second, as she always did, with the club shaft parallel to the floor. She took a short quarter-step to her right to ensure she'd clear the corner of the bed. In that pause she took quiet joy at the light reflecting off the club head into Sammy's eyes. The horror of what was about to happen. Knowing he could not stop it.

He glared at her, knowing intuitively that any merciful hesitation or doubt she might normally have displayed would not take place today.

A year ago, her personal best had been ninety-three miles an hour. Surely she broke one hundred on this swing. Even accounting for deceleration on the upside trajectory, the impact against Sammy's jaw had to be pain beyond comprehension. His teeth shattered like ice and sprayed the floor with a foamy pink cocktail of blood, air, and spit.

Amy pulled the club back again when Sammy dropped into a heap. Much better. She hated swinging on an uphill elevation.

The club head whispered past Sammy's face, though he never saw it. His eyes had rolled back as far as the muscles could stretch. The room's cool air was high-voltage to the dozens of raw nerve endings that snaked out from where his molars had been. Blood poured from the sockets of his crushed teeth, and splintered bone fragments sliced through his skin. He might bleed to death without medical assistance, not that it mattered. She wouldn't let him live long enough for that to happen.

She swung again. It was a good swing. A professional's swing. The impact against Sammy's skull reminded her of Hawaii a few years earlier. The SBS Open at Turtle Bay in Kahuku. That wet, muffled, shell-cracking collision when coconuts fell out of the trees onto the concrete cart paths. Same type of noise. She settled into an exhausted but relieved smile just as she had that day in Kahuku.

Her first LPGA win since joining the tour.

Chapter Fourteen

Mike Seers lifted up the medical examiner's tarp and peered inside.

"Well, he didn't die happy, did he?" he asked.

"You've got to be pretty stupid to try and fight someone with a golf club in her hands," a uniformed officer observed out loud. "Doesn't matter how big you are—respect the stick! And this woman was apparently a pro a few years back."

"That so?" Seers asked.

"On the tour. Even won a couple of them, she said."

"Well, well. Aren't you just full of surprises, Amy," Seers muttered.

He flipped the tarp back over. The house was crawling with people. In addition to Seers and his cadre of officers, there were crime scene forensics specialists and emergency medical technicians. The medical examiner's crew and news media were scattered outside. Everybody was trying to get the story.

When the coroners carried Sammy Clark's body out of the house, Seers went in search of Amy. An EMT emerged from Celia's room with Kathy Maynard, who was carrying the half-asleep little girl in her arms.

"Detective! I don't think she's been touched. Best as I can tell, she slept through everything until the noise woke her up," he said.

"Thank God," Kathy said.

Seers thanked the EMT, who packed up his gear and left. Kathy took Celia back to her bed. Seers turned his attention to Amy. "Maybe we should go downstairs," he suggested.

They descended the staircase to the kitchen in silence. Amy poured coffee from the pot Kathy had brewed and offered him a cup. He held up a hand to decline.

"So a phone call woke you?" he asked.

"Yes, it was my cell."

"*Your* cell? Why would your cell phone be calling your house line in the middle of the night?"

"There's a software program you can download from the Internet that turns a cell phone into a motion sensor. I had it set to call and wake me if Celia came out of her room."

"And you think this . . . Clark fellow got into her room?"

"I don't know."

"Why would he do that?"

Amy turned away, tired of it all. Seers changed his question, unaware of what she was trying to avoid. "Could he have just been in the hallway?"

"I suppose."

"Do you know this man?"

Amy started to answer and stopped. "I know who he is. I know his name."

"That's it?" Seers asked.

"I'm not allowed to talk about what I know about him."

The conflict tore her up inside. Should she tell him or shouldn't she? Either way, someone was helped by her betrayal. It was not a fair decision. Seers flipped his notebook closed.

"I see." He dropped the notebook onto the counter with a thud that made her jump. He folded his arms and leaned against the stove. "Look, Amy. I'm trying to help you here. This guy broke into your home. You were afraid he might have assaulted your child. You thought he was going to rape you, and you still won't talk to me?"

Amy's eyes filled with tears. Seers stepped closer, but Amy instinctively took a step away from him.

"I've seen a lot of rape cases over the years. He doesn't fit the profile. From the statement you gave, it doesn't sound like he was trying to pull your clothes off. What do you suppose that means?"

Amy's head was in her hands. "I don't know!" she cried.

176

"I'll tell you what I think," Seers's volume rose considerably. "I think he came here to kill you."

Amy's sobs wracked her body.

"Why this random guy would come in the middle of the night to kill a young mother in her own home is beyond me. It's beyond me because the only witnesses I have are a sleeping toddler and an assailant whose head was bashed in. Not the most tenable case I've ever pursued!" he yelled.

"That's enough!" said a woman's voice behind him. A clap of thunder ripping through the air seemed to underscore the demand. Kathy had emerged from the hallway in time to hear Seers's rant and see Amy's anguished reaction. Seers turned to her.

"Nobody asked you. I can have you removed if I like."

Kathy jumped toward him, unfazed by the threat.

"And I can tell the FCC you were trying to force a VRS interpreter to reveal information about a caller. To say nothing of the victim support groups who will wax philosophical on police abuse against the victim of an attempted sex crime. Then there's the child advocates! Let's not forget them! Who do you think will create a bigger shit storm on the evening news?" Kathy screamed, inches from his face.

All the shouting reawakened Celia, who began crying again. Another crack of thunder and lightning filled the air. Amy rushed up the stairs to Celia's room and screamed over her shoulder.

"All of you finish what you're doing and *get out!*"

DETECTIVE SEERS sat at his desk. The telephone handset had been glued to his ear for over an hour. District Attorney Richard A. Lamb was on the other end. Ryan, his weeklong slave, sat nearby.

"It's pretty straightforward from what the tech guys are telling me. We brought the cell phone back with us. It checked out," Seers said into the phone.

He listened.

"I stopped by her place a few nights ago. She'd been hearing noises, thought somebody was watching her. She didn't use the word *stalking*, but that's what it appears to have been."

He listened some more.

"Her husband passed away last year. Apparently the little girl's had some trouble adjusting. She went from just night cries to sleepwalking. The mother was concerned she'd get hurt falling down the stairs, that sort of thing."

More listening.

"She's got one of those baby monitors but wanted something that would alert her if the little girl went for a walk or anything. She'd started searching the house at night looking for her daddy."

Pause.

"Yes, sir. Very sad."

Another pause.

"We saw and heard everything happen precisely the way she characterized it in her statement. It recorded everything. Apparently she was not aware of that function. It's clear-cut self-defense."

He listened some more.

"I'd still like to go through his house if you'll authorize it. We need to prove he's been rifling through homes. Might even be able to return some of the stolen money or jewelry from the robberies."

He nodded, apparently getting what he wanted.

"Right. I'll get it written up and sent down to your office. Roger that."

He hung up and exhaled.

"What's up?" Ryan asked.

Lamb gave the OK. "We're going to check out Sammy Clark's apartment," Seers replied.

Ryan rolled his eyes. "I can't believe I've joined the flatfoot ranks."

The ride to Sammy's Dupont Circle apartment took twenty minutes, with Ryan drumming his frustration on the dash most of the way.

178

"This guy is dead, right? What are we supposed to be doing?" Ryan asked in a halfhearted attempt to fill the silence.

"I'm looking for something," Seers replied.

"OK, so what if you find it? You can't arrest a dead guy," Ryan pointed out.

"It's not about arresting someone. It's about recovering something."

"What are we recovering?"

"A Navy Cross," Seers replied as his jaws tightened. Ryan was put off by the abrupt change in mood and dropped the question.

Seers made quick work of informing the landlady Sammy Clark was deceased and they were conducting an investigation. She unlocked the door and stood aside.

"You can close the door when you leave, yes?" she asked.

"Don't you want to stay?" Ryan asked.

"Two cops? The tenant is dead? What do I need to stay for?" she asked.

Seers motioned her to follow them. "It won't take a moment."

She sighed theatrically and walked in with them.

It was a tasteful apartment, though the furniture was apparently included in the rent. Early eighties decor of dark woods and ultramodern furniture. Seers hated it immediately, but Ryan found it very retro.

"Oh man," Ryan said as he dropped into a fat chair of black webbing over a steel-pipe frame, "if you want to get rid of some of this furniture I'll be over tonight to pick it up. This is excellent!"

Seers was happy to let Ryan discuss home decorating and keep the landlady out of his way. He looked through the living room and kitchen. The dining room was set up as an office and contained a laptop computer, a briefcase, several file folders, and a couple of banker boxes.

"What did Mr. Clark do for a living?" Seers called back.

"I'm not nosy," she replied.

Sure you're not, Seers thought to himself—as long as the rent is paid on time, no questions asked.

Seers found nothing out of the ordinary. Just the usual detritus of modern life. In the front bedroom, he checked out the desk, the dresser, and a bureau. He pulled out all the drawers and dumped their contents onto the bed. Nothing.

"Holy shit," said Ryan from somewhere in the apartment. Seers's ears perked up.

"Got something?" he yelled.

"You bet your ass," Ryan replied.

Seers hurried down the hallway into a second bedroom. Ryan stood transfixed in the doorway like a man who'd just been handed the keys to the Playboy Mansion.

"Would you take a look at that," Ryan said admiringly as he walked into the room.

One entire wall was filled with electronics. Wide-screen television. Surround sound stereo. There was a satellite dish near the window pointed toward the southeastern horizon. Ryan ran his fingers over everything.

"This is your *holy shit?*" Seers demanded. "It's a radio. Grow up, for crying out loud."

"A radio?" Ryan screeched. "You think this is a radio? Take a good look, Detective. This wall is more than *both* of us make in a couple of *years.*"

"It's a television and a stereo, Ryan," Seers said, articulating every word carefully, as if Ryan was somehow slow on the uptake. "Would you like to listen to some music?"

He reached for a switch, but Ryan yanked Seers's hand away before he made contact.

"Don't touch that!" Ryan said. "Everything has to go on in a certain order or you'll blow the whole damn thing." He looked around carefully until he found a set of switches along the wall that powered up the various components. He turned on a receiver and CD changer. "Let me spell this out for you, Detective. This is a Nakamichi high-definition plasma screen television. It's a couple of years old. Probably only worth around twenty grand now. Used!"

"What?" Seers replied.

"This amp is even older. Audio Research preamps are widely considered the best on the planet. Really incredible sound quality, like you're in the studio itself," Ryan gushed.

"Hell, Ryan, even I have a CD player," Seers said.

"Ah yes, a CD player. Excellent." Ryan flipped three more switches. "This is Bang and Olufsen. Easily ten to fifteen thousand. Probably the same amount for the turntable, as well."

He reverently turned up the amplifier.

"Behind you are two Electro-Voice subwoofers. Professional, studio-grade material. Countersunk into the walls and ceiling are JBL Cinema Sound component satellites. This guy was an audiophile of the highest order."

A workbench took up the opposite wall of the room. Various components were in tidy plastic bins. A soldering gun, wire clips, and electronic testing tools sat on the bench. Clamped to the bench was an overhead magnifying glass with a built-in light.

"I can't believe this guy's dead. It's a real shame," Ryan said as he pored over the bench. "I'd have loved to pick his brain."

"Ease up, lover boy," Seers said. "You'll frighten the lady. You're scaring the hell out of me already."

"I don't get to play with this kind of quality. This is the best of the best of the best. This is the setup you see at Bill Gates's house. Or Julia Roberts's. People for whom money is no object."

Seers quickly tired of the electronics overview. He walked out, followed by the landlady, who watched over his shoulder as Seers walked another lap through the living room. It certainly didn't look like a burglar's apartment. No burglary tools. No contraband.

"Any chance that stuff is stolen?" he yelled to Ryan.

"No way. All the manuals are here, indexed in three-ring binders. This guy bought every one of these puppies and installed them himself. Beautiful!"

Seers shook his head. Ryan might need a cigarette when he finished in there. But all the high-end hardware had not helped his principal problem: where the hell was that medal?

"What can you tell me about Mr. Clark?" Seers asked.

The landlady shrugged. "He was always pleasant. Very private. He didn't talk much, but he was never rude. Kept pretty much to himself."

No help. She could have been describing her cat. Seers walked around again. No hidden storage that he could find. No reason to suspect Sammy had a secret life. Maybe he should go through the laptop. Might be something there.

"Hey, Ryan!" Seers called. "Climb down from your high horse for a minute and come here."

Ryan walked in with a dozen CDs in his hand.

"Don't get sticky-fingered," Seers warned as he pointed to the laptop on the table. "Can you do the digital dance with that like you did with Jordan's PDA?"

"Sure thing."

"Don't you need a warrant?" the landlady asked.

"Do I?" Seers asked menacingly.

Ryan sat down at the laptop and powered it up.

"Will you have to break the password?" Seers asked.

"I don't know," Ryan said. "Doesn't look like he's got one set at power-up. Most people don't. Only when you try to access the Internet, or e-mail, or some sort of private file do you have to worry about that."

He accessed the hard drive easily. He was correct—no password required.

"Apparently Sammy didn't share his computer with anyone. Guess he figured a password was unnecessary. So let's see what we've got. How about e-mail?"

Ryan opened Sammy's e-mail but found nothing untoward.

"Internet hits?" Seers asked.

"Sure, just a second. Let's check his most recently opened files. See what we find there," Ryan said as he randomly clicked through a few files. A picture that burst onto the screen caused the landlady to gasp so loudly it spun Seers's head around.

"What the . . ." was all he could manage. A naked toddler stared back at him. Her haunting brown eyes bored directly into Ryan's guts.

"Kiddie porn?" Seers asked.

The landlady backed away. "*O Dios mio!*" She made the sign of the cross on herself three times in quick succession.

"Shut it off," Seers told him. "Take it with you and dump the whole damn thing into NCIC when you get back to the office. See if anyone recognizes her. If he was trafficking, we'll turn it over to the bureau."

The FBI's National Crime Information Center was a computerized index of criminal justice data available to federal and local law enforcement agencies nationwide. It compiled and cross-referenced data by type, location, and perpetrator. It also provided forensics information on missing persons, cyber crimes, child trafficking, and other criminal activity that crossed state and national lines.

Ryan nodded his agreement and shut off the laptop before standing back up.

"What the hell is that?" Ryan pointed behind Seers. "I've never seen a setup like that before. There's a coax cable snaking up to it but no computer. Just a cable box. Hey, is that a camera pointing out of the front?" He jumped back as if the device might explode.

Seers immediately recognized it. "It's a videophone," he said quietly.

"A what?" Ryan asked.

"A videophone," Seers repeated. He flipped a couple of buttons haphazardly, and the screen jumped to life. A young man appeared on the monitor.

"Thank you for using All Hands VRS. Can I help you?" he signed and spoke.

"It connects a deaf person to a sign language interpreter for phone calls," Seers explained. He looked at Ryan, who simply raised an eyebrow at him.

"What?" Ryan asked.

"Ma'am? You said you talked to Mr. Clark?" Seers asked.

"Yes, sir," she replied, still shaken by the pornographic picture.

"And he talked back to you?"

"Yes, of course."

"No problems communicating with him?"

"No. Why do you ask?"

"He could hear you clearly, then?" Seers asked.

"He wasn't deaf, Detective, if that's what you mean."

"Then why would he have a telephone system for the deaf? Did he live alone?"

"Yes."

"Girlfriend? Family who stayed with him on occasion who might be deaf or hard of hearing?"

"No, no one! Will this take much longer?" she asked. She was ready to be rid of any reference to or evidence of her former tenant.

Seers turned back to the monitor. The VRS interpreter was becoming increasingly animated over their unresponsiveness. Seers flipped the unit off again.

"What's all this?" Ryan asked as he leafed through one of the folders on the dining room table. Several pieces of paper appeared to have been crumpled up, then unfolded and smoothed out. A few had stains of dubious origin. Seers looked over his shoulder. Ryan appeared to be holding a medical file.

"That might be confidential," Seers pointed out.

"It's not his," Ryan said. "This is some chick. Psychological profile and her prescriptions. Looks like she's in therapy." He scanned a few pages. "Wow. She's got issues. Dead husband. Daughter with a case of midnight wanderlust. She's kind of hot," Ryan noted.

Seers snatched the file from him. His eyes widened at the picture. On top of the thick packet was something labeled a 16PF, used for clinical diagnosis and therapy planning to provide therapists with measures of anxiety, adjustment, and behavioral problems. Several paragraphs were highlighted.

Subject's communication is predicted to be demonstrative and forceful. That is, her sentimental displays are probably uninhibited and genuine. Her emotions are likely to be easily perceived by others and thus are likely to influence the emotional state of those around her. Emotional expressiveness is high.

He skipped a few paragraphs to read another highlighted section.

This person may enjoy observing other people's gestures, moods, and nonverbal interactions. Thus she may feel comfortable interpreting people's emotional and other nonverbal messages. Emotional sensitivity to others is high.

In the margin of the page was scribbled "likely useful for a VRS interpreter." Seers flipped back to the cover page. Subject name: Amy Kellen.

He paged through additional sections with similar highlights. On the last page was an entry entitled Leadership and Creativity.

At the subject's own level of abilities, potential for creative functioning is predicted to be high.

"Who the hell would have something like this on her?" Seers asked aloud.

"On who?" Ryan asked.

Seers reached down and picked up the briefcase. DR. REGGIE BROWN was engraved on a brass nameplate by the handle.

"Son of a bitch!"

HEATH STOOD by a white dry erase board listing Harold Kensington's known associates and their alibis. In one corner of the room, the ubiquitous government office television tuned to CNN played to nobody in particular. As is normal for an election cycle, the talking heads were charging by the word for their time.

"The Democratic slate of candidates is starting to turn on each other," the commentator noted. "What seems clear is that candidates are pulling no punches to find a way into the White House."

Heath listed relevant points about the garage where Brent Jordan's body was found. Secure, deniable, away from town but easily accessible by high-speed roads, room to operate.

"How will the party react to the escalating sense of panic among the candidates? It's no longer us against them—it's more like every man for himself! The political sniping is getting heated . . ." the commentator continued.

On the reverse side of the board, he'd diagrammed the deaths of Harold Kensington, Brent Jordan, Dell Kohler, and Sammy Clark. Each man was connected to family members, work associates, neighbors, memberships in social or business groups, alumni associations, and a host of the other personal relationships people collect over the course of their lives.

Sammy Clark's outline showed connections to people with whom he'd served jail time. Harold Kensington was linked to three past presidents. Brent Jordan and Dell Kohler shared several links in common through the pet services industry, but even their associations were fairly distinct by nature of the clientele they served. The circumstances that linked the four together in relation to their untimely deaths was driving Heath up the wall. Something didn't fit.

He looked at the television but remained lost in thought. He was interrupted by a ringing telephone. Another agent grabbed it and gestured.

"Heath! Telephone."

Heath punched a button on the phone by his side and answered.

"It's Seers. Got a second?" a voice asked.

Heath stared out the window across the Washington, D.C., skyline. "Sure. I presume there will be no charges against Amy Kellen?"

"This a personal or professional inquiry?" Seers asked.

"Bit of both, actually."

"Fair enough. No, she won't be charged, but something far more interesting has happened."

"What's that?"

"We got into Sammy Clark's apartment—found a few surprises."

"Like what?" Heath asked absently.

"A VRS videophone."

Heath stiffened and turned back around to his desk. "In his *house?*" he asked.

"Yep. Landlady said she'd had many conversations with him. Never a hint of being hard of hearing. In person and on the phone, he could hear and speak clear as a bell. He's quite the electronics enthusiast, though. Ryan nearly peed on himself over the high-end toys this guy had."

"That's pretty strange."

"No, that's only odd. I haven't told you the strange part yet," Seers replied.

"What's that?"

"He had a psychological profile on Amy Kellen," Seers said. "Lots of yellow highlighting and some notes in the margins."

Heath stopped everything else he was doing. "Go on," he said.

"Apparently she did talk to a therapist about Kensington's death. She didn't tell him any details, though—only the fact that she watched someone die. Apparently never told him who it was or what the circumstances were."

"That a fact?" Heath asked quietly.

"The files were in a briefcase stolen from one of my burglary victim's homes. In addition to the psych file, this guy had surveillance logs containing her work schedule and babysitter's info. He apparently has been picking through her trash, too. Found some bills, some letters, and similar types of stuff. He's been on her a while."

"Were there files on anyone besides Amy?" Heath asked.

"Yeah, but we found them in the trash."

"Hers was the only one recovered inside?"

"Correct," Seers replied.

Heath processed all the information. It didn't make sense. "Do you think Sammy Clark was your burglar?" Heath asked.

"His fingerprints were in the passenger seat of the Honda where we found Brent Jordan."

"So?"

"So, I figure he and someone else got interrupted on a burglary job. Maybe he delivered the dog and ran into them or something. In any event, he was in possession of an item taken during this rash of burglaries. But nothing else. No jewelry and no cash. I guess he could have just been using the cash to buy the electronics," Seers theorized.

"I doubt that's the case," Heath said.

"Why? Do you think she's into something?"

"No. I don't think she's *into* anything. I think someone was into *her*," Heath said.

"Oh? How's that?" Seers asked.

"Do you know how many people around her have died recently?"

"Can't say that I do," Seers replied sarcastically.

"I count four," Heath finished. He turned to his chart.

"So?" Seers asked.

"What are the odds of all of them being linked to the Deaf community?" Heath asked.

"She's an interpreter! She's around deaf people all the time."

"Only one died in relation to her job as an interpreter. The rest were random or were supposed to appear random."

"You think they're not random?" Seers asked.

"Right now I'm just trying to figure out how they could be related. So far I'm coming up with nothing."

"Concentrate on the first one."

"Why?" Heath asked.

"If they are related, your perpetrator has the most prior planning but the least amount of experience with his first victim," Seers replied. "So what do you think is going on?"

"I don't know. Something's not right. The Deaf community's pretty spun up about it."

"Yeah, well, the *community* doesn't seem to like cops very much. Nobody will talk to me," Seers complained.

"Don't take it personally, Detective. They just don't experience your charming personality the way I do."

"Are you done?" Seers asked sarcastically.

"For the moment," Heath replied.

"Call you back when I know more," Seers said. He hung up the phone.

Heath erased the other names, leaving Harold Kensington alone at the top of the whiteboard.

"OK," he said aloud. "Forget the dog. What would you do if Kensington was zapped the old-fashioned way?"

He scribbled the characteristics of a good sniper onto the whiteboard. Quiet. Intense. Disciplined. He then wrote "The Sniper's Creed" and placed three words in a column.

Stalk. Conceal. Spot.

He looked up at another Secret Service agent standing nearby.

"It's been a while. Do you remember the sniper's creed?" Heath asked.

"Yeah," the other agent replied. "Stalk—stalk the target until you know his pattern.

Conceal—protect and hide your position. Spot . . ."

The phone rang again. He picked it up and tossed the dry erase pen to the other agent. It was Cheryl Corely from downstairs.

"You're not going to believe this," she said. "Washington Metro police downloaded a hard drive into the NCIC. In addition to a couple of kiddie porn pics, guess what it contained?"

"What?" Heath asked, still mulling over Seers's call.

"I was right. Your African e-mail writer was American. Key word being *was*. He's dead. Thought you might want to know he probably won't be much of a threat anymore."

"Who was he?" Heath asked.

"Guy's name was Sammy Clark," Cheryl replied.

Heath stopped mid-breath. "What did you say?"

The other agent tossed the dry erase pen back on Heath's desk. "All done."

"Sammy Clark," Cheryl repeated in his ear.

Heath glanced at the whiteboard's final entry:

"Spot—exploit the target's telltale signs."

The color drained from his face.

"Christ almighty!"

Chapter Fifteen

SEERS INHALED his morning's third cup of coffee. He was no closer to closing his burglary case than he'd been a week ago. But it was the previous evening's conversation with Heath Rasco that had kept him rolling around in bed most of the night.

Heath's dogged questioning of whether or not Sammy Clark was the Georgetown burglar had really chafed him. He wasn't accustomed to having his judgment questioned. *He* was the investigator. Heath was a behaviorist, an academic with a badge. Still, something about Heath's argument chipped away at Seers's certainty. At first it was just annoying. But when he factored in Sammy Clark's apartment, Heath's argument made a lot more sense.

Nothing about the residence suggested Clark was a petty thief. He'd done time several years earlier for stock fraud, so he certainly had the mindset of a thief. But that had been a white-collar crime. The apartment screamed white-collar. Seers could imagine plucking any Wall Street analyst or broker out of New York and dropping him directly into Clark's apartment, and the guy would be perfectly at home. It didn't make sense. Defrauding investors was a long way from breaking windows. Even assuming a pronounced fall from grace, Clark didn't have the skill set necessary to be a professional thief.

"Morning, Detective," Ryan said as he came in. "Two more days and you're rid of me."

"Morning," Seers grumbled. That damned Rasco. If Heath was right, Seers needed to restart his investigation from scratch. Not an appealing idea first thing in the morning.

"That was one hell of a setup that guy had yesterday," Ryan observed. "What will happen to all those electronics?"

"As big a deal as you made of them, I imagine the old lady will be watching *House and Garden* reruns on them. Or in thirty days when they're considered abandoned property, she'll offer them on eBay to the highest bidder," Seers replied.

"Damn!" Ryan retorted. "There's no way I can compete with what some of those eBay bandits can pay. Not on my salary."

Seers stirred. "Can you check that again for me?" he asked.

"I thought you said it would take thirty days," Ryan replied.

"What? Oh, that. Yeah, the electronics would. I was talking about that Navy Cross. Can you check again to see if it's on eBay or any of those other sites?"

"Sure," Ryan said.

He began searching. Nothing on eBay. Same with Craigslist. He checked the classified sections of the *Washington Post* and the *Hoya*, the student newspaper of Georgetown University. He checked several of the databases pawnshops use as clearinghouses to ensure they wouldn't be prosecuted for dealing in stolen items. No Navy Cross.

"Sorry, Detective," Ryan said.

"Damn," Seers muttered. It was a long shot, but he had hoped. Where did that leave him? At the beginning? Begin the entire investigation again from scratch, from day one? He couldn't bear it. Seers dropped his face into his hands.

Wait a minute. What had he told Heath the previous day? Start with the first incident. The bad guy has the least experience with the first incident. Seers pulled out his case file. The first incident had involved the Dix family. Two thousand dollars and a Rolex Mariner watch had been taken.

Nice couple. Young. Teddy and Mary Dix. Quite a blow to a couple just starting out. Two thousand dollars would go a long way with a second baby on the way.

"Detective, I don't think this is going to work. Your bad guy has to know you're looking for him to hock this stuff. He'd be a fool to try selling it locally. The timing isn't right. He's guaranteed to get caught and he's not stupid enough to do that," Ryan insisted.

Seers stopped for a moment.

"What did you say?" Seers asked.

Ryan stammered, "I just mean, I don't mean to tell you how to run your case."

"No, not that part. The other part."

"Timing? I just think you'd have to be a rank amateur to try and sell something locally. We're going to be looking for anyone trying to unload jewelry and stuff. It's too easily traced. Cash makes sense. Jewelry is suicide."

Seers rubbed his chin. Ryan might be onto something. *Timing.* Were the Dixes really the *first* victims? If Frank Stratton's Navy Cross was simply a piece of jewelry, could *he* have been the first case, not Ted and Mary Dix? Seers opened his credenza, looking for the Stratton file.

He spread it out on the table. According to her statement, Sally Ellis reported the break-in at her father's apartment the day after the maid noticed the missing items. But the maid came only every other week. The Dix break-in had been four days earlier. If Stratton's apartment was broken into before that, *he* was the first victim.

"Don't get comfortable," Seers said to Ryan. "We're going out for breakfast."

SEERS PULLED up to the house and parked around back, near Frank Stratton's door. He'd called Sally Ellis on the way. Chris was on a business trip, but she was happy to have Seers come by again.

"Good to see you," Sally said as they walked in.

"Thank you for seeing us," Seers replied. "This is my colleague, Ryan Richter."

"Nice to meet you," Sally said. "Can I offer you some coffee?"

"Thank you. That'd be nice," Ryan said.

"Do you have any news?" Sally asked Seers.

"No, but we're rethinking our investigation. Some things have happened that make us question our original assumptions. Do you think he would mind if we took another look around?"

"I don't think it will be a problem. He's had a pretty good week," Sally replied.

Ryan frowned at Seers, mouthing "what?" as he followed the pair across the back patio to Frank Stratton's apartment. Sally knocked, and a few moments later her father opened the door. He was standing with the help of a cane, but was dressed in pressed khakis and a button-down red shirt. Seers marveled at him. Parkinson's had ravaged his mind and body, but the retired marine still pressed his own clothes. The uniform mindset was hard to unlearn.

"Hi, Dad! Do you remember Detective Seers? He wanted to see your apartment again. Is that all right?" she asked.

Stratton stepped back so the three could enter. Ryan was the last to go in. He suddenly slowed and seemed oddly uncomfortable.

"A *private* apartment, huh?" Ryan asked. Seers was taken aback by Ryan's strange tone of voice. He was also speaking especially loudly. Seers glared at him and walked around the small living space.

"I'm sure we went through this, but refresh my memory," Seers said. "Only the one entrance. No forced entry on the windows. Everything was fine."

"Right," Sally said.

"You indicated the maid first noticed the missing sword," Seers said.

"Sword?" Ryan perked up.

"Yes, that's right. She went over for the usual cleaning she does after the house. She immediately came back here and got me. I was the one who noticed the medal missing."

"Right," Seers replied. "She hadn't been here for two weeks prior, is that correct?" Seers asked.

"Right, Detective. What are you wondering? Do you really believe she's a suspect?" Sally asked.

"No, quite frankly, I don't," Seers replied. Ryan was walking around the perimeter of the apartment and made great efforts to look in every direction. Seers had no idea what he was doing, but it was annoying him to no end.

"Were you not in the apartment at all during that two-week period?" Seers asked.

"Yes. Why?" Sally asked.

"Why didn't you notice the sword missing?"

"I'm not in here that much. And when I am, I'm concentrating on my father, not on the decorations."

Sally tried to answer politely, but her impatience was clear.

"I'm sorry. What I mean is it's hard to get a good timeline if nobody was in here for two weeks," Seers said. "It seems to me that while your father takes his meals in the main house, you might check on him from time to time during the day," Seers said.

"Detective, can I see you outside?" Ryan asked.

"Are you suggesting I don't take proper care of my father? I happen to love him very much!" Sally charged.

"Oh, I'm sure you do," Seers said. "But what if he falls? What if he has a medical emergency in the night and needs help?"

"I'd really like to talk to you outside," Ryan insisted.

"How dare you!" Sally said. "I think it's time you both left!"

"Great idea! Why don't we step outside?" Ryan pulled Seers by the arm toward the door.

"What the hell is wrong with you?" Seers growled.

"What the hell is wrong with you?" Ryan shot back. "You're crawling down her throat and not listening to me. This joint is wired nine ways to Wednesday," Ryan said.

"What?"

"The whole apartment. There are miniature cameras and at least two omnidirectional microphones. And that's just what I could see from a cursory walk around. There could be more. Everything we said and did in there was probably recorded."

Seers looked past Ryan to Sally as she kissed her father and closed the door to his apartment. Ryan made a beeline for the main house.

"Hey! What are you doing? I didn't say you could go in there!" Sally shouted. "Get out of my house!"

"Ryan, get back here!" Seers yelled.

"Yes. Get out! And don't come back! Do you hear me?"

"Ryan! Get your ass out here," Seers yelled again as he chased him into the home, with Sally close on his heels.

When Seers caught up with him, Ryan was standing in front of a television monitor mounted under a kitchen cabinet and was tapping the buttons on a white remote control.

"Ryan! Get your . . ." Seers stopped. He stared at the images on the screen. "What the hell?"

The television screen split into four squares, each showing the interior of Frank Stratton's apartment from a different angle. Seers could see the old man lowering himself back into his easy chair to watch television. The other scenes showed his kitchen, his bedroom, and a reverse angle on the living room. Cameras covered every part of the residence.

"Give me that!" Sally yanked the remote from Ryan and pointed to the door. "Get out!" she screamed.

"She does check on him," Ryan said softly. "She just does it from here."

Sally broke into tears. "You don't understand," she sobbed. "He was so devastated when he got sick. I couldn't let him go to a nursing home. But he didn't want to be a burden on us. He wanted Chris and me to be a normal couple, not worry about an old man who couldn't care for himself."

Ryan gently took the remote away from her and flipped back to the proper channel.

"You set up the cameras so you could watch over him all the time," Ryan said sympathetically. "In case he needed you."

"He raised me alone," Sally sobbed. "My mother died when I was very young. He never once faltered. I wanted him with me . . ."

"Just as he had kept you all those years," Seers finished.

"I don't like deceiving him," Sally choked. "He needs privacy. I respect that. I just don't want anyone taking advantage of him," she declared.

"It's an excellent setup," Ryan offered in a dispassionate forensic analysis to Seers. "You can see him from any angle, but he's still got privacy in the bathroom. The mics will pick up any sound of him falling, or if he has a medical problem. You've got this wired to all the televisions in your home?" he asked.

Sally nodded.

"This is a wonderful thing you've done," Seers assured her. "You're not deceiving him. You're protecting him, including from himself. I'm sure he's happier here with you than he would be in a nursing home. Your husband's a great guy for going along."

"Yes. He is. Thank you," Sally said.

"We should go," Seers said to Ryan.

"I'm sorry I lost my cool," Sally said. "I just miss my dad. Did you get what you needed?"

Seers stared at his shoes. "I'm not sure. I'm still trying to figure out why someone did it. I'm sorry I'm not able to do more."

Ryan handed Sally the remote control and followed Seers to the car. "Now what?" Ryan asked.

"I'm getting too old for this sort of thing," Seers said. "Cell phones that sense babies' movements. Hidden cameras monitoring parents— it's a foreign world to me."

"You're comparing apples and oranges—sensors and monitors are not the same thing," Ryan said.

"How's that?" Seers asked.

"Signal output is totally different. A cell phone call is traceable. Baby monitors are radio broadcasts—they go everywhere. No records or electronic trails of any kind."

Seers had opened his car door but stopped. "What's that?"

"Baby monitors. They broadcast over FM radio frequencies. Same setup these folks have. They're designed for short distances, baby's room to living room or parents' bedroom, that sort of thing."

"Right. And?" Seers asked.

Ryan hesitated, concerned he'd screwed up somehow by commenting. "Well, the signal can actually travel much farther than that," he said.

197

"You mean with a high-powered receiver or something?"

"Doesn't need to be. Remember that teacher in Chicago who picked up the International Space Station on her baby monitor? That's an extreme case, but you get the idea."

"The signal—it includes the audio, too, right?"

"Sure, most times," Ryan nodded.

"It's possible to intercept the signal of someone else's transmitter if you wanted to?" Seers asked, oddly animated.

"Fifty bucks at a Radio Shack gets you everything you need."

"So you could turn a baby monitor into a covert listening device and a parent wouldn't know it?"

Ryan nodded. "Not unless they went looking for it. People put them in place and never imagine the intimate details of their lives being broadcast to the world. My brother's neighbors got an earful of he and his wife conceiving their second child. Now, they'd had a couple of drinks that night and he . . ." Ryan started.

Seers snapped his fingers. "That's how he's doing it!" he yelled.

He walked around the car to Ryan's side as he revisited every one of the burglary cases in his mind. They all had one overarching similarity. Something that tied otherwise completely disparate families together. Something Sally Ellis didn't have. Yet in a way, she did.

"How *who* is doing *what*?" Ryan asked, stopping in mid-story.

"Baby monitors! Every house had a child and a camera to keep an eye on them. They're intercepting the feeds to know who is home, who has a dog, or when people are traveling!" Seers slapped Ryan on the back so hard it stung. "We've got to find the captain," he said as he pushed Ryan toward the passenger-side door.

MIKE SEERS stood at the head of the room addressing the collection of cops, detectives, technicians, and support staff. Ryan Richter was at his side.

"All right, everyone. Grab a seat. I'm sure you're all wondering why you're on duty tonight," Seers began. He nodded to Ryan, who was fiddling with a baby monitor on the bench in front of them.

"Ryan here will demonstrate how we think our burglar is picking his targets."

They watched as Ryan scrolled through several intercepted feeds of babies sleeping, crying, and having their diapers changed. All of the signals were random, live, and coming from homes in the immediate vicinity of the station. Most had no idea they were hosting small television broadcasts directly from their children's rooms to the outside world.

"He knows who is traveling, who is a single parent, and who has an alarm system. My guess is he won't go near a home unless he's certain nobody is there," Seers continued. He nodded to Ryan again, who then scrolled through a series of empty cribs. "It's a perfect standoff surveillance device. When there's no baby and no chatter in the background, he knows the coast is clear. Completely untraceable."

Seers cut the unit off.

"What we are going to do is try to lure him with a few houses we control," Seers said, turning to a tactical map on the wall behind him. "We've arranged with a half dozen families in Georgetown to talk about last-minute travel opportunities within earshot of their baby monitors. In actuality we're putting them up in hotels in the area. Hopefully our baby-dependent bandit will drop by one of these houses. When he does, we collapse on the house. Any questions?" he asked.

An officer raised his hand. "How can you be sure you'll hear him?" he asked.

Seers smiled. "We're placing a few of our own inside the houses."

He put two fingers to his mouth and fired off a piercing whistle. Two police dogs rushed into the room.

"We're placing K-9 units inside some of the homes. If anyone shows up, we'll hear the dogs growling," Seers beamed proudly. It was his idea. Captain Hall stood at the front of the room next to Seers.

"SWAT operators are on call for the week," Hall said. "Now, given that we have K-9 units involved, this is a good opportunity to test out some new nonlethal methods."

Seers rolled his eyes to the rest of the squad room, and Hall threw a SWAT cap at him.

"I'm not saying they're the greatest thing since sliced bread, but we're getting our ass handed to us for relying on heavy weapons. I'd prefer to take this guy down without firing a shot. I need some help on this one, ladies. No shooting unless absolutely necessary. Let's stick it to the media with a story they'll hate—only the *bad* guys did something worth reporting."

"All right. The adult supervision portion of the evening is done," Seers said. "We can't shoot someone we haven't caught yet, so everyone grab a cup of coffee and let's get set for an easy shift. We shouldn't have to do this more than three or four nights to get our guy."

Amy Kellen walked into the back of the squad room. Seers took her aside. "I'm surprised to see you," he began. "Is something wrong?"

"I'm sorry to bother you again, but I wanted to pick up my cell phone. I feel better having it around for Celia at night. I know it's silly, but . . ." Amy said.

Seers stopped her. "No, not at all. You've had a rough time. Anything that lets you sleep well at night is certainly worth doing."

He walked into the evidence room and retrieved the phone for her. "Needless to say, we removed the video of Mr. Clark," he said.

"Oh yeah, I didn't think about that. I've been trying to *not* think about it. Thank you."

She looked around at all the preparations going on. Two officers were packing a net into some sort of ballistic shell. Another was charging his Taser in a docking station. A third replaced the batteries in a set of night-vision goggles. The room was teeming with special weapons activity.

"Looks like you guys are gearing up for a real battle," she noted.

"Oh, no, not at all, actually. Just a little surveillance work," Seers assured her. "We'll be in your neighborhood quite a bit, so don't be concerned if you see cars and dogs and such. We think we've found a way to catch our baby-cam burglar."

"*Baby-cam* burglar?" Amy repeated.

"The homes all have baby monitors. We think he's using them to figure out who has an alarm or a dog."

"Hmm."

"If I might make a suggestion?" Seers asked cautiously.

"Sure."

"Turn Celia's camera off when you get home. Just for a couple of days. We'll be watching all of them, and you'd be surprised what gets broadcast through those things. You've got your cell phone back, and that should be sufficient until we catch this guy."

"I'll do that. Thanks."

"We're placing a few police dogs around to help out. You should consider that yourself," Seers added.

"What?" Amy asked.

"Getting a dog. Great protection, especially for a young woman living alone," he offered.

"I'll think about it," Amy said.

"Why don't you go home and get some rest? If you need anything," he waved his cell phone, "I'll be in the neighborhood."

AMY STEPPED out of the cab and walked up the sidewalk to the front door. After a quick chat with her babysitter, she paid the woman and locked up the house for the night. Kathy had worn her down. And as much as she hated to admit it, she'd had a nice time. Carpool was Kathy's favorite bar in Arlington, and she'd assembled a group from the office for a long-overdue girls' night out. They drank Tommy Bahama rum punch in honor of Amy's former LPGA sponsor.

Amy wasn't drunk, but she'd not had several drinks in one sitting in quite a while, so she had a very comfortable buzz. Her mood was quiet but happy. She'd needed a night out. For a few hours, she'd successfully forgotten about all the problems she'd been dealing with lately. She'd just had fun. They'd toyed with a couple of guys who'd bought them a round of drinks, but the girls all left the bar together. That was rule number one on ladies' night. They left together, no matter whom they met or how cute he was.

The babysitter had run a load of dishes, so Amy put them away. Celia's toys were in their bin, so all she really needed to do before going to bed was kill all the lights save for the small dome light over the stove. She'd gotten into the habit of leaving it on when Celia was still on bottles to prevent the area from being enveloped in darkness when a late-night run down the stairs was necessary.

Upstairs, she flipped on the master bedroom light followed by the bathroom light and exhaust fan. She changed out of her nice clothes and put on a T-shirt and thin pajama pants. She took a long look at herself in the mirror. The guys at the bar had kept telling her how pretty she was. She'd summarily dismissed them, but one guy had kept after her. She looked at herself again.

She was in good shape, all things considered. She'd not been working out regularly since she was no longer on the tour. She'd been eating more, and taking a desk job was a radical departure calorie-wise. She had more weight on her now than she had a year ago, but was certain she could work it off if she tried. After pondering a return to the gym, she turned off the lights, and the entire house was plunged into darkened silence as she climbed into bed.

Outside, the silver Maxima that had followed her back from Arlington pulled out from around the corner and drove away.

Chapter Sixteen

RYAN AND another technician were crammed into the back of a surveillance truck packed full of electronic equipment. A bank of computer monitors took up one entire side of the van, and all of them were filled with baby monitor feeds. Mike Seers opened the back door and climbed in. "Yeah, guys. What's up?" he asked.

"Check this out," Ryan said. "We've been hearing it for a few minutes now."

Seers listened as a dog's low growl bled through a speaker. He saw nothing on the monitor, but the audio feed's dancing LED lights indicated the animal was there and apparently no longer alone.

"Where?" Seers whispered unnecessarily.

"That's Miss Cleo," Ryan replied as he looked over the K-9 roster. "She's at the Darling residence. 3329 Q Street."

Seers stepped outside and keyed his police radio.

"I need SWAT to 3329 Q Street," he said. "Be quick and be quiet." He turned back to Ryan. "You guys follow us over there in a few if this works out."

Seers drove to Q Street and parked one block away from the Darling house. The SWAT van arrived two minutes later and parked behind him. Dark-suited men with rifles, gas masks, and stun grenades spilled out onto the street. Seers walked up to Captain Hall. "Evening, Bill. You guys ready?" Seers asked.

Hall looked over his troops. They were ready. "How do you want to handle it?" he asked.

"I figure we go up the alley in standard cover formation and surround the place. Hang on." Seers keyed his radio. "Ryan! We still good to go inside?"

"Miss Cleo's no longer growling, but she doesn't need to. We can hear movement in the house. *Somebody's* home!"

Bill nodded to the SWAT team. "You heard the man. Two by two down the alley. Lowest possible profile. Let's not telegraph what we're doing. Surround and hold."

A K-9 officer walked up. "Let me know when you want Cleo out," he said, holding a dog whistle.

Seers shook his head. "Leave her alone. We'll try and take this down without accidentally shooting her or letting her take a bite out of them. She's in the kid's playroom and the door is closed. If these guys are any good, they'll go directly for the master suite."

The SWAT team slowly crept down the alley to the Darling residence and went through a back gate. Seers looked carefully at each window of the darkened house. This is where something usually went wrong during an operation. Somebody sees the team just as they arrive, but before they get into position. Sometimes it's the bad guy. Other times it's a neighbor. Occasionally it's a dog. Hopefully that wouldn't be the case tonight.

"Any way to make sure Cleo stays quiet as our guys enter the house?" Seers asked.

K-9 officer David Kemer shook his head. "She's not trained to ignore things—quite the contrary actually. But she's only halfway through the program at this point. Luck of the draw."

"That's what I'm afraid of," Seers said ruefully. Cleo should start barking any second.

But she didn't. SWAT surrounded the house and everything remained quiet. A couple of lights went on next door, and everyone dropped to the ground. Seers couldn't believe his ears. A crying baby! What were the odds? Everyone held their position, and a few minutes later, all was once again quiet. Seers swished his finger in the air, signaling the team to move up to the house.

Bill Hall was the first to arrive at a door. Seers handed him the key, and Hall expertly opened it without a sound. One by one Hall signaled the men into the house.

The lead officer suddenly froze and pointed straight up. The sound of footsteps upstairs. Their burglar was on the move.

Seers motioned Kemer into the hallway. He'd taken off his shoes to keep from making any accidental noise. Kemer walked up to the door and stuck his hand inside. Cleo sniffed once and her tail went into hyperdrive. Kemer gave her two treats and put a leash on to lead the animal outside. Seers breathed a sigh of relief.

One variable removed.

Overhead creaking assured them the burglar or burglars were still around. SWAT fanned out to cover both staircases leading to the second and third floors of the home. This was where things got tricky. If they trapped one burglar on the second floor, but the other was on the third floor, things could get messy pretty quick.

He might panic. He might start shooting—not only at the officers on the street, but also into neighboring homes. That would destroy an otherwise successful raid, and Seers was determined not to let that happen.

Footsteps moved toward the top of the landing. The SWAT team scattered to clear the area at the bottom of the stairs. Everybody was wearing night-vision goggles, so they should have an advantage over whoever was upstairs. Footsteps slowly crept down. Too slowly. Had they made a noise and given away their presence? Seers, still hidden in darkness, peeked around a corner to see a figure standing on the last step, listening for something.

Seers held his breath.

Two prongs leaped out from the darkness to the man's chest. There was a buzz to Seers's right and a faint odor of ozone. The man convulsed, his face contorted in pain. Two officers rushed to catch him.

When the stun gun's electric charge was gone, he collapsed into their waiting arms. They dragged him down the hall as he babbled incoherently. Seers and Captain Hall peered up the stairs. Was there another?

Two officers joined them, and one pointed first up to the next floor, then to his ear. Could they hear anything? Both shook their heads no. All remained quiet.

One of the two officers who had seized the first burglar returned. He made a series of hand signals to Seers and Hall, and showed what he'd pulled off the burglar when he was handcuffed. A walkie-talkie radio. Someone else was still in the house.

Seers looked at Hall and made a series of hand signals. Hall shook his head in disagreement, and Seers rolled his eyes. "We could be here all night," Seers whispered to him.

"I'm not risking anybody and screwing up a textbook arrest by having somebody cowboy their way up a flight of stairs. Forget it, Seers!" Hall whispered back.

Seers glared up the staircase. This could take a while. The burglar might intend to wait them out, not thinking the police would sit around looking for an accomplice. Hall looked outside and made more hand gestures to the second officer, who signaled his understanding. The officer gave Seers the thumbs-up as he slipped past them down the staircase.

"What are you doing?" Seers asked in Hall's ear.

"Using an alternative to violence," Hall replied.

Ryan appeared at the top of the landing with the officer a few minutes later carrying a black duffel bag. He removed something from the bag and placed it on the floor.

Seers looked down to see a small paperback book. Seven inches wide and about nine inches high. It was old, ragged, and looked like it had been around the library a few times. Seers opened his mouth to whisper to Hall, but stopped. The book had moved. Seers blinked. Must be light from the hallway. He leaned over to Hall again when the book moved back. Now Seers stopped and looked closer.

The book's spine unexpectedly separated and rose eight inches into the air. Seers was dumbfounded, but everyone else acted like it was the most normal thing in the world. Ryan was playing with what appeared to be a portable video game console. He looked up from the console to the book, then back again. Seers couldn't make out what was on the screen, so he leaned over a little closer.

"I'll be damned," he said under his breath. Captain Hall's face filled the screen.

Seers's head turned back to see that the book's spine was straight up and pointed at Bill Hall.

"Gives *bookmobile* a whole new meaning, doesn't it?" Hall whispered.

Ryan displayed his characteristic silly grin. Seers shook his head and sat back down.

Ryan fiddled with the controls, and the spine returned to its original position. From any distance over a foot away, it was completely unrecognizable as a robot. Ryan nodded to an officer who picked it up and crept up the stairs to the third floor, placed the book on the top step, then retraced his steps back down. Only after the officer had returned to his hiding place did Ryan tap the joystick to move the robot forward.

The book slowly slid away. Ryan raised the spine camera again to navigate. He came to the first upstairs bedroom. The robot's rubber treads made no noise as it entered the room. A button on the console lit up the robot's tiny infrared light as the unit slowly spun around in a circle.

Nothing.

Either their bad guy had made it into a closet or under the bed, or he was in a different room. Hall motioned for Ryan to try another room. They'd not heard any movement, so the likelihood of a sophisticated hiding place was small. Wherever he was, he'd frozen in place right out in the open. Seers was sure of it.

Ryan returned the robot to the hallway and executed a ninety-degree turn. Another bedroom. From what Seers could see, it was a little girl's room. He leaned over to Ryan and Hall.

"Forget that one, too. Nothing worth stealing in there. Try to find the master."

Hall nodded his agreement and Ryan rolled the robot farther down the hall between doors on either side. Aiming the camera in one direction, he saw a crib, a changing table, and a rocking chair. An infant's room.

Seers smiled. That's no doubt where a baby camera was, too—the trigger that had led them all here to begin with. He waved Ryan toward the other room. It made sense that mom and dad's room would be right across the hall.

Ryan manipulated the little joystick and drove the slim device right under the master bedroom door. He stopped just inside and slowly panned the tiny camera left to right. Seers grabbed his arm and motioned for him to pan back to the right. Standing in front of the dresser, frozen in place, was a man dressed all in black.

Ryan wrinkled his brow. Something didn't look right. He turned the robot around in place and discovered his camera blocked by an object on the floor.

"Let's go get him," Seers said.

"Does he have a weapon?" Hall asked.

"Can't tell. He's got something in his hands, but I can't tell what it is," Ryan replied.

"We've got the element of surprise if we hurry," Seers insisted.

"No way," Hall said. "I'm calling the shots until he's in custody."

Seers leaned back. He hated it when Hall pulled rank on him. Technically, as a captain, he could pull rank anytime, but Bill was normally more than happy to leave the routine police work to others and handle only the SWAT elements.

Seers looked out the window, wondering if they'd have to stay up all night waiting on Mr. Statue to decide when to give up. He checked down the street. People would notice them soon. He was surprised nobody had called the media yet. There'd be no quiet then. They'd better get this thing over pretty quick.

That's when he had an idea.

Seers took the first officer by the arm and whispered in his ear. The officer disappeared back down the stairs for a third time.

"What are you doing, damn it?" Hall asked Seers.

"Letting us all go home before the sun comes up," Seers replied. After a moment, the officer returned with K-9 officer Kemer and a police dog named Prince. Seers pointed up the stairs to the third floor. Kemer looked at Ryan's video display of the target. Hall nodded his approval, and they all slipped back into their respective shadows. Kemer spoke quietly to Prince and pushed him toward the stairs.

Prince walked up the stairs quickly, his nails clicking on the hardwood floor. He didn't bark but instead padded his way down the hallway and out of their field of vision. Several seconds went by with no activity. Seers and Hall exchanged glances.

Ryan moved the robot back a few feet toward the hallway. As he turned the camera around, the screen suddenly filled with teeth, tongue, and fur as Prince ran up.

A man screamed.

Prince growled to drive the man out of the master bedroom. The man tripped over Ryan's robot as Prince nipped at his heels. He regained his footing and sprinted down the hall, then turned and raced down the stairs.

"Freeze!" Captain Hall yelled as he stepped out of the shadows. "Police! You're under arrest!"

The man reached for something in his pocket. As Seers lunged for his pistol, another officer stepped in front of him, brandishing a shotgun. The officer fired a single shot at the assailant.

Seers cringed. But it didn't sound like a shotgun blast. Could the weapon have misfired? He was still pulling his gun from the holster. Bill Hall grabbed it as Seers looked back on their attacker.

"I don't think that'll be necessary, Detective," Hall said.

Seers watched Prince tug on the man's pant leg.

"He could be faking it, playing possum," Seers warned.

"Don't bet on it," the SWAT officer said as he placed the shotgun over one shoulder. "These things hurt like a son of a bitch." He reached down and picked up a small beanbag.

"Nonlethal round," he explained. "But it will make you wish you were dead. Damn things explode the air out of your lungs and knock you off your feet. I think I'd rather be shot for real than hit with this."

Hall pulled up the assailant's shirt to reveal a huge bruise on his chest. The other officer checked the man's breathing and pulse. He stirred.

"Easy now, big fellow," the officer said. "What say we put some bracelets on you before you get all upset with me?" He rolled the man onto his stomach and placed him in handcuffs. As the first officer read him his rights, Hall looked to Kemer.

"Nobody else up there?" he asked.

"He wouldn't have come down if there were," Kemer explained.

"Good enough." He turned to Seers. "Detective, this mess is all yours. Congratulations. I think you just cracked your burglary ring." He shook Seers's hand.

Ryan followed the second officer up the stairs to retrieve his robot. Seers walked into the other room, where the first burglar was still splayed out on the floor.

"What did you find on them?" he asked Officer Damato.

"Police scanner. Retail-quality night-vision goggles—complete crap. Probably why they weren't using them. Small lock-pick set. Walkie-talkies. Gloves. Nylon bags to carry things in. Then there was this."

He gave Seers a handheld television receiver. The back had been removed and additional electronics were soldered into place. Seers stared at the screen. He walked up the stairs and down the hall. He entered the nursery and found the camera on a high shelf on the wall next to the closet. He took three steps forward and saw himself step into the picture on the screen in his hands.

They *were* using the baby monitors.

THE MAXIMA's lone occupant walked up the sidewalk outside Amy's house and stopped behind her trash cans, where the utility boxes were located. A quick snip of the wire severed the phone line.

It was quite late, and both of the house's occupants should be in deep REM sleep—the least likely time to be awakened by a stray sound. Picking the lock on the back door was made simpler with the electronic picker, and it opened silently. He closed the door and relocked it in the event he was not as silent as he hoped. If she looked down the stairs she would find everything as before—but would not find him.

Straddling the staircase, he made his way up the stairs slowly. Creaking wood was impossible to guesstimate, and it would be foolish to be this close to success only to be discovered. Bit by bit, step by step, ascending the staircase to the bedroom hallway was a thirty-minute endeavor. That's why he'd never been caught. He was patient.

Patience was a rarity these days. Young people were always in a hurry to prove themselves, show how smart they were, how tech-savvy they were. He eschewed technology in favor of old-fashioned preparation and experience. It hadn't failed him before; he had no reason to believe it would now.

At the top of the landing he surveyed the surroundings. A thirty-dollar FOIA request at the building inspector's office had gotten him the home's floor plans. Who needed the risk of tripping over shrubs to peek through windows when the U.S. government was kind enough to require builders to place home plans on file? Then they required the inspector's office to make those plans available to anyone who asked. The Freedom of Information Act, or FOIA, was one of the best operational planning tools he could have hoped for.

It was ten paces down the hallway to the little girl's room. He patted himself down one last time. Nothing jingled, nothing rattled. He slid a foot across the first section of carpet and slowly transferred his weight. Then he did it again. No footsteps to be heard.

It was the simplest of methods, and yet one of the most effective. Perhaps that's why it worked. Simplicity. It was hard to screw up unless you moved too fast. Slowing things down interrupts the perception of patterns. That was how people woke up to find intruders in their homes. *Patterns of life*, some people called them. Footsteps in a hallway or the creaking of a staircase. Patterns were how people recognized the most common and routine parts of their lives. Patterns were what he was determined not to have.

Amy's cell phone captured the intruder moving across the floor. The phone's screen displayed "line busy," then reset and dialed again as the intruder slowly shuffled into the bathroom. He removed a bottle of pills from the medicine cabinet and placed it in his pocket. He glanced up and down the hallway quietly as he padded his way down toward Celia's room. Over and over, the cell phone dialed, and each time it concluded with "line busy."

He approached Celia's door and opened it slowly, keeping one eye on Amy's room. He allowed his eyes to adjust to the darkness. Reaching into his pocket, he removed a small vial of chloroform and dabbed it into a handkerchief. Holding it near her nose, he allowed her to draw a few breaths before moving it closer, closer, until it finally rested against her nose. Three full inhales of the magical elixir and she was out.

He listened again for any movement before he picked her up and placed her gently in the black duffel bag, the handkerchief still under her nose. He unplugged her baby camera from the wall outlet and placed it between her feet.

Once again Amy's cell phone noted the movement of Celia's bedroom door and dialed the house. The intruder, focused intently on Amy's door, didn't notice the cell phone's blinking message screen.

He retraced his slow journey down the stairs and paused to give Celia one last whiff of chloroform before unlocking the back door. He slipped outside with her in the nearly pitch black darkness. He pulled the door shut but did not lock it.

Walking down a back alley, he cradled Celia in the bag and quickly covered several blocks. At this time of night, there was no traffic, and the complete darkness made any stray vehicle easily detectable before its driver could see a man dressed in black carrying a sleeping child in a duffel bag.

Through a back door he'd left nearly two hours earlier, he entered an empty house and placed the little girl on the floor. Slinging the black duffel bag down, he pulled out the baby camera and placed it, pointed down at her, on a nearby counter. He had already cordoned off an area giving the toddler a little room to move around in. She'd be within the camera's field of vision for the duration.

However long that might be.

Chapter Seventeen

SEERS WALKED downstairs and gave the portable receiver back to Officer Damato. Two SWAT officers emptied the pockets of the second burglar, who'd come to and was making threats of legal action.

"I'm going to have all you guys on charges!" he shouted. "Who the hell shoots an unarmed man who's not threatening anyone?"

"You don't know how lucky you were, pal," Damato told him. "You sure you're not packing a weapon? Any knives or needles I need to know about? Tell me now, because if I find one the hard way it's assault on a police officer. You'll really enjoy some quality time inside at that point."

Seers picked up the man's wallet. Anthony Stephens.

"That seems familiar," Seers said to Damato.

"His brother's in the other room," Damato replied. "Don't you love a good family operation? *John* Stephens. Maybe they can be roomies in the joint."

John and Anthony Stephens. Seemed really familiar. Like he'd seen their names somewhere. In the paper, maybe? He couldn't quite place them. Their faces meant nothing to him, just the names. It had been a long day. Maybe he was mistaken.

"Anything on them?" Seers asked.

"Nothing worth discussing," Damato replied.

Seers poked through the two piles. Car and house keys. Wallets. A handkerchief and comb in John's pockets. A lighter in Anthony's. Then he noticed the address on John's driver's license. Brookfield Avenue.

Seers blinked several times. Brookfield Avenue was familiar, too. Whom did he know on Brookfield Avenue?

214

Damato prepared Anthony for transport to the station and was about to hustle him from the house. Seers stood in front of him. The younger man's defiance, even after getting caught, suggested he wasn't too bright. Maybe he could use some of Heath's techniques again.

"So what the hell did you guys do with all that stuff you took?" Seers asked.

"We didn't take nothing!" Anthony said. He kicked at Seers.

Damato yanked back on Anthony's restraints. As he fell back on his heels, several necklaces swung out from his shirt.

"Suppose those might belong to someone else?" Damato asked. He opened Anthony's shirt and found two gold chains. One held a gold coin, some sort of Spanish currency—the kind seen on television news stories when marine salvagers find a long-lost sunken treasure ship. The second held a gold cross. The third necklace wasn't gold. It was the metal chain used by soldiers to hold their dog tags. Dangling from the chain was a black Navy Cross.

"Hold it!" Seers snapped. He bridged the gap between them in seconds and reached into Anthony's shirt. Despite the young man's convulsive moves to stop him, Seers grabbed the Navy Cross. He flipped it over. CAPTAIN FRANK STRATTON: 1983.

That was it. Brookfield Avenue. The street Chris and Sally Ellis lived on. Seers gripped the medal and yanked. His face flushed red and the tip of his nose touched Anthony's nose.

"Uncuff him," Seers said quietly.

"What?" Damato asked.

"You heard me."

Anthony blinked. He didn't understand what was happening.

"Hang it around your neck, huh? That how it works?" Seers hissed. "How about if I hang you around *my* neck? How would that be, tough guy?"

"Detective, I really should take these guys downtown," Damato said.

"Want to screw around with an old marine? How about me? I'm old. Not as old as he is, but try that shit with me, huh?" Seers's chest pushed Anthony backward, and Damato was forced to catch him.

"Get this shithead off me," Anthony said to Damato.

"Come on," Seers implored. "You can wipe up the floor with me. Tell you what. I'll take the cuffs off and these guys will all leave. Just you and me. You get past me and you're both free to go. How's that sound?"

Anthony's eyebrows flew up. Seers looked like a crazed animal as he seethed with rage. He sweated profusely as his chest heaved with deep breaths. He grabbed Anthony's shirt with both hands, the medal still in his grip. Damato broke in between them, but Seers pushed him aside with an elbow.

"Knock it off, Detective! Let him go. Mike! Let him go!"

The two other officers helped pull Seers off Stephens. The young man's vitriolic tirade began anew, and he threatened a lawsuit against all of them. Damato hustled him outside and left Seers alone in the middle of the room with the medal in his hand.

"I APOLOGIZE for the late hour," Seers said quietly. "Are you sure it's all right for me to come in?"

Chris Ellis stood in the doorway and gestured for Seers to enter. Sally was walking down the stairs tying a robe around her nightgown.

"I'm sorry," Seers stammered. "It's too late for me to just be dropping by on a moment's notice. I should have waited until tomorrow."

He held a large brown bag nervously behind his back and tapped the top with one finger. Chris hadn't overlooked the word *Evidence* stenciled down the side. Seers was uncertain, a feeling not common to him. Was he overdoing it by coming by at such a late hour? He still had a mountain of reporting to write up and had simply bolted from the scene when Damato found Anthony Stephens's car a couple of blocks away.

"Not at all," Sally said. "You were very excited on the phone. It's not a problem. Did you have some success?"

Seers looked out across the back patio to Frank Stratton's apartment. "Is he still awake?" he asked.

Sally looked at the television as Chris clicked the remote control. Frank Stratton was sitting in his recliner, feet up, watching television. "He's right where he always is. Dad's a night owl."

"Do you mind?" Seers asked.

The three walked across the patio, and Sally conducted her usual ceremony of knocking on his door before cracking it open and calling inside. She entered first, with Chris and Seers staying outside.

Seers knew she wanted to make sure her father was prepared for visitors in a manner befitting a Marine Corps officer—keeping his honor and dignity intact. She reappeared in the doorway and motioned them inside. Seers walked up to Stratton and dropped to one knee next to the man's chair.

"Sir, I have a few items that I think belong to you," Seers said softly. He opened the evidence bag and withdrew the Mameluke sword. He reached inside his jacket pocket and removed a handkerchief. He reverently unfolded it to reveal Stratton's Navy Cross. He looked back at Sally, who was already dabbing her eyes with a tissue. "No bullshit speeches, no political crap about a grateful nation. Just a retired gunny at your service, sir."

Sally whispered to Chris and disappeared into the colonel's bedroom for a moment before returning. She pretended to be engrossed in the Washington Nationals game her father had been watching. Seers's voice dropped to barely above a whisper.

"I lost friends that day, sir. You protected the guys who were digging them out. That means a lot," he paused, wiping away a tear. "I'm calling every one of their families to tell them what you did."

The old colonel's face was flushed. His lips were moving but out of sync as he labored to push the words out of his mouth, though the result was incoherent. A single tear escaping his right eye told Seers that Parkinson's hadn't yet won. Marines *always* find a way.

Seers stood up before his emotions got the better of him. But he didn't know how to leave. Saluting seemed trite. He grasped the retired officer by the hand and looked him right in the eye. "Thank you, sir," he squeaked.

Seers turned and walked out, not at all embarrassed by his red eyes and runny nose. Chris nodded respectfully, not wanting to interfere with their private moment. Sally was nowhere to be seen. Seers was across the patio to the driveway before he heard her voice.

"Detective?"

When he turned around, she was right behind him. Her eyes were red and puffy, too, and there was a tissue still in one hand. She clutched something else with the other.

"Dad was the unit's commanding officer when he retired. I think he'd like you to have this."

She handed him a large coin. Seers turned it over in his hands.

It was Stratton's Commander's Coin. The Marine Corps logo was emblazoned on one side, the unit's crest on the other. The words COLONEL FRANK STRATTON were engraved on the bottom. Seers swallowed back the lump in his throat.

Commander's Coins were a highly coveted token of a leader's recognition for the contribution of an individual or unit. They were about the size of a half-dollar. Dirt cheap to produce, but unquestionably one of the most useful management tools the military had ever conceived.

Commanders had wide latitude in presenting a coin to anyone, military or civilian, whom they felt deserved recognition for a job performed above and beyond the call of duty. It enhanced a unit's esprit de corps and was quite a point of pride. You were *somebody* when you got a Commander's Coin.

Seers held the brass token as carefully as he would a newborn child. He stammered for something to say, but the words simply weren't there.

"I know it doesn't mean as much coming from me," Sally said.

"Actually, it does. Maybe even more. Thank you," he said. Without a second thought, he hugged this woman he barely knew.

A SCREAM shattered Amy's slumber. She flailed around wildly and tried to make sense of what was happening. She fell out of the bed completely, banged into the dresser, and clawed at the duvet to get on her feet. The Callaway iron was already in her hands.

In the hallway, Celia's cries were so loud that Amy covered her ears while still gripping the club. She fought to clear the fog of waking up to her daughter's nightmarishly distorted screaming.

"Celia!" she called.

Amy opened her daughter's bedroom door. She squinted, uncertain if Celia might be hiding under the covers, or under the bed itself. Checking both, she realized her daughter was gone.

The pale walls of the hallway appeared distorted as Amy struggled to regain her faculties. She saw her cell phone's lighted screen and yanked it off the table.

"Busy signal?" she whispered as she realized Celia's cries were coming from downstairs. The *bottom* of the stairs. She dropped the cell phone and raced down two at a time. "Baby! Did you fall?" she yelled.

She flipped on the light at the bottom of the staircase, but still no Celia. She turned to the kitchen. "Celia! Where are you?" Amy cried as she walked into the kitchen.

Amy's heart sank. Her daughter's tortured face filled the screen of the baby monitor she'd turned off hours earlier. The volume was cranked up to the maximum.

"Celia!" Amy screamed.

A gloved hand grabbed her from behind and slung her across the kitchen.

"She's fine," a voice said. "But I think it's time you and I had a conversation of our own."

Amy looked up at the intruder from the floor. "Who are you? What are you doing in my house?" she demanded.

He bridged the distance between them and hauled Amy to her feet. "I'll ask the questions," he said and shoved her into the refrigerator.

Amy managed to run out of the kitchen and ran from room to room as Celia's cries poured from the monitor. "Celia! Where are you?"

The intruder followed her, laughing. "You don't think I left anything to chance, do you?"

Amy grabbed a phone. She tapped the return several times when there was no dial tone. Now she understood the cell phone's "busy signal" reference. The phone line had been cut.

The cell phone! When she ran past him toward the stairs, he slapped her hard across the face and knocked her to the ground.

"You don't really think I left anything to chance, do you? I hate to repeat myself. Isn't that a point of pride among interpreters? Getting it right the first time?"

She blinked at him. The voice. The accent. "I know you," she said slowly.

"Do you now?" he asked.

"I know you! You're *Lenny*. That sick son of a bitch bought porn from you!" she spat.

"Quite an ear you have. It is indeed me. Lovely to meet you in person at last," he teased.

"I knew that wasn't real," she growled.

"Really?" he patronized. "And how's that, my dear?"

"Deaf guys don't order porn of a little girl screaming!"

He was put off, not expecting the accusation. "Hey, you know, I never considered that! You're quite bright for someone so new to her career."

"What do you want?"

"I want to know what you told the police."

Celia's distorted cries filled the air. Amy felt like she was breathing through thick pudding, every labored breath requiring another pound of energy as her mind raced for a solution.

"Nothing! I told them nothing!" she said finally.

He grabbed her hair and wrestled her to the floor. He raised a hand to strike her when Celia inexplicably stopped crying. They both froze.

Slowly, moving in unison, they peered over the counter facing the baby monitor. Celia filled the screen. But she was no longer crying. *She was signing.*

"Call the police," Lenny muttered.

"Mommy needs help," Amy followed.

"She knows her address?" Lenny said.

"That's my girl," Amy whispered proudly.

Lenny dropped her and stormed out the back door.

Amy tripped across the kitchen threshold and fell to the floor. She turned back to momentarily stare at the threshold. A roll of thunder crashed overhead. She opened the cabinet above the refrigerator to take out Jeff's pistol and chased after Lenny into the night air.

Still clad in her nightclothes, Amy pursued him down the alleyway several blocks to an empty house. Lenny shoved the back door open, but Celia and the baby camera were gone. Amy walked in with the pistol leveled at him.

"Where is my daughter?" she asked. Her voice had deepened with adrenaline-fueled fury.

"I don't think that's going to help," Lenny said calmly.

She was still searching for the right thing to say when a brown Labrador retriever stalked in the open door behind her. Lenny exploited her momentary distraction and escaped through the house and out the front door. Amy was frozen. Kensington's death was too raw, too recent, for her to allow this animal near her or her daughter.

"Celia! Are you here, baby?" Amy called out.

She aimed the wildly shaking gun at the dog. The animal skulked off, head down, back out of the house. Amy raced around the house.

"Celia!" she yelled. "Celia! Where are you?"

There was no sign of her.

Searching the entire house room by room, Amy realized her daughter was gone and that the man who had taken her had disappeared, too. The stress of the past year—Jeff's death, a new career, Kensington's death, Sammy Clark—all piled on top of her. She dropped slowly to the floor. How could she have let her daughter down? How could she have let someone just walk in and take her, then taunt the fact that he could do so with impunity? What kind of mother was she?

The bedroom door slowly creaked open. Had Lenny returned? Amy was wild-eyed, pointing the gun, waiting for a clear shot. She didn't want to kill him. Just wound him. Leave him able to talk so she could find out where Celia was. The door opened slowly, allowing a stab of light to cut into the room. But it wasn't Lenny. It wasn't Celia.

The Labrador peeked in cautiously and looked around. Amy dropped the shaking gun down at him again. The dog withdrew and returned a moment later with Celia's blanket in its mouth. He walked over tentatively and dropped it at Amy's feet. She scooped it up and pressed it to her face. For one long inhale, she had a fleeting link to her daughter. The dog walked back to the door and turned to her.

"OK, Lassie! It's your show," she said.

With the blanket in one hand and the gun in the other, Amy followed the Labrador out the back door and down the alleyway, crossing several side streets to a large Victorian home. As the dog leaped onto the back porch, Amy was close on its heels.

It took over an hour to clean up the mess and return the Darling family to their home. Seers walked them through everywhere the police had been, making sure nothing was broken or missing. He knew some people loaned out their homes for police purposes only so they could sue afterward, saying the cops had broken things, stolen things, or just generally made the house suddenly unlivable. They always required a signed legal release beforehand, but that never seemed to stop some people from at least trying to sue.

When the Darlings were happy, Seers cleared everyone out so they could put their two children to bed. He wrote a five-page report sitting in his car and jotted a few notes for follow-up when he interrogated his suspects the next day.

He savored having the eight-hundred-pound gorilla off his back. There'd be another one tomorrow, of course. There always was in law enforcement. There's no shortage of dirtbag criminals in the world. But today, the good guys had come out on top.

He'd awakened the chief and the commissioner, and neither one had complained. Both were delighted he'd finally cracked the burglary case that had gotten them so much negative media attention. They promised a letter of commendation for his personnel file. That would go a long way at his next promotion board.

Seers put away his report and flipped the Commander's Coin through his fingers. When he'd been in uniform twenty years earlier, no one could have pried that sucker from his fist with the Jaws of Life. Today, though, he was a different person. He appreciated Sally's gesture, especially since he'd been only seconds away from blubbering like a baby. But he also knew the coin didn't really belong to him. And he couldn't live with that.

Seers walked over and yanked open the big back door of the SWAT team's surveillance van. "What are you still doing here?" he asked, his voice loud and booming for such a late hour.

"That son of a bitch broke my robot," Ryan replied angrily. "It's not much good to us if we can't see." Ryan had the device disassembled on the truck's workbench, and was rewiring the camera to the top of the elevating spine. Seers looked over his shoulder.

"I don't think he stepped on it on purpose. Prince had the guy cornered. Must have scared the piss out of him," Seers said.

"I'm talking about Prince," Ryan said. "Damn dog broke my robot. Animals and electronics don't mix, man." He soldered a wire back into place.

Seers smiled. Ryan was the ultimate kid with a new toy. "I'm sure you'll get it squared away," he said. "Listen, I need to talk to you about something."

"Shoot," Ryan replied, still bent over the bench.

"Over here, please." Seers's tone was firm but friendly. He didn't want Ryan to get the idea that something was wrong.

"Sorry," Ryan said as he turned around.

Seers was sitting in the other technician's chair, right next to him. Ryan jumped, not expecting Seers that close.

"This . . . is for you," Seers said. He dropped the coin into Ryan's hand. "Do you know what a Commander's Coin is?"

"Sure. Where did this come from?" Ryan asked.

"It came from a retired marine colonel. I couldn't have solved this case without your help. I wouldn't have recognized all the stuff you saw. The electronics. What they could do. That would have all slipped by me. You earned this. I'll be telling Captain Hall and the commissioner what you did tomorrow." He shook the young man's hand strongly, a real handshake.

"But wait. He gave it to you. What do you get out of it?" Ryan asked.

"Something far more priceless," Seers said as he stood.

This was one of the best days of his entire life. This is what marines do. Protect people. He was delighted to ensure that the families knew what Frank Stratton had done. But he couldn't have done it without Ryan's help. "I'm heading out. You going to be long?"

"No. I'm about done. I'll spend most of tomorrow squaring the rest of this away."

"OK. I may want a few of your surveillance tapes when I interview those guys tomorrow," Seers said.

"No problem. I'll have it all ready."

"See you then," Seers said. He slapped Ryan on the back as he walked out. He stopped short when he heard a woman cry out. "What was that?" he asked.

Ryan didn't look up. "We're still picking up baby-cam feeds. They've been arguing for about an hour. He sounds like a real dick. I didn't place the voice at first, but I knew I recognized it."

Seers listened. He didn't recognize the voice immediately, either, but he did recognize the language. He hadn't heard profanity that creative since he'd left the corps.

"Do I know him?" Seers asked.

Ryan reached over and turned up the volume. "From what I can tell, it's Chris Billings," he replied.

"The DNC chairman? Are you sure?" Seers asked.

"I can't swear to it, but it looked like him earlier, and sure as shit sounds like him now."

The language coming out of the speaker was rough. Seers shook his head. "I don't have time for this," he said finally.

"We taped all of the feeds tonight," Ryan said. "What do you want to do with it?"

"Lose it. We were after burglars, not political assholes," Seers replied. "Let's not give anyone fodder for a conspiracy theory or a special prosecutor."

Ryan stopped the tape. As Seers turned to climb out of the van, another monitor caught his eye. He moved closer to the tiny screen. It was a toddler using American Sign Language. She looked familiar.

"Celia? Is that you?" he asked aloud. He stared at the screen, but the reception was fuzzy and full of noise. The image flickered in and out with white static. "Amy, I told you to turn the damn thing off."

As he stepped outside the vehicle, the police dispatcher paged him over the radio.

"Seers—go ahead," he replied.

"Detective Seers, there's an emergency call for you," the dispatcher said. He walked a few steps away from the surveillance vehicle for privacy.

"Emergency?" Seers repeated. "What kind of emergency?"

"I'm not sure. Just a second." The line crackled and beeped. "Go ahead, caller."

"Detective Seers? It's Carol Burdick from All Hands VRS."

"Ms. Burdick? What's the problem?" Seers asked.

"We have a call you should be aware of," Carol said.

"I thought you couldn't share information about your callers to anyone."

"That's true—but the call is to the police."

"So why are you calling me?" Seers asked.

"She asked for you by name. It's Amy Kellen's daughter, Celia. She says her mommy is in danger!"

Seers ran back to the surveillance van and jumped in. He could see the child still signing furiously on the monitor. "Is she wearing princess pajamas?" he asked.

"Yes," Carol replied. "How did you know that?"

Seers leaned out of the van and waved furiously at Bill Hall, who was finishing up with the last of the remaining SWAT officers. "Captain Hall!" he yelled. "Get everyone geared back up! We've got more to do tonight!"

Ryan appeared behind him with the soldering iron still in his hand. "What's going on?" he asked.

Seers keyed his radio. "Dispatch! I'm taking the SWAT team to Amy Kellen's house!"

Chapter Eighteen

As the SWAT team took up positions, Seers stood next to Ryan's truck listening to the police radio.

"I'm around back—the door is wide open and a light is on inside. No signs of anyone around," Sergeant Williams reported.

"Stand fast. We're coming to you," Seers said into the microphone. He motioned for two officers to follow him to the back of Amy's house. They linked up with Williams near a holly bush.

"Signs of life?" Seers asked.

"No, nothing," Williams replied.

"Let's take this nice and slow. There's a little girl in there, so mind what you shoot at," Seers cautioned.

They slowly entered the house. Seers tripped again on the kitchen threshold. It took two very loud stomps before he caught his balance. He swore as he grabbed the counter to steady himself. The SWAT officers glared at him. So much for a quiet entry.

Signs of a struggle were everywhere. Items knocked over. Spilled kitchen supplies. A chair on its side. A baby monitor on the countertop popped and hissed. They slowly approached it like itinerant moths to a hearty flame, searching for signs of a trap.

Celia was still signing on the monitor. Seers turned the volume down to a normal level. More SWAT personnel slipped past them and checked every room, cubbyhole, and potential hiding place. The attic. Under the stairs. Amy's car in the garage. There was no sign of her and no sign of the little girl signing on the monitor in the kitchen. Seers pulled out his radio.

"Dispatch! We've cleared Amy Kellen's home. There's nobody here."

The dispatcher replied immediately. "The watch commander is here. Just a moment."

"Seers!" he barked. "What happened to the baby who signed for help?"

"She's still signing! We see her on the monitor, but she's not anywhere in the house."

"So where the hell is she? How did she call in?" he demanded.

"Detective Seers?" Carol Burdick called hesitantly. "I'm sorry to interrupt, but Celia's not calling from Amy's house."

"Where is she?" Seers demanded.

"We can't trace the call," Carol explained. "The FCC won't allow us the technology to do it. We have no way of knowing where she is."

"You've got to be kidding me," Seers said.

"I recognize that room," Kathy Maynard said quietly in the background.

"Where? Where is it?" Seers asked.

"She can't be there," Kathy said. "She *can't* be."

"Where, damn it? Where?" Seers yelled.

"I think it's Harold Kensington's house!" Kathy said.

AFTER CALLING the SWAT team out and packing them up again, Seers had one hand on the steering wheel and one hand on his radio as they raced the four blocks to Harold Kensington's home.

"Ms. Burdick, are you still there?" he called on the radio.

"Yes," she replied.

"I want you to ask Celia where her mommy is."

"I'm sorry, Detective. I can't do that," Carol replied.

"Why the hell not?" he shouted. "I thought that's what you people did for a living!"

"That's not what I mean. That is what we do. But Celia can't see me."

"What are you talking about?"

"The monitor on her end of the call isn't on," she said.

"Meaning what?"

"She's signing blindly. She can only send a message out. She can't receive one."

AMY FOLLOWED the Labrador to an opulently decorated office. Celia was boxed into a corner by a credenza and an office chair. Amy yanked the chair away and swept her daughter up into her arms. "Oh, baby! Mommy missed you so much! Are you OK?" Amy cried.

Lenny suddenly burst in behind her and snatched Celia away. He promptly dropped her to the floor. "Well, well. Aren't we just full of surprises?" he asked.

"Leave us alone!" Amy screamed.

The Labrador clamped down on Celia's pajama shirt and half dragged the little girl from the room.

Amy drew the pistol from her pocket but hesitated, afraid of hitting her daughter. Lenny wrenched the gun away. She glanced at the baby monitor camera sitting on the credenza, and Lenny promptly smashed it against the wall. "Don't ever play poker, lady. You can't bluff," he taunted.

"Why are you doing this to us?" Amy cried.

His demeanor and face softened. "You really didn't tell them anything, did you? Everything we put out there and you didn't say anything! Sammy was right after all. He said you were the perfect one."

"Perfect what?" Amy pleaded.

"If only that idiot judge hadn't released the dog before it could be put down."

"Put down? You mean killed!" Amy said.

"Yes! Killed! Don't you know the first rule of assassination is kill the assassins?" he asked.

Amy repeated the word like it was poison. "*Assassins?*"

"How does it feel to realize you've just altered the course of history?" he asked.

Amy paused. "The election?"

"If you kill a president you go down in history, but you still go down. Kill the man behind the candidate *before* he's elected and you *change* history," he said.

"What does this have to do with me?" Amy asked.

"Billings wanted a surefire means of keeping Thompson from getting the nomination. Getting rid of Kensington was the easiest, least risky way to achieve that," Lenny replied.

"His death wasn't an accident?" Amy asked.

Lenny's head slowly shook back and forth. "Without Kensington, Thompson doesn't stand a chance," he said.

"Oh my God! You killed him?" she asked.

"Oh no, my dear. *You* killed him!" he replied, in a cold, dark voice.

Amy was horrified. "Me?"

"He insisted on controlling the exact time and place—ensuring there were no witnesses and no help. But he couldn't physically be there. He needed a solid alibi."

"How? What?" Amy babbled.

"Finding a similar-looking dog? That was easy. Training him to attack based on an innocuous phrase like 'I don't understand'? Simple."

"*I* killed him?" Amy repeated in disbelief.

"We couldn't just drop him off and wait for it to happen. There might be a room full of people, someone might save him. The authorities would know the dogs had been switched. No, he had to die alone. How can you watch a man die without actually *witnessing* it?" he asked.

"Video relay," Amy whispered.

"A surrogate, that's right! He's not a witness because he didn't see anything. He contacted the authorities after the fact, but what happened on the call is protected by our good friends at the FCC!" Lenny said.

"All those calls. The porn. The thefts. It was all a setup?" she asked.

"We've been on you for weeks. Hal's favorite interpreter. You knew his preferences, his mannerisms, and his quirks. When you told him you were going to work for All Hands, we knew he'd want to use you for that as well."

"He trusted me," Amy stammered.

"Yes, he did. A little bit too much, I think."

"He was always very careful about what he said publicly. But on the phone, in his own house . . ." she couldn't finish the sentence.

"He let his guard down," Lenny said.

"Yes."

"So did you. We had a remote psychological profile done on you. Quite sad. I know about your husband. I know you're in therapy."

"So are a lot of people," Amy replied.

"I know about Glenn Whitaker and his campaign manager. I was there that night. You could have told his wife, but you didn't," Lenny said.

"You had me hired for Whitaker's rally? Why?"

"How did it feel?"

"How did what feel?" she asked.

"You walked in on him screwing her in the shower while his wife was out campaigning. How'd it feel to watch him exploit her like that when you've got no one?"

"None of your business," she struggled to get to her feet, but he pushed her back down with the barrel of the gun.

"See! Keeping your mouth shut! That's what we needed! It's one thing for the FCC regulations to be so strict. It's quite another to find an interpreter with unquestionable integrity. One totally committed to following the rules without question. But we had to be sure that no matter how repulsive something was, you wouldn't rat. So we threw drugs at you, porn, whatever it took, and you passed all the tests with flying colors. You, my dear, were the perfect wingman for a sniper team, especially when the other member, that damned dog, can't talk. If they'd put him down as planned, we'd all be having a much better day."

"I think I'm going to be sick," Amy said.

"Now the problem is, what to do with you," Lenny said.

"Me?"

"The stress was too much for you. Kensington's death—not being able to say anything. Anybody could crack. You just couldn't take it," Lenny said.

"What are you talking about?"

"Staging a suicide is different from staging an assassination."

"Suicide?" Amy squeaked.

"Can't have too many similar deaths at once. Too noticeable. That damn Brent kid wouldn't go along with the plan—not much to be done about that now. The dog? Well, accidents happen. Yours is going to have to be a suicide. No way around it."

Amy was sobbing now. "Please. Just let me go. I can't say anything to anyone."

"I'd planned to wait a few weeks, let things calm down—make it clean and quiet."

He reached into his pocket and pulled out the prescription tranquilizers from Amy's bathroom medicine cabinet. "You felt guilty about not stopping it, couldn't live with it. You had to die here where he did."

Amy pushed the pill bottle away. "Everything I heard is protected," she cried. "I can't tell anyone. Please just let me go."

"Can't take the chance. You're the last assassin!"

A clap of thunder shook the house. Lenny couldn't open the childproof cap with one hand and was forced to set the gun down. Amy seized it and raced down a hallway, slinging furniture behind her to slow him down. She rounded a corner—and slammed straight into Dan Banducheck, who was coming up from the basement with an arm full of boxes.

"Mr. Banducheck! What are you doing here?" she said in surprise.

Banducheck was also startled. "I'm boxing up campaign files. Why are you here, Amy?" he asked.

"We've got to get out of here! Someone kidnapped my daughter and brought her here!" Amy yelled.

"Who kidnapped your daughter? What are you talking about?" Amy tugged on his arm. "I don't have time to explain! We've got to get out of here! Please help me!"

"Calm down! Calm down!" Banducheck exhorted, ducking away from the gun she was waving around. "Let me have that." He carefully took the gun from her. "Start slowly and talk to me. What are you doing here?" he asked again.

"My daughter is here somewhere!" Amy said. "Please help me! I need to call the police!"

"Amy, you're not making any sense! Please just sit down. I'm sure there's an explanation for all this."

Lenny appeared behind her. Banducheck stepped in front of her, placing himself between Amy and Lenny. "What are you doing in here?" he demanded.

Lenny stared at Banducheck but didn't speak.

"I'm talking to you!" Banducheck bellowed.

"I heard you!" Lenny replied and started toward him. "I'm not the deaf one. Remember?"

Banducheck took a step forward with the gun still pointed at Lenny's stomach.

"Would you mind keeping her under control, or do I need to do that as well?" Banducheck asked. He flipped the pistol around by the trigger guard and handed it to Lenny.

"Just finish and I'll handle this," Lenny said.

"Like you've handled everything else?" Banducheck replied. "That's a real comfort."

Amy blinked in disbelief. Lenny was once again pointing the gun at her. He gestured for her to stand. She looked desperately at Banducheck. "You're with *him*?" she asked incredulously.

"Why the hell did you bring her here? I told you to come get me when you're finished," Banducheck said, ignoring Amy.

"I didn't bring her here. I followed her and some damn dog."

"Get your dog and your other loose ends and get lost. I'm still looking."

"I don't believe this," Amy said. "He was your friend."

"He was my boss, and a political dinosaur at that, nothing more," Banducheck retorted.

"He trusted you," Amy replied.

"And I trusted him to do what I needed done. I guess we were both disappointed."

"Just remember who took care of things," Lenny said menacingly.

"Don't worry. It will all get worked out. Just don't screw this up," Banducheck assured him. Looking at Amy, he continued, "Billings wants to be Whitaker's vice president. Been waiting twenty years for Kensington to die so he could run for office instead of just being the party manager. Guess he thought Whitaker was his last best chance. Nobody expected Thompson to con Harold out of retirement for one more campaign," Banducheck said.

"Vice President Billings will be a shoo-in for the nomination when Whitaker leaves office," Lenny said.

"But I still haven't found any pictures," Banducheck said.

"It's got to be Billings with someone's wife, or a Chappaquiddick thing, or . . ."

"I don't know what it is," Banducheck interrupted. "All I know is it was enough to keep him from running for any elected office since he was a state assemblyman back in Jersey."

"That was a long time ago. People forget," Lenny said.

"Yeah, well, it was serious enough to keep him on the sidelines for twenty years. Chris said every time the party suggested him for a public office, Hal would just glare at him. It was like this secret sign between the two of them. Chris got the message clear as day—if you run, those private pictures become public. Hal played hardball, no doubt about it. Maybe there's not a statute of limitations on whatever it is. Maybe a felony-type thing. Anyway, I still haven't found it," Banducheck said.

"Billings must have learned a thing or two from him. He had me shoot stills and video of Whitaker with his hot blonde campaign manager," Lenny said.

Banducheck's eyebrows flew up. "Jackie? Son of a bitch! He was passing my information to her?" Banducheck asked.

"Oh, you didn't know that, huh? I guess the boss is careful about who he shares the important plans with," Lenny taunted.

"You're hilarious. He'll dangle Jackie over Whitaker's head like Kensington was dangling something over his. She was spying, sharing her pillow talk, so now he owns both of them," Banducheck said.

"A honeypot operation," Amy whispered.

Both men were taken aback and momentarily fell silent. Lenny reacted first.

"Ha! Even she knew about it! He doesn't tell you anything, does he?" Lenny laughed.

"You were doing the same thing, reporting on Kensington! You were both whores! Don't think you're any better just because you've got a law degree."

"Eat shit," Banducheck replied.

"You've got to be the dumbest lawyer on earth," Lenny continued. "He sent you to the courthouse to ensure your client was executed, and they released him instead!" Lenny laughed.

"Shut up, you asshole," Banducheck said.

"No wonder you don't practice law. So, did you let him get into your 'briefs'? Did you dress up in lacy underwear for the old man?" Lenny asked, prancing slightly as he mocked Banducheck.

"That stupid bitch won't live to see the convention once Whitaker names him VP. Just one more loose string to be tied off."

A crackle of lightning dimmed the lights. Amy used the momentary distraction to run back down the hallway toward the office. Lenny was quick on her heels, with Banducheck a step behind him. She managed to get the office door open, but at the cost of her two-second lead. Lenny grabbed her just as Banducheck slammed into both of them. All three wrestled for control, grunting and pulling in multiple directions—until a shot rang out.

Amy jumped, though Lenny was still gripping her arm tightly. Banducheck had hold of Lenny's arm. Amy had one hand on each.

For a second, all three stared at each other in the silence that enveloped the room.

Banducheck gradually sank to his knees. A pulsing flow of dark red blood poured down his pressed white shirt.

"You stupid bastard," Banducheck said.

Amy lowered him the rest of the way to the floor and knelt beside him. "Oh my God! He needs an ambulance!" she cried.

Lenny stumbled back to the wall, gun in hand, in shock. The whole plan was dying on the floor in front of him.

"I don't believe this! You miserable shit! I can't take you to a hospital! You've screwed us both!" Lenny cried.

"Billings will have your ass. You won't be safe anywhere," Banducheck gurgled. His panicked eyes darted around the room. He breathed heavily, with a strange whistle escaping his lips. He looked at Amy. His mouth moved but didn't form anything intelligible. His eyes rolled back.

Banducheck was dead.

Lenny barely held onto the gun—he was a man on the edge of losing control. His eyes scurried from side to side as his mind raced to find a way out of this mess.

"What do I do now?" he shouted at Banducheck's lifeless body. "What do I do now?"

Chapter Nineteen

"PLEASE. JUST let us go! Everything is still protected," Amy said quietly.

"Protected?" Lenny yelled. "This is not protected! You're an eyewitness to a murder!" He waved the gun around as he paced. "How am I going to dispose of both of you? What the hell can I do with this many bodies? I've got to leave the country. Banducheck's old man will have an army of goons after me if I stay. I'm screwed! I'm totally screwed! I can't believe this!" he ranted.

Amy stepped toward him and immediately faced the business end of her husband's gun.

"I've no choice. I've got to kill you both," he said as he stared down the barrel at her.

Amy raised her hands toward him slowly. "You can't kill my daughter. She's a child, a baby."

Lenny shook his head. "Can't have any witnesses. Can't risk it," he said.

"Celia hasn't seen anything. She's not even here. She's gone," Amy pleaded.

Lenny looked around. He'd forgotten the Labrador had taken off with Celia. "No witnesses," he said in a monotone. "Can't leave anyone."

"Please! I'll make you a deal," Amy begged. "Spare my daughter and I'll take the fall for Mr. Banducheck."

Lenny stared at the body lying on the floor. "Can't. Just can't. Not believable," he lamented.

"It's *my* gun," Amy said. "I have gunpowder on my hands, too! They'll believe it! But you can't hurt my daughter! You have to let her go." She gingerly reached down to the floor and picked up the prescription bottle. "Do we have a deal?"

"You have to take them all," he demanded.

"You have to dial 911 so someone comes for her. You can't hurt her—she can't hurt you."

Lenny only nodded. Amy stared at him, struck by the irony of her circumstances. She had to commit suicide to save her daughter's life.

Suicide. Damnation. Would the same God who'd taken Jeff away now take Celia's mother away as well? Amy had never been able to adequately explain to Celia what had happened to Jeff. That was probably the main reason Celia was sleepwalking. If there was a possibility Daddy was alive and simply lost, Celia would go find him.

Who was going to explain why her mother was gone, too? How screwed-up would Celia be after this? Would she be sleepwalking through some orphanage looking for both parents?

"This is not something that requires a great deal of thought. Either do it," Lenny said, leveling the pistol at her head, "or she can join you. Unless you think I won't do it and I have to do her first." He started for the door.

"No!" Amy cried. "Please, no! She's done nothing to you. Please," her voice faltered.

Keeping the gun trained on her, Lenny walked to the bar, poured a glass of Scotch from a crystal decanter, and slammed it down on the counter in front of her next to the pills. "All of them. I regret I don't have much time." His jaw muscles were clenched and his eyes weirdly dilated.

"Can I at least see her once more?" Amy whispered.

Lenny didn't hesitate. "Not a chance. I've got to get out of here in time to have someone discover what's happened. Do you want her to walk out or be carried out?" he asked.

Amy's shaking hands picked up the pills and the Scotch. She glanced toward the next room, unable to believe her daughter's crying would be the last memory she would have of her. And how could she trust Lenny to not kill her anyway?

"You're thinking too much," Lenny said. "Do I need to just go do it? As you point out—your hands are covered in gunpowder. The police would believe you killed your daughter and yourself."

Amy shook her head as she held the glass and pills.

"Is that what you want?" he yelled at her. "Do you want me to do it? Make it easy on you?" He stepped over her toward the door again.

"Stop!" she screamed. "I'll do it!" She dropped a few pills into her mouth and washed them down with the Scotch. She'd never had straight Scotch before—it took her breath away.

"Again!" he demanded, one hand still on the doorknob.

She chased a few more pills down with the Scotch. Pills and Scotch. Again. And again. Five swallows. That was all it took to swallow twenty-six pills. One for each year of her life.

She didn't have much to show for it. A dead husband. A career that had crashed before it got started. A daughter who would spend years in therapy. How did it all go so wrong? Where did everything jump the tracks?

She and Jeff had had such wonderful plans. A professional golfing career—a few years on the tour, then settle somewhere warm where she could be a full-time instructor. No travel. Time for family. It was perfect. She had the skills. He'd stepped in with his new business degree as her full-time manager and had negotiated her endorsement contract with Tommy Bahama. He'd been working on several others. It had all been going quite well.

The pregnancy had been unexpected. It was hard sticking to a regular birth control regimen given all the travel for the tour. Rookies had to pay their dues. Late nights talking with journalists. Early mornings with a swing coach. Somehow, some way, she'd missed a pill. It was a few years earlier than they'd planned. But Jeff had just rolled with the punches.

He'd taken care of Celia while Amy got back into shape and requalified for the tour. Tommy Bahama was delighted to pick right back up with the endorsement. They were quite a team. Jeff signed contracts with one hand and rocked Celia's bassinet with the other.

His office—and her nursery—were one long series of hotel rooms. Amy had known they couldn't keep that up for long, but as a new mom and new golf pro she'd needed a support system nearby. It had been great fun.

Amy leaned back against the wall as she watched the man who was slowly killing her similarly lean back and relax. She was tired. Very tired. She didn't think anyone in their mid-twenties could be this tired. In a few minutes the pills would render her unconscious, and she would sleep forever. She just hoped that somehow her daughter might still have a nice life. As messed-up as Celia's childhood would certainly be, Amy hoped her sacrifice would pay off later.

Another clap of thunder echoed overhead. A momentary flash illuminated the room. Lenny hovered nearby like a shark waiting on injured prey to die before moving in for the feast. She blinked away a blur of tears.

"Shouldn't you be calling by now?" Amy asked.

"No rush," he replied. "She's not going anywhere."

Celia's distant cries deepened Amy's anxiety. What had Dr. Brown told her? Celia would eventually call out for her rather than for her father. Ironic that it was finally happening now that she was powerless to do anything for her except die.

The storm no longer scared her. The crashing thunder and flashes of lightning didn't hold sway as they once had. She would join Jeff soon. Perhaps in the afterlife they could watch over their daughter together. She accepted her fate and was waiting for the darkness to overtake her.

A thunderclap directly over the house made Lenny jump. Amy savored his fear—it was satisfying to see him cower. She looked out the window at the approaching storm. Another bolt of lightning spread across the sky. In that instant of illumination she saw a man kneeling behind a tree across the street.

She cocked her head at the window. Was she hallucinating? Was she seeing things as the last bit of consciousness slipped from her grasp? Was this what a slow and internalized death was like?

Another celestial burst. She saw him again. Dressed in black. A baseball hat. Some sort of hunter's vest. He had a long stick across his lap.

Another booming clap jolted her as the accompanying flash revealed similarly dressed figures scurrying in the street. More men in black. Their sticks were pointed at the house. She suddenly understood.

It was Mike Seers's SWAT team.

Her eyes cut to Lenny, who was pacing around, bordering on panic, and back to the window. No helpful flash showed itself. How did they know she was there? What were they waiting for?

"Mommy?"

Celia opened the door from the hallway and stopped—startled at the sight of Dan Banducheck lying in a pool of blood and Lenny with a gun pointed at her mother.

"So much for that plan," Lenny growled as he pushed off from the wall.

"Celia! Run!" Amy screamed.

A guttural shriek then exploded from somewhere within her, and Amy tackled Lenny at the knees. She pulled him to the floor and hugged his legs tightly. He kicked himself free and pressed the gun against her head as he stood. But she had the desired result. Celia was gone—another chance to live. Hopefully her mysterious canine friend would protect her.

But the Labrador suddenly returned, barking wildly and baring its fangs until Lenny swung the gun toward it as a stream of obscenities flew from his mouth. The dog retreated back into the hallway. Lenny leaned against the credenza to catch his breath.

Amy pulled up into a sitting position and looked down. She was lying on a huge red stain on Harold Kensington's Persian rug. Blood! This was where Kensington had died. How appropriate that she was going to die in the same place.

She'd left him there. Surely as if she'd been standing in the room, she'd done nothing and let that old man die. This was karma. The crime scene technicians would write procedural papers on this one. Maybe the *SVU* writers would see the headlines, and Mariska Hargitay would film an episode based on the incident. What's that expression? *Ripped from the headlines?* She'd be a headline for a week or so, then fade away into obscurity. Just another statistic in crime-torn Washington, D.C. Bad enough her sports career had petered out. Now her life would, too. Her heart would stop on the exact spot where Kensington had taken his final breath.

Amy looked up into the camera of Harold Kensington's videophone. A red LED light stared back at her. *The unit was on!* Glancing furtively over at Lenny, she pushed the power button on the monitor to reveal Kathy and Carol's frightened faces filling the screen. Her heart pounding, Amy signed quickly, "Come get Celia—Thompson in danger."

Lenny's head had popped up when the monitor came on. He noticed the VRS unit for the first time, moving his gaze quickly from the monitor to the red LED to Amy. She turned around defiantly.

"Celia must have turned it on! They've seen everything!" she said.

He saw how Carol and Kathy were pointing at him. Kathy jumped up and down in her seat, and Carol yelled into the telephone headset. He darted out of camera range and turned to Amy.

"I guess there's no point in worrying about a clean and tidy suicide now, *is there?*" he shouted as he pointed the pistol at her head. Amy cringed, anticipating the shot.

The Labrador abruptly leaped from the doorway and sank its teeth into Lenny's hand. The dog pulled Lenny around the room, causing him to lose his balance. The animal's eyes nearly glowed. His fur stood on end and his legs quivered.

Another crash of thunder and lightning shuddered through the room. It was as if Stephen King were directing the weather.

While Lenny was unable to fight back, Amy crawled to the sink of the wet bar. With great effort she shoved a finger down her throat. Over and over, she threw up little red pills. It took three episodes before she was completely purged, when only foul-tasting bile remained. She was unsteady, her adrenaline at odds with the first of the now half-dissolved pills.

"Mommy!"

Celia ran back into the room.

The pistol fired wildly as the Labrador fought Lenny for control. Objects on shelves exploded and the overhead light shattered, plunging the room into darkness. Amy grabbed a Congressional Golf Course golf ball from Kensington's desk. She had only one shot at this, and she hurled the ball with all her strength. She threw herself on top of Celia and thrust both hands into the VRS camera.

Carol and Kathy stared at the screen, mesmerized as the action played out. They saw Amy's gestures but had no idea what they meant. With the overhead light gone, the VRS monitor was the only ambient light source and gave Amy's hands a ghostly, disembodied appearance.

"A minute ago she signed 'Thompson in danger,'" Kathy said.

"Did you hear that, Detective?" Carol Burdick said into her headset.

"Yeah, I heard it. Somebody find Heath Rasco at Secret Service and tell him to stash Thompson until we know what the hell is going on!" Seers yelled.

Seers and the SWAT team dropped to the ground when shots rang out from the house. Seers keyed his radio again.

"Anyone see what's happening?" he called.

"Can't see anything," SWAT commander Bill Hall replied. "Too much lightning to use night vision. We can't see a thing."

"I see shadows in front of a window, but nothing definitive," Damato said.

"Can anyone see Celia?" Seers yelled.

"Amy has her," Carol replied. "But we don't understand what Amy's trying to sign. It doesn't make any sense."

"What do you mean?" Seers asked.

"She's holding up both hands. One is shaped like a fist and the other is a pistol!"

What could she be trying to say? Seers repeated Carol's words under his breath. Suddenly his eyes widened.

What had her psychological profile said? *"At the subject's own level of abilities, potential for creative functioning is predicted to be high."* Seers understood.

He pushed Bill Hall to the ground and tore away the SWAT team leader's sniper rifle. He set the weapon on the roof of the car and flipped the safety off. As he peered into the laser scope, he pressed the microphone button on the radio.

"Take the shot! Anyone who's got a shot take it now! Now!"

THE GOLF ball shattered Harold Kensington's double-paned office picture window. Startled, the Labrador released his grip, and Lenny popped upright, still holding the gun.

A fortuitous flash of lightning exposed the interior of the room. Two bullets ripped into Lenny's chest, and a third dotted his forehead. He dropped to the floor next to Banducheck. Each man's dead eyes stared into the other. The Labrador raced off.

"I've got a dog out here. Should we tag him?" a voice asked over the radio.

"No, damn it! Hold your fire! We're going in!" Seers yelled back. He dropped the rifle and chased after the SWAT team as they entered the house.

"Damn it, Seers! I'm in charge of field operations! What the hell do you think you're doing? We don't use lethal force unless we've got confirmation from a spotter that you've got a clear shot," Hall shouted.

"I *have* a spotter," Seers said defiantly. He tore through the house and burst into Kensington's office. The light from the hallway spilled into the room. Amy was on the floor rocking Celia in front of the videophone. Seers sank down next to her and put his arms around them both.

"Captain Hall? Meet my spotter—Amy Kellen."

POLICE BARRICADES and crime scene tape surrounded Harold Kensington's house once more. A growing crowd of neighbors talked in hushed tones, pointing and theorizing endlessly about what was going on. Again.

On the perimeter of the crowd, a man in a hooded gray pullover slowly moved away from the pack of pajama-clad residents. He pulled a Sidekick from his pocket and pounded out a text message.

Got him, he typed.

He slid down the railing of a concrete staircase to the street below and stopped with his back to the hill.

AT THE Democratic National Convention, Heath Rasco felt a vibration on his belt and took out his Blackberry. The screen read "Got him." He stepped into an anteroom for privacy.

Any problems? he texted back.

Nope, came the reply a moment later.

Heath walked down the hallway to another Secret Service agent and whispered in his ear. The agent opened a door and Heath walked in, still texting.

Celia OK? he sent.

Not a scratch, came the reply.

Nice work, Heath sent after a moment's thought.

You too, came the reply.

Police officers encircled Chris Billings on the stage of the Convention Center as Heath walked up from a different direction to Philip Thompson backstage. He directed Thompson to watch.

Chapter Twenty

S EERS WALKED Amy and Celia outside, where Officer Damato was removing a child carrier from the trunk of his patrol car to strap it down in the backseat.

"Apparently Anthony Stephens accidentally picked up the video feed from the surveillance cameras his neighbor uses to monitor her father's apartment. He showed it to his brother, and they got quite a charge out of getting into the guy's apartment without being caught. Took a few personal items and realized they could exploit baby monitors to identify burglary targets that had much better stuff to steal."

"What does any of this have to do with me?" Amy asked.

"Well, that's where you become a victim of circumstance. Anthony Stephens did time in a federal pen a few years back, and his cell mate was a gentleman of your acquaintance."

Amy frowned, not at all clear what he was talking about.

"Sammy Clark! Anthony must have told old Sammy what he and his brother were up to. Clark realized it was perfect for this job Lenny and Banducheck wanted done. His fingerprints were in the vehicle where we recovered Brent Jordan's body and found Champ."

"Are you sure?" Amy asked. "Why me?"

"We found a videophone at his house," he told her. "There was also a psychological profile on you, stolen from Reggie Brown's briefcase. He figured you were the perfect way to signal a four-legged assassin, and everyone involved would have perfect alibis. But you *knew* he wasn't deaf, didn't you? Or, you at least suspected it. And you never said anything even after he was dead."

"I'm not saying anything now, Detective," Amy replied.

"No, no you're not. I'll make sure my report indicates that."

"Thank you!" she said, smiling.

"Kensington was a victim, but he was just the means. The *target* was Thompson. We've torn the place apart—we can't find any photos of Billings or anything else that appears to implicate him in a crime. If such a thing existed, it must have died with Kensington."

Amy merely nodded.

Seers ran a hand through his hair in exasperation. "Our friend Heath was right. He and I go after very different types of bad guys. This is way out of my league. Give me burglars any day! Hard to say how much the Secret Service will publicly reveal about all of this."

Amy shook her head, glad to finally have the whole ugly incident behind her. She was looking forward to going home and getting some well-deserved rest.

"Give Detective Seers a good-night hug, pumpkin," Amy told Celia.

Seers hugged her. "Good night, sweetheart. You did your mommy proud tonight."

Celia signed thank-you to Seers's delight as Amy placed her in the patrol car.

WHEN CHRIS Billings was taken into custody and handcuffed, the uproar in the Democratic National Convention bordered on anarchy. Watching the events unfold brought the entire crowd to its feet. In the maelstrom, Heath Rasco pulled Phil Thompson down into a chair.

Knowing the candidate's limited proficiency in sign language, Heath chose his words carefully, his hands directly in front of Thompson's face. The crushing crowd provided more than adequate privacy. Quickly, and with as little detail as he could manage while making the story understandable, Heath described the entire scenario, beginning with Harold Kensington's murder.

Yes, he said, *murder.*

Heath related how he had come to suspect foul play when Champ turned up alive but the dog groomer was dead. He confessed to handing Jim Skelton, the man from the animal shelter, a business card on which he'd scribbled "text me in ten minutes" on the back. He described how Skelton had texted *How can I help?* while Heath and Seers drove Amy back from the kennel. He'd told them it was his boss who'd text-messaged him.

He described Sammy Clark's amateurish break-in at Amy's home, likely not expecting the shy young mother to be as dangerous off the course as she once had been on it. But Heath suspected Clark was either supposed to fail and get caught or that he'd have been eliminated as soon as he returned to his handlers.

He described giving Skelton a crash course in street surveillance to keep an eye on Amy at night, when she was most vulnerable. He described how Skelton had watched Lenny take Celia from the house and had been torn as to what to do—stay with Amy or go with Celia. He chose the latter, and took Celia to the one place he knew she would be safe: Harold Kensington's home.

Thompson swallowed hard at the mention of his lost friend and confidant. Heath paused. Thompson regained his composure and motioned for Heath to continue.

"Anticipating that Lenny or others were expecting to see her, Jim turned the baby camera back on to Celia. He also activated Kensington's VRS unit and dialed the police," Heath shared.

"Why?" Thompson signed.

"He stood behind both cameras, the baby-cam and the VRS unit, and waved to Celia. Made funny faces at her. When she finally calmed down, he signed to her and she repeated back to him. Standard practice for learning sign language," Heath explained.

Thompson was thoughtful for a moment. "With the baby monitor and videophone running, he knew someone would respond," Thompson signed.

"Right!" Heath acknowledged.

"Nice!" Thompson signed and gestured for more.

"Jim directed the dog's actions using sign language. Her name is Lucy. She warned him when the police were arriving and gave him time to slip out the back door before SWAT surrounded the house. He remained there as my eyes and 'ears,' so to speak," Heath joked.

Thompson leaned back in his chair, enjoying a serene moment of gratitude as the crowd around them raged. "Harold was right about you," he yelled aloud over the noise.

"How's that?" Heath shouted back.

"He said you'd make a hell of a field agent."

JIM SKELTON looked up at the stone staircase and pulled the gray sweatshirt hood off his head. His sweat-soaked hair was spiked out in every direction. He wasn't used to all this stuff. Not that it hadn't been fun. He pulled a whistle on a chain around his neck from inside the sweatshirt. He put it to his lips and blew. The evening silence remained unbroken.

He grinned and put a set of earphones in place as he took off in the direction of the Key Bridge. The earphone plug dangled uselessly at his side. A prop purely for show purposes to anyone in the area who might see him. Just another Georgetown health nut out for an evening jog. He took out his Sidekick and fired off another text message.

CELIA REACHED into her pajamas and handed a thin metal disc to her mother. Amy moved into the light to examine it. The reflection off the stamped brass plate temporarily dazzled her. As she blinked, clear movement in the distance caught her attention. A lone jogger crossed the Key Bridge with a dog racing to catch up. A dark brown dog. A chocolate Labrador retriever.

"Is everything all right?" Mike Seers asked.

HEATH RACED along the Potomac River toward Georgetown. The flashing blue lights of the Secret Service–issued Chevy Suburban cleared the traffic ahead of him. He held the Blackberry with one hand while driving with the other.

She's pretty cool for a terp, it read.

A 'terp' who risked her daughter's life to keep a deaf guy's secrets, Heath tapped out slowly.

That Clark guy wasn't really deaf, came the reply.

Harold Kensington was, Heath noted.

True. I guess she's one of us now.

That she is, Heath texted back.

So are you going to ask her out or what?

Heath negotiated a corner as he searched for the proper answer: *What do you care?*

If you don't, I might, came the response.

Heath considered this for a moment before he texted: *Enjoy your run.*

JIM LAUGHED at Heath's final entry and put the Sidekick away as he trotted across the bridge. The Labrador slowed down to look back one last time. A big white Chevy Suburban was speeding up the hill toward the blue police lights. The dog turned and raced after Jim.

Amy watched as the dog ran to catch up with the jogger. She reread the dog tag her daughter had handed her: "Lucy." Flipping it over, she read the inscription: "H. RASCO, ARLINGTON, VA."

She looked back at the bridge.

When she'd first visited the kennel to see Champ, Jim Skelton had been working with a chocolate Lab. They had both been there again when she'd identified the real Champ for Heath and Seers a few days later.

It was Lucy. The same dog that had led her to Celia. The dog that had whisked Celia from the room when Lenny showed up. The dog that had clamped down on Lenny's hand to allow Mike Seers a clear shot.

"Where did you find this, pumpkin?" Amy signed silently to her daughter.

"Funny man!" Celia laughed.

"What man?" Amy signed.

"He talk doggie!" Celia replied.

"Did he talk with his hands to the doggie?"

Celia nodded.

"Did you take this from the doggie?"

Celia's guilty grin answered for her.

Amy watched the Labrador get smaller in the distance. She stared for a few seconds as the realization of what had been going on became clear. She'd just gotten a bit of help from the Deaf community.

"Amy! Is everything all right?" Seers repeated.

"Yes," she replied as she put the dog tag in her pocket. "I was just thinking about something and wanted Celia's opinion."

"What's that?" Seers asked.

Amy watched Lucy disappear on the other side of the Key Bridge.

"Maybe you were right," Amy said. "Maybe I should get a dog."

"I think it's a good idea," Seers offered.

"Champ needs a good home."

"I think that's a wonderful idea!" Seers exclaimed.

They both looked up as a white Chevy Suburban threaded its way around the emergency service vehicles and stopped in front of Damato's patrol car. Seers nodded to Heath as he climbed out. He clipped the Blackberry to his belt.

"Sounds like you guys had a busy night, too," Heath said as he walked up.

"You've been busy?" Seers asked.

"I'd say so," Amy observed irreverently.

Seers frowned. He squinted at both of them. "Something I should know about?" he asked suspiciously.

"Of course. The nomination was tonight," Heath observed.

"Oh, right," Seers said dismissively. He walked off.

Amy smirked at Heath, a clear tell, but said nothing.

"Do you need a ride home?" Heath asked.

Amy smiled. "Thank you. That would be nice." She unbuckled Celia from the car seat and Heath moved it to his car.

"I'll bring this back, Detective," Heath said. Seers waved without

251

stopping his conversation with Damato. Amy buckled Celia into the back of the Suburban.

Heath had left the engine running, and the radio was on. An announcer broke in with a big news story—an audio clip of Chris Billings allegedly abusing his wife.

"Billings was just arrested at the Democratic National Convention in front of thousands of people and led off in handcuffs. This could be huge, folks. We may be watching history in the making," the announcer gushed. Amy ignored the broadcast.

"I made a decision," she said. "I've decided to adopt Champ."

"Really? That's great," Heath replied.

"I thought you'd like it. Maybe we can walk our dogs together sometime."

"What makes you think I have a dog?" he asked.

"Oh, a little bird told me." Amy tossed Lucy's dog tag on the front seat as she slid in back next to Celia.

Heath cleared his throat nervously. "Maybe we should talk about that little bird. Can I buy you a drink or something?" he asked.

"No thanks," Amy said. She nodded toward Celia.

"Right. She needs to get home."

"How about a cup of coffee at my place?" Amy asked.

Heath looked at her in the mirror. "That'd be nice," he said. "It's not too late?"

"No, but I have to do one quick thing first," Amy replied. "And you can help me."

Heath's face denoted his confusion. "Oh? What's that?"

Overhead the storm was breaking up. The moon pierced the gray blanket and burst over the car. Thunder was barely perceptible in the distance as it moved east. Amy wouldn't be afraid of storms anymore. That she was sure of.

She was ready to let go, to let Jeff rest in peace. Maybe she would be at peace now as well. She tickled Celia under the chin—maybe she could show Celia how to do the same.

"I've got to fix the threshold in my kitchen," she said finally.

"Tonight?" Heath asked incredulously.

Amy smiled silently into the growing moonlight and said good night to the brown-eyed guardian angel looking back at her.

"Yes. Tonight."

Acknowledgments

WHERE TO begin with my thanks and praise? Certainly my little sis deserves some, serving as the muse for this entire idea. She was Mom and Dad's trophy-winning baby, a lace and ribbons pink crusader in a house overwhelmed with dissected frogs, green army men, and perennially scattered Legos. Like any legend, she was known by many names: Pee Wee. Tink. Lizardbreath. These were the honorifics for the little voice in our ears whenever trouble came calling—the collective conscience of the Waters boys—our heart and soul. Love you, kiddo.

This book would still be millions of random 1s and 0s if not for the inspired efforts of Ivey Wallace at Gallaudet Press. Innocently answering her phone one day, she was blindsided by some yammering writer in Florida who cold-pitched her about a novel he'd written. She didn't hang up (though I wouldn't have blamed her if she had) and she took a chance. She has my eternal gratitude.

I also appreciate my cadre of shadow-warrior interpreters and Deaf community experts—Rebecca S., Erika B., Matt K., and Meghan B. Even the difficult parts were fun—all because of you guys. Let's do it all over again for the sequel!

Any accolades belong exclusively to the folks listed above.

Any problems, issues, oversights, or just generally jacked-up, dumb ideas are all mine. I hope you can see past my many failings and enjoy the story.

—T. J. Waters
St. Petersburg, Florida